THE
SILENT
ONES

BOOKS BY K.L. SLATER

THE SILENT ONES

K.L. SLATER

bookouture

Published by Bookouture in 2019

An imprint of StoryFire Ltd.

Carmelite House
50 Victoria Embankment
London EC4Y 0DZ

www.bookouture.com

ISBN: 978-1-78681-774-7
eBook ISBN: 978-1-78681-773-0

PROLOGUE

The two girls skipped down the narrow side street, hand in hand. The council houses all looked the same around here, boxy and grey. Only the doors were painted different colours.

'B. O. R. I. N. G,' they chanted in time with each springing step.

The afternoon sun warmed the backs of their necks and arms as their feet scuffed satisfyingly against the cracked grey asphalt, scattering gravel off the kerb and into the gutter.

When they neared the house at the end, they slowed down and walked the last few yards, looking around them furtively.

They had to be careful, because people were nosy. Everyone knew other people's business in the small, sleepy village, and the girls didn't want to get into trouble for straying this far from their grandparents' home.

Luckily, it was just after lunchtime and they were on a side street with hardly any cars around. Most of the adults who lived here were at work, with only the older people and young mums with babies at home during the day.

It was quiet here on Conmore Road, although the girls had spotted one or two people pottering around in their back gardens with watering cans, or dozing in their front rooms in comfy chairs.

Nobody appeared to have noticed the children, both barely taller than the fences and hedges that edged the small front gardens.

One held open the peeling wooden gate, whilst the other girl slipped through, stepping on to the short weed-strewn path that ran down the side of the dwelling. They'd been to this particular house a few times before and knew better than to try and gain access at the front door.

The old woman often forgot to lock up at the back of the house. Sometimes, she'd told them, she only realised the back door had been unlocked all night when she came down to make herself a cup of tea in the morning.

Her name was Bessie, and she was much older than the girls' own grandma, Joan. She liked to tell them stories about her secret work during the war, decoding messages intercepted from the Germans.

The girls hadn't believed her at first, but then she'd shown them actual photographs of her sitting at a large, very odd-looking machine, her slim fingers poised above the mysterious buttons and levers.

In the pictures, Bessie wore her blonde hair swept back from her forehead, set in neat waves around her smooth, round face. You could see she had make-up on, possibly even red lipstick, although it was difficult to tell from a black-and-white photograph with creases in it.

Truthfully, the girls found it hard to imagine it really *was* Bessie, seeing her as she was now: that soft, wrinkly face and the twisted fingers that sprouted at odd angles from swollen knuckles.

Still, they enjoyed hearing the stories, and Bessie was good at telling them, always including lots of interesting detail. Yet she was useless at remembering anything else. The last time the girls had called, she must have asked a dozen times if they'd like a malted milk biscuit and a glass of home-made lemonade.

In the end, one of the girls had decided to help herself, but she'd found the biscuit tin devoid of anything save a scattering of stale crumbs, and there was no lemonade in the fridge at all. Only a mouldy bit of cheese and a tub of margarine.

They'd been annoyed, and when they'd raised their voices, a tear had slid down Bessie's face. She'd said she must have thought she'd bought the stuff in and then forgotten that she hadn't.

Who did that? It was crazy.

Anyway, they had nothing else to do today, because it was a staff training day at their primary school. Sometimes school sucked, but then it was boring around here without it to fill most of the day.

'Let's go and have some fun with Bessie,' one girl had said to the other, and although the second girl didn't want to make fun of the old lady, she'd known better than to disagree.

To be fair, when Bessie got confused and thought the two girls were actually women she used to work with, it *was* quite funny.

As they'd suspected, the back door was unlocked.

They walked boldly into the kitchen without knocking, and wrinkled their noses against the stale odours and the smell of damp.

They found the old lady in her chair, snoozing. She looked thinner than when they'd seen her during the spring bank holiday week a couple of months earlier. On the small lamp table next to her were a few pound coins and a small piece of paper. To pay the milkman, she'd explained to them before.

Pressing her finger to her mouth, the girl with the ponytail tiptoed up to the chair and bent forward so her mouth was right next to Bessie's ear.

'WAAKE UUUP!' she yelled.

She shouted so loudly, the other girl jumped back from the doorway in alarm.

Bessie let out a strangled yelp and lurched forward, tipping right out of her chair. The girl with the ponytail howled with laughter, bent over double, her eyes shining with mirth.

'Oh! Oh no… please, help me…' Bessie pleaded, rocking slightly on her back like a dazed swatted fly.

The girl snatched at Bessie's arm and roughly tugged at the pretty ruby and gold ring on her right hand before slipping it into the pocket of her shorts. Bessie had once told them it had belonged to her mother, but it was too nice to be stuck on the finger of an old lady who never went out.

'I need the bathroom,' said the girl at the door, and hastily walked away. She wanted to leave now; it had all got out of hand and this wasn't what she called fun. But her cousin seemed to be enjoying it. She would try and think of an excuse why they should go home.

When she got back from the bathroom, she gasped when she saw the blood seeping steadily from the side of Bessie's head. It pooled neatly on the worn, patterned carpet and sank into the grooves around the corner of the cream tiled fire surround.

'What happened?' She swallowed down a knot of panic.

'It… it was an accident,' her cousin stammered.

The girls backed out of the room and had just stepped into the kitchen when they heard it… a scuffling sound, like the movement of feet.

They froze as a shadow loomed in the hallway and advanced towards them.

Had Bessie jumped up and started coming after them covered in blood looking like a zombie from a horror film?

Alarmed, they let themselves out of the kitchen and darted around the side of the house until they were out in the front garden again.

Behind them, through the open window, they felt sure they heard Bessie laughing.

They were halfway up the street, heading back home, when they heard the sirens.

DAY ONE

1

Juliet

I offload the last armful of red and blue toddler painting smocks and push the empty delivery box away with my foot, sinking down on a nearby chair.

'I thought we'd never get to the end of that lot.' I stick out my bottom lip and blow air up onto my face, damp wisps of hair flying off my forehead, as I think about the mountain of other stuff I have to get through today: I offered to pick up Mum's prescription from an out-of-town pharmacy, and then I have to wash Josh's football kit for his away match the day after tomorrow.

'You know, we could take somebody on part time to help with stuff like unpacking.' Chloe, my sister, cuts into my thoughts. 'Our time could be spent far more productively and you might not complain about being exhausted the whole time.'

Compassion isn't one of my sister's strong points. Now I regret telling her in a moment of weakness that the doctor has put me back on my medication. Just until I can feel I'm back in control of everything, feel less overwhelmed.

'Maybe we can look at taking on help in another year or so.' My best friend Beth is the obvious choice for the job, but I refrain from voicing that, as she and Chloe can't stand each other. 'Are you coping with the admin?'

Chloe isn't just an employee, she's also a director of my business, InsideOut4Kids, so she'll hate me for checking up on her, but this stuff is important.

Top of her to-do list is our insurance renewal, and some quarterly expenses paperwork the accountant asked for over a week ago now. As the main shareholder, I make it my business to keep a discreet eye on what needs doing.

Every time I ask her if she's OK, I simply get a stock 'yes thanks' in reply, so I'm reluctant to ask. But Chloe has always been one to take the path of least resistance, even when we were children. She'd always rather Mum buy a cake than help her bake one. So I feel I have to keep tabs on the stuff she's doing, because it could make or break the company.

'I'm on top of my responsibilities, thanks for asking,' she retorts. 'The fact remains that we spend a lot of time sweating the small stuff that someone else could easily take on.'

I try to appeal to her logical side.

'Like Beth says, for now we need to plough any spare cash back into the business. I can't afford to do anything to jeopardise this order now I've put the house up as collateral. We talked about all this, remember?'

Chloe folds her arms and shoots me a belligerent look.

'Yes, *Mother*, I do remember,' she snipes back. 'But let's at least make decisions off our own bat. The business actually has sod-all to do with Beth bloody Chambers.'

I should have known better than to mention Beth again, but her knowledge and advice have been invaluable to me as I try and build the business. In fact, if Beth hadn't encouraged me to go for it, to take a chance, I probably wouldn't have had the confidence to start up in the first place.

We began eighteen months ago from my spare bedroom, getting our trademark kids' clothes made by local home workers and selling them on eBay.

Now we have a sophisticated website complete with shopping cart function and we sell clothing wholesale to independent shops up and down the country. Six months ago, we moved out of my box room and rented a local industrial unit.

We have big plans to expand by selling to Europe in the next twelve months, and there's still a sense of celebration in the air after we recently won a very lucrative contract for major Dutch wholesaler Van Dyke.

Pretty rapid by anyone's standards, though still not quick enough for Chloe, judging by her comments today.

But she's not the one who has remortgaged her house to fund the merchandise to satisfy this big new order.

'Sir Alan Sugar never got anywhere in business by being cautious.' Chloe's is a big fan of *The Apprentice*. 'We need to talk about these issues seriously, Juliet. If we moved production to Bangladesh or India, we'd double our profits overnight.'

Her phone rings and she glances down at it on the floor between us. The screen lights up with the words 'No Caller ID' and she ignores it.

'Remember what we said when we started out?' I sigh. 'Fairly paid work for local people, and we get vibrant, happy clothes made with care. Not a load of tat churned out by some poor soul trapped in an unregulated sweatshop.'

We'd had to go abroad for the Van Dyke merchandise but we still chose to go ethical over the cheaper sweatshop options.

Chloe rolls her eyes and picks up her phone, the screen still lit up from a text notification. She dabs a fingertip on it and reads the message.

I try and read her expression and wonder idly if she's seeing someone again. There's been nobody really special since Jason walked out on her and my niece, Brianna, five years ago, but she does use online dating sites in fits and starts and occasionally tells me about her dates.

But Chloe's face remains deadpan as she presses a button so her phone screen turns black again. She seems oddly distracted, still staring down at it when there's nothing to see.

'Do you want to have a proper conversation?' I suggest.

'About what?' Her fingers begin to drum on her thigh as if she's thinking about something else entirely.

She's dressed in old jeans, which she's paired with a faded blue T-shirt and a cropped cream cardigan. Her reddish-brown hair is pulled back into a smooth ponytail and she looks effortlessly groomed in a sort of laid-back way.

She is all sharp angles now, but for the wrong reasons. Her perfect nose, cheekbones and jawline used to match her toned body, with its wide shoulders, narrow hips and slim legs. But that was before she lost so much weight. Now her head looks a bit too large, out of proportion with the rest of her. There's her bony clavicle, the protruding tendons in her neck and the once perfectly fitting skinny jeans that now bag a little around her bum and thighs.

In contrast, I am shorter and rounder, my features less distinctive. I do make the effort to tame my dark corkscrew curls before I leave the house each morning, usually by twisting my hair up in a messy bun, but bits of it constantly make a bid for freedom throughout the day.

Our daughters are similarly different physically too.

'Chloe, do you want to talk about the reason why you can't seem to focus on anything I'm saying?'

She hesitates and glances at me, and I think for just a moment that she's actually going to open up to me, but then her eyes glaze over again.

'Maybe, just not now.' She blinks and picks up her phone again, scrolling unenthusiastically through her Facebook feed. 'But you're not the only one who gets to make decisions around here. Remember that.'

I sigh, stand up and brush bits of red cotton from my jeans.

'I'll add the new stock to the system in the back office while it's fresh in my mind,' I say, picking up the mood.

'Put the kettle on while you're in there, will you?' Chloe calls just as her phone rings again.

I pop into the tiny kitchenette and wash the packing dust from my hands, drying them on the small hand towel. Then I reach into my handbag on the counter and pull out my phone.

Three missed calls, and they're all logged as having no caller ID. Immediately I think of my ten-year-old daughter, Maddy. I hope there hasn't been a problem at school and it's the office trying to get in touch with me. I can't think of anyone else whose number isn't in my phone who would be so desperate to speak to me.

My eight-year-old son, Josh, is away on an overnight school trip to Hathersage in Derbyshire. But I know everything is OK with him, as the teacher sent a group text to parents after breakfast confirming they'd had a good night at the youth hostel. They were heading to an adventure survival centre before returning to the school for pick-up this afternoon.

Josh will be beside himself with excitement when Tom collects him later. He'll be bubbling over with exaggerated stories of how brave he was in the forest survival tasks.

We have no worries about Josh, but Maddy… well, she's a different story.

Her behaviour has been somewhat challenging at home lately. She seems to suddenly have a smart answer to everything, whether it's a request to tidy her bedroom or a suggestion that she get her homework done before tea.

On top of that, she's not been sleeping well for the last few weeks. I've been meaning to take her to the doctor, just for a general chat and check-up, although I wasn't too concerned until the other night, when I heard her moving around in her bedroom past midnight. When I got up to see if she was OK, I found her bed empty. She was sitting downstairs in the living room, in the dark.

'What's wrong, sweetie?' I sat on the arm of the chair and stroked her hair.

Usually she'd lean into me, talk about what might be bothering her, but not this time.

'Nothing's wrong, Mum,' she told me in an irritated tone. 'I just can't sleep, that's all.'

Tom didn't think there was anything in it when we had a quick chat about it in the morning, but it was the main reason we agreed to spend some quality time together as a family this summer.

Now we've landed the big contract with Van Dyke's, I can't really take a full week off for a holiday abroad, as Tom initially suggested. But we've agreed to organise more days out to National Trust attractions, and we're going to try and book a long weekend at the coast at the end of August.

Tom has been really busy in his new job, too, working extra hours voluntarily to get up to speed with the infrastructure at the vast distribution centre where he's trying to make his mark.

Between his new career and my business, it hasn't left a lot of time for us as a family *or* a couple. I couldn't remember the last time we'd had a night out, just the two of us.

I stare at my phone screen again, at the missed calls that could be from school. But then that theory implodes as I remember with a jolt that Maddy's not even *at* school, because they're having yet another of those blasted staff training days.

I dropped her off at Mum's this morning to spend the day with her cousin, Chloe's daughter Brianna. It's a measure of where my head is at the moment, that it slipped my mind at all.

BANG, BANG, BANG.

Someone is hammering on the side door of the unit that we always keep locked.

BANG, BANG, BANG.

They knock harder still.

'Police! Open up,' a deep male voice yells.

I rush out of the kitchenette to find Chloe already standing by the door, her hand pressed up against her throat. Our eyes meet, and in that single glance, the shadow of a thousand terrible scenarios flashes between us.

BANG, BANG, BANG.

The noise is deafening, urgent. It infuses my entire body with a primal sense of terror that sets every nerve ending on edge.

'OK, OK, I'm coming,' I call, rushing over to the door. My hands shake as I fiddle clumsily with the latch. When the door flies open, I stagger back.

There are two uniformed officers there, both male and wearing grim expressions.

'Mrs Juliet Fletcher?'

I nod, and they look at Chloe questioningly.

'Chloe Voce,' she offers faintly.

'We need you both to come with us to the station,' the taller one says, looking around the interior of the unit. 'I take it you have the means to secure this place?'

'Yes, but… what is it?' I say. 'What's happened?'

'There's been a serious incident and we need you both to come with us right away.' The other officer sounds as if he's been rehearsing the line.

'Why both of us?' Chloe says, and I can hear the fear crackling through her words like a burning wire. 'Is it our parents? Has something happened to Mum or Dad?'

'Is it our girls?' I say, my voice faltering.

'It's your daughters, ma'am,' the taller officer confirms. 'There's been a serious incident and we need you to come with us to the station.'

'Oh God!'

Chloe gasps and I press my back against the wall. An unwanted vision of Maddy running into the road, chasing a ball into the path of a racing vehicle, clouds my mind.

'Are they… are the girls OK? Has there been a car accident?' I don't want to hear the answer, but I have to know.

'It's not a car accident,' the shorter officer confirms.

'So nobody's hurt?' Chloe blows out air. 'Thank God for that.'

'Your daughters aren't injured, but as I've already said, there *has* been a serious incident. Rest assured you'll be told everything when you get to the station.' He coughs. 'I'm afraid we can't answer any more questions at this point in time.'

The officers glance at each other, and I feel a blistering heat settle over my chest. It creeps up into my neck and face and scorches my flesh from the inside.

Whatever has happened, it's bad. I can feel the weight of it bearing down on us. Police officers aren't usually this brusque or evasive. Especially where kids are concerned.

Chloe grips my forearm as I reach wordlessly for the key hanging on the wall hook. She's blinking back tears of the same raw panic and dread that are currently forming a huge knot in the pit of my stomach.

But I can't say anything to make her feel better, because as I grab my handbag, pull the door closed and check that it's locked, I somehow instinctively know, deep in my bones, that once we leave the lock-up unit and go with them, things will never be the same again.

2

The interior of the police car is stifling, and the pungent odour of hot plastic from the equipment-crowded dashboard irritates my throat as I try to take calming breaths.

The driver opens the two front windows slightly before driving out of the industrial park. Our lock-up unit is so close to home, I walk there and back every day. It takes me no more than fifteen minutes each way.

My throat and mouth feel bone dry and my head is thrumming with a thousand possibilities, none of which make any sense. It's hard to reconcile what the officers are saying: that the girls aren't hurt but they've both been involved in a serious incident.

Relief and panic squashed together in one sentence.

I text Tom rather than call him. It's a big day for him, and I'm hoping this problem with Maddy can be resolved quickly.

On way to police station... Maddy ok but involved in some kind of incident. Will call when I know more but come if you can x

The car passes the familiar streets my sister and I used to play on during our own childhood. We move smoothly past the village library, staffed mainly by volunteers and open only three days a week, where I'd go to research my homework. Further down the road, the primary school sits neatly fenced and squat in its position set back from the street. It's the safe place our girls would usually have been on a Monday afternoon.

The police radio crackles periodically with unfathomable voices, and each time it does so, Chloe squeezes my hand and I look at her and press my lips together.

'It'll be OK,' she mouths, just like she'd reassure me when we were kids if Mum was on the warpath or I'd lost something I needed for school.

I used to believe everything my older sister said then, but now... now I'm not so sure it really is going to be OK.

We approach Conmore Road, which is about a ten-minute walk from Mum's house. I sit bolt upright as we pass it, lengths of blue and white police tape fluttering in the light breeze like wedding ribbons. Uniformed officers place bright orange cones strategically to close off the road to pedestrians and traffic.

There are police officers clustered past the tape at the far end of the road, next to police vehicles and a stationary ambulance with flashing blue lights. A couple of photographers loiter on the edge of a group of local rubberneckers, pressing up against the tape.

'What's happened up there?' Chloe gasps, but there's no response from the front.

She pats the pockets of her jeans and pulls out her phone.

'It can't be anything to do with the girls,' I whisper as Google's home page loads on her screen. 'They wouldn't stray that far from Mum's house.'

She doesn't respond, and I look down and see her fingers gripping the phone so tightly, her knuckles have turned white.

'Is our mum at the police station too?' Chloe's tone is frosty as she addresses the two officers. 'Have you told her what's happening? She's supposed to be looking after the girls today.'

Hesitation from the front, then: 'I'm not sure, ma'am. We can establish that once we get there.'

'Mum will be beside herself if nobody's told her where they are.' Chloe presses her fingers to her forehead and closes her eyes. 'She's got enough to worry about.'

She clicks into her contact list and calls a number. After a few seconds, she rolls her eyes and speaks quickly to what is obviously our parents' answerphone.

'Mum, Dad, it's me. The police came to the lock-up unit; apparently the girls are at the police station, so we're on our way there now. I'll call as soon as I know more.' She ends the call. 'Just in case no one's told them yet.' Chloe sends a withering glance to the front of the car.

I wonder what she meant when she said Mum has enough to worry about. She could be referring to her health problems, but it sounded like it was more than that.

Mum doesn't confide in me the same way she does Chloe. I don't know why; it's just the way it's always been – perhaps something to do with our ages and the fact that Chloe is two years older than me. Mum's firstborn, her unofficial favourite.

Two years shouldn't add up to the difference it has made in our lives, shouldn't carry the extra weight our mother silently attaches to it. Yet the realisation and the unquestioning acceptance of it has always been there inside me like a bone-deep ache.

'Sounds like some kind of break-in and attack on Conmore Road,' Chloe murmurs, staring at her phone screen. 'You'd think the police would need all their resources there, instead of rounding us up.'

I realise I have another text to send. I'd arranged for Beth to come over at 2 p.m. to look through some new footwear samples with me.

I tap at my screen.

Hi Beth, sorry, something's come up, can't make our appt now. Will be in touch soon. J x

'Who are you texting now?' Chloe whispers, leaning in to read my message. Her face darkens. 'Not her again. Why do you have to involve her in everything?'

I ignore her, pressing send and tucking my phone back in my handbag. To me, Beth is like another sister; to Chloe, she's an irritation she'd rather not have around. And the feeling is mutual.

Sometimes I feel like I'm caught between a rock and a hard place with the two of them.

The police car bears left and we pass the row of small shops – the butcher's, a hair and beauty salon, the off licence – before continuing along Forest Road.

My house stands about two thirds of the way down on the left. It's a red-brick semi with a long, narrow back garden that Tom and I stretched ourselves to buy twelve years ago. When Tom lost his job, we had to face the fact that we might lose our home too. Thankfully it never came to that.

Later, when this mess has been sorted out, I'll relish walking into the cool, airy hallway with the new wooden floor we had laid earlier this year. I'll slip my shoes off at the door and head directly into the spacious kitchen with its oversized island that I'm always grumbling has become a dumping ground for dirty dishes, junk mail and a hundred other things that get parked there instead of being put away.

Perhaps I'll open the French doors slightly and stand there for a few moments enjoying the breeze on my face, feeling grateful that normal life has been resumed.

It's those little routines that reassure me, anchor me, and it's what I'm craving right now. Ironically, it's also the exact same stuff I sometimes take for granted when I find myself wishing life was just a touch less mundane.

Another few hours at work today and I'd have been back home, having picked Maddy up from Mum's. I'd put tea in the oven and try and get a bit more work done so I'd be ready to ask Tom all about how his interview went.

Finally, the management promotion he's been waiting for since taking a job several levels below his last position is here. Today is his big day, his chance to shine before a panel and increase his salary by a hefty eight thousand pounds a year.

The houses begin to blur as the police car speeds up a little.

I check my phone, but there's no reply from Tom yet, and when I open the message, I see he hasn't read it. He's probably still in his interview, as he said he'd let me know how it went.

But Beth has sent a quick reply.

No worries. See you tomorrow. B x

When we first left the unit and they told us the girls were unhurt, I thought I'd be fine dealing with whatever has happened, but the longer we're in the car, the more I can feel the tightness between my shoulder blades. I really hope Tom can get over to the police station soon.

My hurried text message will probably panic him, but I had to let him know what was happening. There'll be plenty of time to tell him how it all came about later, when both Maddy and Josh are tucked up safely in bed and his interview is behind him.

'Which station are you taking us to?' Chloe demands, her voice brittle. She sounds upset, but I can tell she's festering angrily underneath that, silently convincing herself that the police have got it all wrong. 'Are you allowed to tell us *that* at least?'

'We're heading for Hucknall station.' It's the officer who is driving who replies. 'They're holding your daughters there for the time being.'

'*Holding* them? At ten years of age?' Chloe says scathingly. 'Haven't you lot got enough crime to keep you busy without herding up little girls? I thought this country was supposed to be in the grip of a knife crime epidemic.'

'Chloe, just leave it.' I can't see the sense in riling the only two people who know anything about the situation, and I'm feeling more jittery by the second.

But I do know what she means. What can two ten-year-olds have done that's so bad, really? Thrown stones at a passing bus? Shoplifted sweets from a local store?

Hardly a reason to detain them at the police station.

Maddy and Brianna are essentially good kids. Granted, when they're together, they can get up to mischief just like any other children their age.

Shutting Mrs McKinney's grumpy cat in Mum's old coal shed overnight when it scratched them, and flooding the dance school toilets with two older girls last year crosses my mind. But those were hardly *serious incidents*. They let the cat out the next morning when they heard that Mum's neighbour had been up all night searching, and another child reported the flooding before any real damage was done.

On both occasions, they were full of apologies.

The two of them are more like sisters than cousins. They've grown up together; there's only a couple of months between them in age. They go to the same primary school in the village, are even in the same class. I think even poor Josh feels the odd one out when the three of them spend time together at Mum's house.

I take pleasure in witnessing their closeness. I hope they can enjoy their sibling-like relationship without the complications that have blighted Chloe and me in the past.

They must be so upset right now. Terrified, in fact.

Thank goodness they're together and have each other's support until we can get there to end this nonsense and bring them home.

3

The police station

The police car had swiftly become a suffocating vortex of tension and unspoken words. Chloe's temper was being severely tested now. She could feel herself teetering on the edge of giving the two uniformed tossers who had been sent to find them a piece of her mind.

She had enough drama in her life right now without all this malarkey to deal with, but at least the staggering incompetence of the police was a welcome distraction from her troubles.

Who on earth turned up at someone's workplace unannounced to tell them they were holding their young daughters, and then refused to say why? It was an absolute farce.

The local newspaper would have a field day with the whole sorry tale, and Chloe intended making sure the *Herald* knew every pathetic detail once she had Brianna safely back home again.

She knew her colour was up because her cheeks were hot to the touch. The tendons in her neck felt like guitar strings stretched to breaking point. It was a sure sign that the mother of all tension headaches was on its way, and she'd had more than her share of *those* over the past few months.

Truthfully, she'd been stressed out even before the police had arrived at the lock-up.

After reading the last text message that had come through just before they almost battered the door down, she'd finally admitted to herself that she had no option but to talk to her sister.

She'd exhausted all other options and it had to happen soon, before things spiralled completely out of control.

But how would Juliet react? How would Chloe herself react if the situation was reversed? She really didn't want to think about that.

They'd enjoyed a much more supportive relationship since they'd started working together, and despite her mother's cynicism about Juliet's business capabilities, Chloe didn't want to threaten that.

Juliet was complex; who knew how her mind worked? It was in her nature to attempt to control every detail, trying too hard to make things perfect for others.

Chloe had felt a twist of irritation when she'd spotted her sister texting Beth Chambers. Beth had hung around their family like a bad smell since they were kids, formed some pathetic kinship with Juliet because she'd lost her brother in a car accident when she'd been fifteen.

As Chloe had pointed out to Juliet many times, it was hardly the same thing that had happened to Corey, but Beth's sob story obviously struck a chord with her sister, and whatever Chloe had to say about the woman always fell on deaf ears.

Their mother's opinion was that Juliet had turned into an irritating people-pleaser, and the car journey bore witness to this. Her eyes were silently pleading with Chloe not to make a fuss, so as not to offend the police officers.

Good old Jules, maintaining the status quo, keeping everybody happy whilst everything fell down around her ears. She seemed to notice nothing unless it actually slapped her in the face.

A big part of Chloe wanted to tell Juliet everything, without censoring it. Her sister would either cope or not. Period. Life was sometimes unpalatable and you just had to find the strength to deal with it or go under. She of all people understood that.

Still, for now they had to pull together to sort out whatever mix-up had occurred with the girls. Once they arrived at the police station, Chloe was determined to get the facts. She wasn't going to be put off by small talk or more of the officers' irritating vagueness.

One of the policemen opened her car door and Chloe emerged silently, her face still dark with everything she was suppressing.

'Are you OK, Chloe?' Juliet asked nervously when she clocked her sister's sour expression.

'I'll be *OK* once I know exactly what's happening around here, instead of having to make do with a load of senseless answers from Dumb and Dumber,' Chloe seethed.

Juliet gulped and glanced at the glowering officers, who had clearly overheard the comment.

The police station foyer was thankfully almost empty save for a pockmarked teenager in a baseball cap and hoodie, who didn't glance up from the game he was playing on his phone as they walked past. The only other person in the vicinity was the duty officer, who sat watching their arrival from behind a Perspex security screen, her fingers poised above a keyboard in anticipation.

'We're bringing in Juliet Fletcher and Chloe Voce… they're the mothers of the two girls,' one of the officers told her in a quiet voice.

The duty officer hesitated, glancing up at Chloe and then at Juliet. Was it Chloe's imagination, or did her eyebrow rise just a fraction in apparent disapproval before she began to tap at the keys?

Christ, she was almost starting to feel like a criminal herself.

They were led through a keypad-protected door into a long, stark corridor lined with linoleum and glossy white walls. Scuffed unmarked wooden doors led off to rooms every few yards.

The leading officer slowed his pace before stopping and opening a door on the left. The small, airless room was sparse inside, furnished only with four hard plastic chairs and a small table holding a withered pot plant and a dusty-looking jug of water.

'If you wait here, someone will be with you very shortly,' the officer told them.

'But how long will it be?' Juliet pleaded, her face pale and drawn. 'We still don't know what's happened.'

'Where are Brianna and Maddy?' Chloe's tone was steely in comparison. 'We have a right to see them without any further delay.'

'Someone will be with you shortly,' the officer repeated, closing the door behind him.

'Damn. I meant to remind them to check that someone has contacted Mum.' Chloe's nostrils flared. 'I hope she's listened to her answerphone messages.'

Juliet picked up the dusty jug and poured the water into the parched soil of the plant pot.

Chloe watched her closely. Mum was right: Juliet never seemed in the least bit concerned about her. Joan was in her mid sixties now, and it took next to nothing to spark off her anxiety. This whole misunderstanding with the girls could set her back big-time unless it was handled properly.

And then they'd all suffer.

4

The door of the small, stuffy room opened unexpectedly and both women sat up straight as Tom appeared with an accompanying officer.

'I came as soon as I could,' he gasped, rushing over to Juliet. 'What's happened? Where is she?'

Chloe watched as they embraced, Tom's broad shoulders and biceps straining against the material of his navy suit jacket. He glanced over at her, nodding an acknowledgement.

Juliet pressed her face against his chest in such an intimate way, Chloe felt like she ought to look away.

'We still haven't seen the girls,' she wailed.

Tom kissed the top of her head and closed his eyes briefly, and Chloe remembered when Jason used to do the same to her if she got upset. It was a long time since she'd had a man show her such soothing, reassuring concern.

'You OK, Chloe?' Tom asked when Juliet led him to the seating area.

'Oh yeah, I'm champion, Tom,' she replied sourly.

Tom and Juliet exchanged what they thought was a discreet glance, but Chloe caught it anyway.

Juliet touched her husband's cheek. 'How did the interview go?'

'Really well. But we can talk about all that later, when we've sorted this mess out.' He looked at both women. 'What exactly happened before—'

He broke off mid sentence when the door opened and a well-built middle-aged man with swept-back sandy hair walked in. He wore a slightly crumpled brown suit and a tired mustard tie, and had an easy confidence about him, his florid cheeks making him seem jollier than his serious expression suggested.

Behind him was a bird-like young woman in her mid twenties, dressed in a black trouser suit and white blouse with flat black pumps. Her movements were precise but nervy, and from the second she stepped into the room, her eyes darted backwards and forwards between Chloe and her sister as if she was trying to get the measure of them.

'DI Conor Neary,' stated the man in a thick Irish accent and held out his hand. Chloe felt glad of his directness after the ambiguous manner of the two uniformed officers who'd driven them here. 'And this is my DS, Rachel March.'

They all shook hands and the detectives sat down opposite them. DI Neary glanced at a piece of paper in his hand and established who were the parents of which child.

'So what's happened?' Tom said briskly. 'Where are the girls?'

'Brianna and Madeleine are with a specially trained female officer right now,' March said officiously. 'They're quite safe and you'll be able to see them very soon.'

'Maddy,' Juliet said. 'We call her Maddy.'

Neary leaned forward, elbows on his knees. He laced his fingers together and Chloe spotted faint nicotine stains. When he spoke, his voice was heavy with a grave regret.

'Mr and Mrs Fletcher, Ms Voce. I'm sorry to tell you that your daughters are here because we believe they were involved in a very serious assault that took place this afternoon on Conmore Road in Annesley.'

'Oh God, are they OK?' Juliet stood up abruptly and Tom touched her arm to still her.

'The girls are safe, yes. They are both physically unhurt.'

She sat down again, her posture stiff.

Chloe spoke next, making an effort to keep her voice steady. She didn't want to show any weakness.

'Our mother, Joan Voce, was looking after the girls today, as it was a school staff training day. Does she know what's happened? That the girls are here?'

'Your mother and father have been informed and will make their way here soon. Apparently your mother is feeling unwell and needs to rest first.'

Chloe and Juliet glanced at each other. If Joan was in bed with one of her migraines and making her usual demands, then it might've been far easier for the girls to slip away without Ray noticing.

'Our priority was to contact you, as the girls' parents,' DS March continued, referring to her notes. 'May I ask if you have spoken to Brianna's father?'

'Brianna's father is not in touch with her,' Chloe said sharply.

'I see.' March made a note before looking up again. 'It seems the girls were quite a way from your mother's address at the time they were apprehended; about a ten-minute walk, we've estimated.'

'They wouldn't stray that far from Mum's,' Juliet offered limply.

'So who was assaulted, and why are Maddy and Brianna being held here?' Chloe asked bluntly, thinking about the police incident tape they'd seen as they passed the end of Conmore Street.

'What happened exactly?' Tom added.

Chloe locked her back teeth, feeling her nostrils flare as she renewed the pledge she had made to herself. She would not veer from her intention now she was finally here. All the other problems in her life had paled into insignificance, at least for now.

'Officers were called by a neighbour to a house in Annesley, where they found an elderly woman who had been assaulted.' DI Neary locked his fingers tightly together. 'We don't yet know the severity of her injuries and we're still waiting for an update from

King's Mill Hospital. Suffice to say she's being treated in intensive care as we speak.'

'Who is this old lady?' Tom asked.

'A Mrs Bessie Wilford,' March answered, consulting her notes. 'She's eighty-one years old.'

'Remember Dad's friend, Charlie Wilford, who died?' Juliet frowned and looked at Chloe. 'Wasn't his wife called Bessie?'

'I think so,' Chloe murmured. 'I know Bessie went round to Mum's house a few times after Charlie died, but not for a while now, as far as I'm aware. The girls might have met her there.'

DS March scribbled something down on her pad.

'Were our girls witnesses to the assault?' Tom edged forward on his seat.

The senior detective cleared his throat and DS March began jiggling her foot.

'We have reason to believe your daughters had just left the house when the officers arrived,' Neary said simply, unclasping his fingers and looking at them all in turn. 'It's possible one or both of them may have assaulted the victim.'

'Now hang on a minute!' Tom said forcefully.

'That's the most ridiculous thing I ever heard!' Juliet let out a strained laugh. 'Why on earth would they attack an old lady they barely even know?'

'There must be some mistake,' Chloe echoed. 'They're just ten years old, for God's sake. It's not possible. You need to—'

'There is strong evidence to suggest they were involved in the assault.' DS March frowned.

'What *evidence* exactly?' Tom snapped.

'First things first, Mr Fletcher. There's something else we must address urgently to ensure we deal with this in the best interests of the girls.' He hesitated. 'Something I hope you'll all be able to assist us with.'

The three of them stared at the detective.

Neary cleared his throat, a guttural sound that seemed to fill the small room.

'Both girls are refusing to speak,' he said. 'They haven't yet uttered a single word.'

5

The detectives left the room, but not before emphasising their concern.

'We'll give you a few minutes to process what's happened,' March said, as if that was how long it might take for the horror to sink in.

'Then we'll talk about the girls' self-imposed silence,' Neary added. 'It's vital we break through that as soon as possible. It can only hamper their defence.'

The sisters looked at each other. Juliet began to weep quietly and reached for Chloe's hand. They held onto each other, saying nothing, while Tom hung his head wretchedly.

A hard, sour nut had wedged itself in Chloe's throat the way it always did when something bad happened to her. It meant she couldn't feel or articulate any emotion that sat below it, and that suited her just fine.

'What are we going to do?' Juliet whispered. 'This could ruin their entire lives.'

'We fight,' Chloe murmured, pulling her hand away. 'We fight with everything we have to get them out of here.'

'I agree,' Tom said grimly. 'These things have a habit of getting out of control very quickly when they're looking for a scapegoat.'

'It makes no sense whatsoever.' Chloe stamped her foot in frustration. 'Let's not forget we don't have to accept everything those detectives tell us. They're obviously mistaken.'

'But I don't get how the girls came to be there, at Bessie Wilford's house… on that street even.' Tom frowned. 'And where were your mum and dad while all this was happening?'

'We've still got a lot of unanswered questions,' Juliet agreed. 'Mum and Dad should be on their way here soon, so hopefully they'll be able to shed some light on it all.'

The detectives returned with lukewarm tea in soft-walled polystyrene beakers. Neary handed out the drinks.

'We'll need to interview the girls,' March said. 'But before you see them, we'll have to remove their clothing for forensic examination. We can give them something else to wear until you bring some of their own clothes in. Is that OK with you?'

'I suppose so. Yes.' Juliet sounded dazed; Tom simply nodded.

'When can we see them?' Chloe said, her voice a little shaky despite her best efforts. 'We have a right to make sure they're OK.' How long were the girls likely to be here if the detective was talking about their parents going home to get clothes for them?

'And a lawyer,' Juliet added. 'We'll need to contact a lawyer.'

'Of course. We can arrange for you to make phone calls in a private office.'

Chloe's stomach roiled. She found herself silently praying that Brianna continued to keep her mouth shut if there was anything that could be used against them, although the thought that they were actually involved in a crime like this was ridiculous.

There must be some other explanation as to how they'd become tangled up in this appalling mess.

Chloe knew her daughter could sometimes speak without thinking. Maddy was the smarter of the pair when it came to words… more calculating. She did better in school assessments, which you might expect given that she had both her parents around, spending lots of time with her. Brianna didn't have that luxury.

Chloe felt a mixture of emotions about this. She was furious with Jason, who had simply turned his back on Brianna when he left for a new life abroad. Their daughter had been just five years old at the time and yet he had never tried to get in touch again. She was angry with herself for picking such unsuitable father material. But often, although she'd never admit it to anyone, she also felt jealous of Juliet's neat little family.

'Pending your arrival, the girls have been in the care of DC Carol Hall, who specialises in the care of juveniles in custody. She confirms that they seem to have made some sort of vow of silence between themselves. Not only are they refusing to speak to officers, they're not communicating with each other.'

Chloe frowned. That didn't sound like Brianna at all. She was a gregarious girl, who wore her heart on her sleeve. It was getting her to quieten down that was the problem in class, according to her teacher.

Neary continued. 'We're in the process of collating the notes from the attending officers, but as I mentioned earlier, we know both girls were at the house. Hopefully, once they begin to talk, we'll be able to establish further details and find out precisely what happened. In the meantime, collection of forensic evidence is paramount.'

'Are we going to be able to take them home after the interview?' Juliet asked.

'I'm afraid not. We're entitled to hold them for twenty-four hours, and a further twelve hours can be added to this if the crime committed is of a serious nature.'

Tom folded his arms. 'I think we want to call our lawyer now.'

Twenty minutes later, they followed an officer deeper into the bowels of the building.

Juliet had contacted Bryan, the solicitor they used for business purposes. Bryan, in turn, had contacted a criminal lawyer he knew of. It was preferable to simply googling a suitable local legal firm.

'The lawyer is on her way. Don't let them interview the girls before she gets there,' Bryan advised her. 'Don't you tell the police anything, either.'

Chloe felt like she was in one of those police dramas on TV, but there was nothing fictionalised about the awful mess Brianna was in right now. She could feel concern bubbling away in her guts, but she pushed the emotion down again.

She glanced sideways at her sister and brother-in-law walking beside her and felt a familiar pang, wishing she had someone special to share her worries with. She'd suffered a massive drain of confidence when Jason had left her. It might have been five years ago now, but sometimes it still felt as raw as if it were only yesterday. He'd broken her heart, and although there had been other men – a handful even lasting for a few dates – she hadn't found with anyone else what she'd had with Jason. That depth of passion and understanding.

Tom had always been a man of few words, but to Chloe, Juliet seemed uncharacteristically quiet, already beaten. Yet this was the very time they needed to show strength and not compromise one iota.

All siblings had their irritations with each other, but right now, Chloe felt protective towards Juliet, like she used to when they were kids. She leaned in and squeezed her arm as they walked, and Juliet pressed her lips together in a grateful but sad little smile.

They'd get through this, Chloe felt confident of it. And once they had, perhaps it would be easier for her to find a way to finally sit her sister down and tell her the awful truth.

The officer slowed and stopped at a door on the right, tapping before pushing it open.

He stepped aside to reveal Brianna and Maddy sitting side by side. A plump woman in casual civilian clothing with glasses and permed brown hair stood up and smiled.

'Here we are, girls,' she said brightly. 'I told you your families would be here soon.'

Brianna jumped up and ran full pelt to Chloe, crashing into her and nearly knocking her over. Chloe wrapped her arms around her, buried her face in her daughter's hair. She smelled different. Strange.

They'd taken her clothes for forensic examination, and the ones they'd provided hung too big on her. Chloe knew she'd hate that. Brianna was always picky about what she wore. Cheap-looking stretchy grey leggings bagged at her ankles, and a blue and brown striped long-sleeved tunic covered most of her hands. It was about as far from Brianna's usual clothing choice as they could have got.

She could hear Juliet crying, and when she looked up, Tom was sitting with Maddy on his lap, holding and rocking her like she was a toddler again. Her niece sat perfectly still, like an oversized doll. While Juliet sobbed, Maddy stared ahead at the wall, her eyes wide and haunted. It was creepy to witness.

Chloe's own heart ached, like it had split in two, but she had to stay strong, had to set an example for Brianna.

Maddy had both her parents to rely on for support; Bree only had her.

She loosened her grip on her daughter and gently tipped her chin up so she could study her forlorn face. She saw with revulsion that there were tiny blood spots dotted around her cheeks... Could it be the old woman's blood? Somehow she managed to keep her expression impassive.

'What happened?' Juliet asked Maddy between sniffs. 'How come you were so far away from Grandma and Grandad's house?'

'You can tell us the truth, but you mustn't say anything to the police until the lawyer gets here, do you understand?' Chloe told Brianna.

The girls glanced at each other and then immediately looked away again.

'Come on, Bree.' Chloe squeezed her daughter's shoulder. 'Tell us why you were at Mrs Wilford's house. Did you know her from Grandma's? You've never mentioned her to me before.'

'What happened, princess?' Tom stroked Maddy's hair. 'You have to tell us so we can sort this out.'

A tap on the door and a young uniformed officer opened it and stuck her head through.

'Your lawyer has just arrived and we've briefed her on events so far. You can see her for a few minutes before we begin interviewing the girls. She's ready for you now, in the juvenile interview room.'

6

The village

Dana Sewell thought every day about the girl who'd died, but the nights were the worst. In the cold, empty early hours, Collette Strang came to her, her pleading fifteen-year-old eyes boring right into her heart like a laser.

Dana had arguably done more than anyone else: she had listened to Collette, she'd believed her when she said she'd had nothing to do with her best friend's overdose. But Dana had also dithered and been too late in taking action, and for that she would never forgive herself.

She'd ignored the orders of her superiors and the police and driven over to the Strang family home, banging on their door at nearly midnight. At her insistence, they'd gone upstairs to wake Collette, and found she'd hanged herself in her own bedroom.

Dana had acted *unprofessionally*, the board of trustees had told her. Hadn't followed *official procedure*. They'd seemed more concerned about that than the fact Collette had taken her own life.

Dana had been thinking of moving away from the area for a while now, but couldn't seem to find that final push to do so. But she knew she couldn't stay in the village much longer, bumping into Collette's family and other locals who knew everything that had happened with the case.

Since her suspension from duty, she'd had plenty of time to think. Too much time, if truth be told. She couldn't seem to galvanise herself to get her act together, to move on.

At the end of her spell of deep thinking, when for days on end she'd often seen no other living creature apart from Heston, her cat, she had decided to get out of family therapy altogether. Retrain and embark on a fresh career.

She just had to decide exactly when to go and what that new path might be.

And then, just a month ago, a series of unexpected events had changed everything.

First, the academy trust internal inquiry had concluded she was not at fault after all. They offered to reinstate her, which, with great effort, she politely refused instead of giving in to the satisfaction of telling them where precisely in their nether regions they might stick their offer. But she did accept a small severance payment they offered as a gesture of goodwill.

Two days later, Conor Neary had telephoned and asked if she'd be willing to partner with Nottinghamshire Police and work on selected juvenile cases on a consultancy basis. This she had readily agreed to, having worked with Conor on many occasions prior to her suspension.

Finally, the local newspaper, the *Herald*, had featured her in an article about how Nottinghamshire Police were engaging young people in various initiatives throughout the county and building a trusting relationship in the process. They also gave a brief outline of the Strang case and the outcome of the inquiry.

The dirty looks in the street and snide comments behind hands from those villagers who had heard only scant details about Collette's death seemed to disappear overnight.

But the best thing by far that had happened was that two weeks ago, Dana had met someone at the gym. In Lizzie she felt a real connection and that was where she wanted to focus her energy and build their relationship. For the first time in her life, work was no longer her number one priority.

She had only just finished a consultancy job at the end of last week with Notts Police, running workshops with young people who had been involved with gangs. So far, the jobs had been sporadic, so to get a call so soon afterwards from Conor Neary had surprised her, his western Irish lilt dripping down the line like honey into her ear.

'I've a proposal for you, Dana. Something I think only you can do.'

'I'm a sucker for your charm, Conor, you know that,' Dana said sourly but with a smile. She'd known Conor long enough they completely 'got' each other.

In the midst of her career troubles, Conor had been one of only a handful of colleagues who'd stood by her. He had spoken out in support of her and rallied to her defence when the media approached him for comment.

In the event, none of it had done any good – Dana was suspended anyway – but she was grateful for his loyalty and wouldn't forget it.

'Seriously, I think this case has your name all over it.' He continued, not joining in with her banter which was unusual. 'Have you heard about the attack on the elderly lady in the village earlier today?'

'On Conmore Street,' Dana confirmed. It would have been hard to miss it. The news was all over Twitter, Facebook *and* the local BBC television news. Some lowlife had attacked an eighty-one-year-old woman in her own home.

'That's the one. It's a very nasty incident.'

Dana felt a spike of sadness for the elderly victim and her family even as understanding dawned as to why Conor might be desperate for help.

Small, gossipy villages were breeding grounds for vigilante action that could quickly spiral out of control. Angry and upset, local folk who knew the victim and her family personally didn't usually bother themselves too much with the small detail of solid, proven evidence. They tended to make their minds up about what had taken place and then quickly forge ahead with an act-first, think-later approach, intent on seeing justice done.

Neary would be more than aware of this, as would his boss, Superintendent Cath Fry. Speed was always of the essence in apprehending the culprits in a sensitive crime of this nature and perhaps he was after her insider knowledge of the village.

Conor sighed on the end of the line. 'I'm not sure how long we can keep a lid on this, but we've got two ten-year-old girls who look good for it, Dana.'

She sucked in breath. Her own niece, who lived in Yorkshire with her sister and brother-in-law, was just ten.

'But there's something else. Both girls attend Annesley Wood-house primary school.'

Neary's line of thinking was now clear, but a prickle of appre-hension settled over her skin. Was a high-profile case in her home village the right one to involve herself in just as things had finally settled down?

The trust that employed her as a family therapist had around twenty schools under its control throughout Nottinghamshire. Annesley Woodhouse school was one of them. Until her suspen-sion, Dana had spent roughly half a day a week there, counselling kids and getting involved with local families who needed support.

'What are the girls' names?' She felt her scalp tighten, afraid of his answer. What if she'd counselled one or both of them? So young, with their whole lives ahead of them. Dana couldn't help but get close to the families she helped and she didn't think she could bear to see any of them in terrible trouble like this.

'Maddy Fletcher and Brianna Voce.'

Dana breathed a sigh of relief. They weren't among the kids she'd already worked with closely, though the names did sound familiar.

Last term she'd conducted family and social skills workshops for Year 5 and 6 pupils, and the two girls would almost certainly have been among her groups of ten- and eleven-year-olds.

DI Neary didn't wait for a response. 'I know it's problematic because you live in the village, so we approached a couple of local freelance therapists we thought might be able to help us, but they won't touch the case with a bargepole. Public feeling is running high; they've both said it could wreck their reputations. That and the fact that it looks like an open-and-shut case.'

Dana could hear the tension in his voice. The frustration.

'What's your take on where you're at right now in the investigation?' Dana asked. 'Straight up, no fluffing.'

'Honestly? Time's running out and we need to get to the truth. It looks a straightforward case, but there's something that just doesn't sit right with me about the whole thing, and I'd really appreciate your input.' He paused a moment. 'Thing is, we've got rather a big obstacle we need help getting over, Dana.'

'Which is?'

'Both girls are refusing to speak.'

'What?'

'I know it's a big ask, but I don't want innocent kids blamed for something they didn't do because the super is piling on the pressure for us to move quickly.'

Dear God. Dana felt her resolve start to crumble. The parallels to her last case were too similar to ignore.

When it came to her trauma buttons, Neary certainly knew exactly which ones to press.

7

Juliet

The lawyer introduces herself as Seetal Bhatia. She is a plain-looking woman in her early thirties, with short black hair and no make-up. She's dressed in a navy skirt suit with flat navy shoes and she has a friendly round face with large brown eyes that look permanently startled.

She explains to us some facts we already know about the case before moving on.

'It looks as though they might have some pretty worrying evidence, from what I can gather at this early stage.' She consults her handwritten notes.

'What sort of evidence?' Tom asks.

'Early forensic observations, though nothing official yet.' Seetal seemingly has no filter when it comes to stating the facts, yet I find her candour reassuring in the midst of everyone else's vagueness. Perhaps now we'll actually have a chance of finding out exactly what happened in that house. 'According to the summary I've been given, they suspect the blood and other body matter that's spattered on both girls' clothing came from the victim.'

My stomach lurches. '*Other* body matter?' The viciousness of the attack does not fit with my ten-year-old daughter who cries at

Disney films and who begged me to arrange to adopt an African elephant as one of her Christmas presents last year.

In fact, the mere suggestion that she could carry out such a heinous crime would be laughable if it wasn't so horribly real.

'We'll look at that in detail when we have the forensics back.' Seetal moves swiftly on. 'Do you know anything about this apparent vow of silence between the girls?' She hesitates. 'Have they ever done this sort of thing before?'

'Never,' I say emphatically. I look at Tom and he shakes his head.

'Not to my knowledge,' Chloe agrees.

'You'll get the chance to speak to the girls privately before their interviews,' Seetal says. 'I'll introduce myself to them first, but in the short time you have, it's vital you try and get them to open up to you, tell you the truth about what happened earlier today. They need to know they're doing themselves a disservice by remaining silent. We can't protect them unless we know exactly what we're dealing with here.'

The juvenile interview room is relatively pleasant compared to the stark grubbiness of the others we've encountered so far.

The floor is covered in a wiry dark grey carpet. A couple of incongruous brightly coloured floral prints adorn the walls, and a limp potted yucca sits forlornly in the corner. The digital recorder and the official-looking notepad and pens on the teak-laminated table, though, are an indication that we're not here for the fun of it.

As Seetal busies herself getting her paperwork in order, the tension in the room is palpable. I check my phone and see I have a text message from Beth. I click into it.

Everything OK?! Weird rumours ripping through the village like wildfire… and online, too! Is Maddy OK? B x

That damn village grapevine. It's faster than the Internet for spreading gossip. I send a quick text back.

Problems. At police station with Tom, call you soon x

It's not much of a reply, and I can't say we're OK, because we're not. I have to stay focused on what's happening here.

When I click on my Twitter icon, I see I have eighteen notifications. *Eighteen!* I only usually have one or two at the most. Against my better judgement, I load up the list of tweets the business has been mentioned in.

@Jezhallam76
Is it true your kids have bashed up an old lady @ InsideOut_4Kids? #BessieWilford #Disgusting
@dartfanatic180
Does anyone know if it's true about the daughters of the women who run @InsideOut_4Kids? #Annesley #BessieWilfordAttack

I turn the screen so Tom can read it over my shoulder, and hear his sharp intake of breath. Chloe is looking down at her own phone, and her face looks pale and shocked, so she's probably reading similar things.

'Have you remembered that Josh is back from his trip later?' I say in a low voice to Tom, and he nods.

'I'll go and pick him up,' he says. 'I'll have to bring him back here, with my mum and dad being away.'

I really don't want to bring Josh here to the police station, but we might not have a choice. Tom's parents are on a Mediterranean cruise, and Josh won't be going to *my* mum and dad's at any point until this mess is all sorted out, I know that much.

I close the Twitter page with a shaking finger just as the girls are ushered in. I feel Tom's body tense next to me as he tries to rein in his emotion.

The tweets are instantly forgotten when I see my Maddy looking so vulnerable. She's small and pale, like a startled doe. Brianna looks wild, as if she's ready to bolt.

As we agreed, Seetal speaks first. She shakes hands formally with the girls and introduces herself in her no-nonsense way.

'Your parents have asked me to come here to help you both. I'm not a policewoman, I'm a lawyer. That means I'm on your side and anything you tell me is confidential, just like if you were to talk to a teacher at school. Do you understand?' She looks from one girl to the other. 'We want to get you back home as quickly as possible, so it's very important you listen carefully to what your parents have to say to you, OK?'

My heart sinks when there is no response from either Maddy or Brianna. They both sit still and wide-eyed as if they're competing to see how long each one can hold their breath.

'You can give them a hug before the interview starts,' Seetal says, turning her attention to her yellow legal pad.

We all jump up and rush over to our girls, lost in the precious moments of holding them close without the need for words.

I press my face into Maddy's hair and breathe in her smell as Tom wraps his arms around us both. There are other smells there I can't identify, odours that don't belong to my daughter at all, picked up from the musty surroundings of the police station and their temporary clothing.

Maddy's small hands grip me hard, her fingers digging into my back as if she never wants to let go. I take her by the shoulders and prise her gently away until I can see her face.

Her usually sparkling blue eyes are bloodshot, her glowing pink cheeks sallow. She stares at me silently, as though imploring me to help her. She isn't speaking, but she's still letting me know how distressed she is.

'Tell me what happened, sweetie,' Tom whispers. 'We can't help you if you don't tell us the truth.'

The intensity of her stare doesn't waver, but still she doesn't reply.

I try to get through to her. 'Whisper in my ear, Maddy. Just tell me what happened. Did you hurt the old lady?'

Silence.

Tom's voice is low and urgent. 'We know you wouldn't have hurt her on purpose, but maybe there was an accident? You were scared and—'

I have a brainwave. 'You can nod your answer. Or shake your head. Did you hurt the old lady by accident, sweetie?'

Nothing.

I glance across the room at Chloe and Brianna, locked together. Chloe is speaking in a low voice, too low for me to hear, but I can see that Brianna's lips aren't moving at all.

I bend forward and whisper as quietly as I can in Maddy's ear, 'Did Brianna hurt the old lady? Just nod once, or shake your head.'

I sit back and watch her, a dull thud starting up inside my skull. She maintains eye contact, but does not move or make a sound.

There's something there that wants to get out, something she's desperate to tell me. I can see it. *Feel it.*

Fear, dread, sadness… she's trying to convey one of them, but I can't identify exactly which.

Maybe it's a little of all of them.

8

DC Carol Hall whispers something to Chloe, and she and Brianna stand up and follow her out of the room. I try to catch my sister's eye, but she keeps her gaze to the floor.

The two detectives walk in and sit down without looking over at us. March scribbles something on a pad and shows it to Neary, and he nods.

I feel Tom's hand envelop mine, but I can only stare blankly into space. I feel numb, distanced from everything that's happening around me.

The bitter, nasty words I read on Twitter are still bouncing around my head, and that was just a quick glimpse. Goodness knows what is being said on Facebook. I'm not sure I want to know.

Here in this room, I can feel… not exactly hostility, but a sense of revulsion. The very air seems dense, thick with the unspeakable truth of what had happened to that poor old lady.

Maddy sticks close to me, her upper arm and thigh pressed against me the whole time.

I am her mother. She expects me to protect her, keep her safe, and I can't. I can't whisk her away from here to gently tease out the truth of what happened to Bessie Wilford, and I can't stop all those vile online comments and judgements.

I feel utterly helpless, and judging by his expression and continual frown, I'm pretty sure Tom feels the same way.

Carol comes back in and gently ushers us over to chairs that have been placed opposite the two detectives. She herself sits at the back of the room near the door, while Seetal silently takes her place to my left, a little apart from the straggly row the three of us form.

Neary starts with an introduction about the interview, and explains that it's all going to be recorded. He's talking about how they need to establish beforehand that the girls understand the difference between telling the truth and lying. It sounds like nonsense.

I try really hard to take it all in, to absorb his words, but I can't drag my eyes away from my daughter's washed-out face and the puffy dark circles under her eyes.

Last October, there was a Halloween disco held in Annesley Village Hall. Maddy dressed up as Wednesday Addams and I applied white face powder and dabbed slate-grey eyeshadow around her eyes to give her that authentic Addams Family look.

Today she has no need of any such makeover to look exhausted and drawn. I reach across and squeeze her hand, but she doesn't respond.

'Mrs Fletcher?' Neary's voice penetrates my thoughts.

I jump a little and bring my attention back to the room.

'He's asking if it's OK to start,' Tom prompts me.

'Sorry, yes. Yes, that's fine.' I uncross my legs. Chloe would be annoyed at me for behaving so politely, saying all the right things... saying more than I need. But I can't help it. We're different like that.

DS March kicks off the interview.

'So, Maddy. Like DI Neary says, it's important we make sure that you fully understand the difference between a lie and the truth. For instance, if I was to say that you're wearing a red top, would that be the truth or would it be a lie?'

Maddy glances down at the long navy-blue tunic they gave her when they took away her clothes for forensic examination. It's a bit tight at the tops of her arms and it pulls a little across her belly.

She doesn't answer the detective, but March is undeterred. 'Let's try another one. If I said that DI Neary *isn't* sitting next to me right now, would that be the truth or a lie?'

Maddy shifts in her seat, squeezes her eyes shut as if she's silently instructing herself to keep her words inside. I swear I can feel the tension rolling off her in waves as I watch her fingers grasp and pull at the bottom of the dull long-sleeved T-shirt.

Neary clears his throat.

'Maddy, earlier today, officers were called to the house of Mrs Bessie Wilford on Conmore Street.'

Maddy looks up at him. Two dark pink spots begin to bloom on her pale cheeks.

I glance at Tom, but his eyes are fixed on our daughter.

'Maddy, can you tell us what happened to Bessie Wilford?'

Her chest rises and falls faster now, but she looks away from the detective. Away from me and her father.

'The officers found Bessie badly injured on the floor,' Neary continues. 'How did she get to be there, Maddy?'

Maddy twists the hem of the tunic into a small point. The pink spots on her cheeks are bigger now, and a faint sheen of perspiration has appeared on her upper lip.

'How was Bessie when you first got to the house?' DS March takes over. 'Was she unhurt?'

'Perhaps she did something to make you both angry,' Neary adds.

'I don't think leading questions are the way to go here,' Seetal warns.

Maddy slumps a little further down in her chair. She must be feeling overwhelmed. Confused. I feel like I ought to intervene, ask them to go a bit slower. But we've got to get to the bottom of this mess, sort it out so we can take her home.

That poor old lady is seriously ill in hospital, and someone put her there. Her family must be beside themselves too. But I would bet my life, without any hesitation at all, that my daughter was not the one responsible. She simply isn't capable of doing something like that.

And my niece, Brianna? Of course I don't think she'd do anything so terrible as to deliberately attack an old lady, but she has got Chloe's temper. I've seen her shout back at Chloe, and even throw stuff around.

Last Christmas, when she and Maddy were playing a game of Operation in Mum's front room, we all ran in, alarmed, at the sound of screeching.

'She stabbed me with the tweezers when I won,' Maddy howled, showing us the angry red snick on her hand.

'I never!' Brianna insisted.

Granted, it was nowhere as serious as attacking an old lady, but nevertheless, people can do some pretty bad things in anger.

'Was Bessie OK when you first arrived at the house?' Neary repeats.

Maddy slides her flat hands onto the chair under her thighs and stares at the floor in front of her feet. Her loose ponytail shifts slightly as she rocks gently on the seat, as if she's trying to reassure herself. I want to prompt her to answer, to say something to fill the gaping hole that is swallowing us all up. But before the interview started, Seetal instructed Tom and me not to speak at all unless one of the detectives addressed us directly.

'Maybe you had nothing to do with Bessie's injuries at all,' March continues, and Maddy looks up. 'Did you help her, once you saw she was hurt?'

It's far too warm in this room. You'd think they'd have a fan going or something. I'm starting to feel a bit queasy.

'What did you do, Maddy? What did you do when you saw she was badly injured?'

Maddy's bottom lips wobbles, and then the tears come. A trickle at first, but in no time at all she is gulping and gasping for breath, and her face is wet and completely scarlet.

Tom shuffles in his seat and pats her leg as Carol brings over a box of tissues. I take a couple and dab gently at Maddy's face.

'It's OK, sweetie, you're doing so well,' I whisper to her.

Seetal turns to Carol. 'I don't think Maddy can carry on like this. She needs a break.'

I hear DS March's voice then, cold and officious.

'Interview suspended at three fifteen p.m.'

I slide my arm around Maddy and we follow Carol out of the interview room and down the corridor. It's cooler out here, but I still feel sick, and my heart is racing. It was so traumatic for Maddy in there, and we're no further forward.

'I don't know what I expected the interview to turn out like, but it wasn't *that*,' I whisper to Tom, and he nods grimly.

I thought they'd go easier on her, be less formal. The creeping sense of unease that started in my solar plexus now fills my entire body.

Maddy's silence is unnerving. That she's capable of keeping up a brick wall even against me and Tom makes me shiver.

Carol stops walking and opens a door. Just before I follow my husband inside, I look back along the corridor and see Chloe and Brianna about to step into the interview room. I wish I could speak to them, so we can talk amongst ourselves about what happened in that house.

Our eyes meet for a moment and I shoot my sister a meaningful look to try and warn her; to convey how awful it's going to be to see her child put through the wringer.

But Chloe turns her head away and steps inside the room. And she doesn't look back.

9

The police station

The room felt hot and sticky as Chloe entered, but still, she'd been glad to escape Juliet in the corridor. She couldn't handle that plaintive look of hers, not today.

This was no place to show weakness, and she intended to fight the allegations against Brianna tooth and nail. *Both* sisters needed to fight with everything they'd got, but Chloe could already see the doubt etched on Juliet's face, and she couldn't afford for that to undermine her own strength.

She squeezed her daughter's hand as they took their seats under the gaze of the two detectives. She noticed that the female officer had already slipped off her tailored black jacket, and Neary had loosened his grubby tie.

'Are there no windows in this place?' Chloe said tersely, her eyes swivelling around the room. What a dump the station was; everything she laid eyes on was make-do and in desperate need of an overhaul.

'Sorry,' DS March replied without real concern. 'We'll try to locate a fan for later.'

Later? Chloe had been hoping this interview would be it and then they'd be heading home. She opened her mouth to challenge the comment, but then thought better of it when Seetal shot her a look.

That fussy woman Carol crept into the room and closed the door quietly behind her, then perched on the edge of a hard chair and sat expectant and still, blinking comically like a plump bird. She looked about as far from the description of a competent officer as Chloe could imagine.

Some people thrived on the drama and misfortune of other people, and Chloe strongly suspected Carol was one of them.

Brianna still hadn't uttered a word. She looked so small and vulnerable sitting there faced with the two detectives. Only the people who knew her best realised that her bolshie exterior was a facade. It broke Chloe's heart that she couldn't just scoop her daughter up and protect her from all this.

Chloe folded her arms and listened to the nonsense DI Neary was reeling off. Something about establishing Brianna's understanding of what it meant to tell the truth as opposed to telling lies. Bree might be young, but she was no fool and deserved better than to be patronised.

Chloe turned her scathing gaze on Seetal, their lawyer, sitting there scrawling on a pad and saying nothing. As good as useless for her eye-watering two-hundred-pounds-an-hour fee.

The interview proper began. A constant barrage of questions, good-cop bad-cop style.

Neary: Did Brianna hurt Bessie?

March: Did she try to help Bessie or think about raising the alarm?

Neary: How long did the girls stay at the house?

'Did you actually see Bessie fall, Brianna?' March asked.

Brianna looked down, bounced the heel of the ill-fitting navy lace-up shoes they'd given her on the floor.

'This is important, Brianna,' the detective continued. 'Was Bessie OK when you got to the house? Did you speak with her?'

It felt to Chloe like the detectives were trying to trick Brianna in some underhand way, getting her to admit to something she might later regret. Had they asked Maddy exactly the same questions?

She tried in vain to catch Seetal's eye.

Brianna remained silent, staring at her fidgeting foot.

'She's obviously confused on that particular point.' Chloe sat forward and glared at the detectives. In the absence of the lawyer saying anything constructive, she wouldn't just sit there mute and let them distress her daughter.

Neary's tone gained an edge. 'Miss Voce. Can you please let Brianna speak for herself?'

Seetal touched her arm and nodded in agreement, silently reminding Chloe that she wasn't supposed to speak. Some lawyer they'd selected in her.

'I'm just saying, it's clear she's feeling confused!' Chloe's face burned. This was her daughter, and she couldn't possibly be involved in hurting the old lady. She wouldn't let them shut her up so they could try to put words into a little girl's mouth.

Brianna took a breath. A strained, expectant hush settled over the room. Both detectives sat up straighter in their seats Chloe's throat tightened.

But her heart sank when the silence continued. This wasn't like her daughter at all. With Brianna, what you saw was what you got. When she felt sad, she'd cry; when she was angry, she'd shout, and when she was worried, she'd say so.

Maddy, on the other hand, was a sulker. Many a time Chloe had seen her refuse to speak to Jules and Tom when she was in one of her moods. She could be a stubborn girl. She could be sneaky, too. Like the day they'd all gone to Scarborough back in May. The girls and Josh had built sandcastles and appointed Grandad Ray as the judge. He'd picked Brianna's. Maddy had smiled and congratulated her cousin, but later, as they all left the beach and headed towards the fish restaurant on the promenade, Chloe had looked back to see her trampling Brianna's sandcastle into the ground.

When she'd raced to catch them up, her mood had brightened considerably.

Brianna's heel began thumping on the floor again.

'Take your time, Brianna,' March urged her. 'You're doing really well.'

Brianna began to cry. She looked up at Chloe with swollen, bloodshot eyes.

'Right, I think that's enough.' Chloe stood up and bent forward, cradling Brianna's head in her arms. 'We're getting nowhere fast here. What happened to Bessie Wilford was obviously some kind of tragic accident. You *must* be able to see that my daughter isn't capable of anything remotely violent.'

'Ms Voce, I have to insist that—'

The tap on the door startled everyone. A uniformed officer craned his head into the room and beckoned Neary over.

Carol sprang up from her chair and offered Brianna a box of tissues, but Chloe waved her away and reached into her own pocket to pull out a used one.

'She can't cope with this pressure for much longer.' She glared at DS March, who sat back without comment and watched her with a neutral expression. 'She's confused and very upset about what happened. This line of questioning is too rushed. Too aggressive.'

'Perhaps a break is in order,' Seetal finally piped up.

As Chloe dabbed her daughter's watery eyes, too furious to speak, she registered that the senior detective had returned to his seat, but she didn't look up at him. Her priority was to get Brianna out of this stuffy room and back home as soon as possible.

She would also suggest to Juliet that they find another lawyer. This time, one who actually did something to justify her fee.

Out of the corner of her eye, she spotted Neary whispering something in his colleague's ear. The corners of DS March's mouth twitched downwards in disapproval. Neary exhaled noisily and ran a hand over his thick sandy hair.

'We will take a short break,' he said gravely. 'Carol will get the girls something to eat and drink and then we'll need to continue with—'

'Surely you can see she's had enough for today?' Chloe snapped, jutting her chin out as she stroked Brianna's fine hair. 'Look at the state she's in – it's obvious she didn't do anything wrong. So as her parent, I say no more.'

Neary held her stare. 'That, I'm afraid, Ms Voce, is no longer your call.'

10

Juliet

The door to the family room opens and DC Carol Hall comes in.

'I'm going to look after the girls. I'll get them something to eat and drink while you all take some time out,'she says, laying her hand supportively on my upper arm. 'Just holler through to the desk sergeant if you need me.'

Tom nods. 'Thank you.'

I'm beginning to warm slightly to the woman, although I can tell that for some reason, something about her really irritates Chloe.

I give my daughter a hug as she passes. Tom reaches out and ruffles her hair.

'Stay strong, kid,' he says in the silly voice they use with each other at home, but it rings hollow and Maddy doesn't react.

She doesn't sob, doesn't cling, doesn't beg me to stay with her. She just takes Carol's hand.

This whole process has changed her in a terrifyingly short length of time. Her behaviour is totally out of character in a way I wouldn't have believed possible only this morning.

I can see an awful desperation in her eyes, a pain I just can't reach or soothe better. She's ten years old. She's not equipped with the tools needed to get through this relentless pressure; she doesn't know how to steady herself, control her emotions.

It's crushing me to watch her slowly fading away.

Conversely, when I look at my niece, Brianna, she seems to have an innate ability to distance herself from what is happening. Her eyes look slightly unfocused, as if she's managed to detach herself from the sharp edges of reality. She kisses her mother and leaves quietly, holding Carol's other hand. She doesn't seem nearly as distressed as Maddy.

The three of us watch silently as they leave the room. There is something about two angelic-looking children being accused of such a terrible, savage crime that feels wrong on a visceral level.

It's just not right. It can't possibly be right.

When Tom pops to the bathroom, I check my phone. There's a group text from school.

Hathersage trip update: your child will now require picking up at 3.30 p.m. prompt from school please. Many thanks.

My heart hammers. It's two-thirty now, so that's only another hour now that they've brought the pick-up time forward from the original four o'clock.

Soon we'll have another child to try and protect from all this. At least while Josh is with his friends on the trip, he's away from this circus of horrors. Plus I'm worried something important will happen here and Tom will be delayed getting to the school in good time to collect him.

My phone buzzes as another text from Beth comes through.

There are people in your front garden, looking through the windows!! Pls let me know asap if you're all OK. B x

I shiver. Who are these people trespassing in our front garden? Locals? Or ghoulish out-of-town onlookers?

When Tom comes back into the room, I show him Beth's message.

He shakes his head, colour flooding his cheeks. 'Cheeky buggers. I'll be going over there soon to get changed; I'll chase them all away before we bring Maddy home.'

I think *cheeky* is the wrong word. It feels more menacing than that to me. The thought of people trampling through our personal space totally freaks me out.

But in a way, it's the least of our problems.

'Also, school have texted,' I tell him. 'Josh needs picking up at three-thirty now.'

'I can do that when I've been to the house.' He's calm and confident, and it helps. I pinch my tight left shoulder, trying to alleviate the tension that has gathered there. He checks his watch. 'I'll need to get going shortly. I've only got an hour until Josh gets back.'

'I feel so helpless,' I say. Tom sits down next to me and slides his arm around my shoulders, massaging my neck. 'I don't know how we can help Maddy when she won't even talk to us.'

'What I want to know is when Mum and Dad are going to get here,' Chloe remarks. 'It could take hours before Dad manages to shoehorn Mum out of bed, even for an emergency like this. We need some gaps filling in as to why the girls were at Bessie's house in the first place. I'm going to ask the front desk if they know what time they're due to arrive.' She starts to walk out and then turns back. 'Oh, and I've left another message for them to bring spare clothes from their house for the girls so no need for you to bother, Tom. That's if they listen to their voicemail before leaving.'

She leaves Tom and me alone.

'I don't know how Mum is going to handle all this.' I chew my thumbnail.

'I'm worried how *you're* going to handle it,' Tom tells me. 'We have to make sure we're there for Maddy every step of the way. She needs to know we believe she's innocent, Jules.'

I nod, and when I look at him, I realise his gaze is loaded.

'What?' I say. 'Why are you looking at me like that?'

'Because I want to make sure I've got through to you. *Maddy* is our priority now. Not Brianna, not Chloe or your mother. Just Maddy.'

'Obviously!' I shake my head, irked. 'I don't know why you even feel the need to say that.'

'I'm saying it because I know how easily your family can sway you. Chloe and your mother are the worst when they get their heads together, so don't give them the time of day if they start. Don't be their fall guy, Juliet.'

My nostrils flare. I've no intention of causing tension with my mum and sister at a time like this.

'I'm just saying,' Tom continues, 'I think you've paid enough years of penance for what happened. They'll bleed you dry if you let them.'

'You know, I really don't need this.' I stand up and walk a circuit of the tiny room like a caged tiger. 'Maybe this is a chance to get closer to my family. We need to pull together, not bicker about the past.'

The door opens, and Carol's head pops around it.

'Your parents have arrived, Juliet. Your sister is with them in room 15A, just down the corridor on the left.'

'Thanks,' I say, and walk past Tom and out of the room. Finally, Mum and Dad are here and can hopefully shed some light on the situation.

Tom catches up with me just as I reach room 15A, and I feel his hand on my shoulder. I turn and whisper to him.

'Don't wade in with both feet, Tom. The last thing we need is Mum's anxiety flaring up again.'

He looks hard at me and presses his lips together.

11

The door is already slightly ajar, so I push it open a little more and see that Mum is sitting next to Chloe, their heads close together. They're speaking urgently, in voices too low for me to discern what they're saying.

I step inside the room and Tom closes the door behind us. Mum looks up quickly and reaches for my sister's hand.

'Here's Juliet now,' Dad says needlessly. 'Any more news?'

'Not yet.' I kiss Dad on the cheek. His face is smooth from a recent shave, and I can smell toothpaste.

'Thank God you're both here.' Mum offers me her cheek before turning her attention to my sister again. 'We got Chloe's message and brought the girls some clothes.'

'I can't bear seeing my baby like this, Mum,' Chloe whines softly. When Mum's around, she seems to regress to a teenager again, but she needs to stay strong for Brianna.

'Try not to think about it, love,' Mum tells her gently. 'Everything will sort itself out, I'm sure.'

It doesn't sound as if Mum quite understands the gravity of the situation.

'All right, Tom?' Dad stands up and shakes his hand. 'Rum business, this. Terrible.'

Tom nods, a muscle flexing in his jaw.

'Tell you the truth, we can't get our heads around what's happened,' Dad says, his face haggard and pale. 'Where's Josh?'

'He's on his way back from the Hathersage trip.' I say. 'Tom's got to go and pick him up from school shortly.' I notice Mum hasn't spoken to Tom yet.

Tom ventures a few steps further into the room and says pointedly, 'Joan. How are you doing?'

Mum shakes her head sorrowfully by way of reply and continues to stare down at her hands.

'I was due a trip up to Edinburgh tomorrow to see my old mate there but I've cancelled it now,' Dad says softly, his voice fading out as he seems to realise nobody's really listening. We're all caught up in our own little worlds of denial and dread.

Tom sits down in Dad's chair, next to Mum.

'I know this is as hard for you both as it is for us, but we're trying to understand what's happened here,' he says softly. 'I need to ask you a few questions, is that OK?'

Mum looks over at Dad.

'This has already sent her anxiety soaring, Tom. She's been in bed with one of her headaches most of the day,' Dad says in a confidential manner, as though Mum can't hear him. 'Think the world of those girls, we do. We're gutted this happened on our watch.'

Mum is in charge of the kids when they're over there; she kind of directs Dad to carry out certain duties so he'll have coped on his own if she's been in bed resting. As with everything else in their lives, it's Mum who's boss.

'They said the detectives will need to talk to us too,' Mum says fearfully. 'I mean, what can we tell them? We didn't even know they'd gone over to Bessie Wilford's house, did we, Ray?'

Tom presses his lips together as Dad shakes his head sadly. 'What her husband Charlie would make of all this, I can't imagine. Friends since school, me and Charlie were, you know.'

'How did the girls know Bessie?' I ask.

'She'd pop round the house now and again, but it's been… oh, at least a couple of months,' Mum says. 'She'd talk to the kiddies if they were around, ask them how they were doing at school and suchlike, but that was it. Rumour in the village has been that she's losing her marbles.'

Mum taps the side of her head and I shake mine in mild disapproval. Her comment is disrespectful and cruel but my parents are of another generation. I know from previous times I've challenged their language and views, I might as well save my breath.

'I think if we just recap on timings, we can make sure we all agree on the early part of the day and you'll feel more prepared to speak to the detectives,' Tom says affably. 'Juliet, you dropped Maddy off this morning at your mum and dad's house, yes?'

'About nine o'clock,' I confirm. 'Maddy darted straight upstairs to Brianna's bedroom.'

Chloe and Brianna still live with Mum and Dad. They moved in for a few months after her husband, Jason, left her, supposedly so she could get a deposit for a new place together. Five years later, they're still there.

Mum told me a year ago that it was time Chloe got her own place, and Chloe told me Mum had said she'd like them to stay.

'I left for work at nine thirty, and the girls were playing quite happily in Bree's room.' Chloe sniffed.

'I was making Joan's breakfast when Juliet dropped Maddy off,' Dad adds. 'I saw Chloe leave for work while I was downstairs, too.'

'And… where were you, Joan?' Tom prompts.

'She had a bit of a headache and stayed in bed later than usual, didn't you, love?' Dad looks at Mum and then back at Tom, lowering his voice a little. 'If truth be told, she's been under the weather the past couple of days.'

Mum starts to sob quietly. 'I'd give my own life to keep those children safe,' she says to nobody in particular. 'I watch them like a hawk when they're out in the back garden, you know. And I always check out of the window when they're playing on the street, make sure I've got sight of them.'

Mum and Dad still live in the quiet cul-de-sac where Chloe and I grew up. They've been there since they got married forty years ago and have known most of their neighbours for as long. All the grandchildren often play out together, and everyone watches out for each other.

'I heard Maddy suggesting to Bree before I left for work that they play outside,' Chloe remarks lightly.

'And that's where they told you they were going, isn't it, Mum?' I say kindly. 'They said they were going out to play on the street.'

Mum nods and looks at Tom. 'I saw them out there, too. There weren't any other kids with them, but the girls were bouncing a ball across the road to each other.'

Tom nods. 'And that was what time, approximately?'

'I'd say… probably about twelve,' Mum tells him.

'I went out to call them in for a sandwich at twelve thirty after your mum went up to bed,' Dad says. 'No sign of the little scamps then. I went to the gate and looked up and down the road, but there was nobody out.'

'I thought they might have popped in to Maureen and Arthur's for a glass of juice when he told me,' Mum murmurs.

'And did you check?' Tom asks carefully. 'If they were next door, I mean?'

Mum fusses with her hanky.

'I went round there about twenty minutes later,' Dad says quickly. 'We didn't think there was any rush, you see. Always been as safe as houses, our road.' He looks at me and then over at Chloe. 'These two used to play out all day long when they were little, Tom.'

My husband's expression says it all, and I find myself cringing inwardly. The last thing I want is for Mum and Dad to think we're criticising them, but it sounds as if the girls have been given carte blanche to do pretty much as they please.

I've never thought to question how my parents supervise Maddy when I'm not there. Why would I? They managed to raise my sister and me without any trouble, so it's never felt necessary or appropriate to question their capability.

Plus, it isn't as if my kids are with them constantly, unlike Brianna. Granted, Mum does look after Maddy and Josh on staff training days and some school holidays, or occasionally if I have to work early or late, but Tom and I try really hard not to palm them off on my parents all the time like my sister does.

Now it seems blindingly obvious that it might have been prudent to have a general chat with them about safety and how things have changed since we were small. And I could easily have quizzed Maddy about what the three of them get up to when Tom and I are at work.

I'm awash with regret. If only I'd thought to check this stuff, explain the sorts of dangers kids face today, maybe this whole terrible situation could have been avoided.

Tom stands up, and I can see he's finding it hard to swallow down his thoughts.

'I'd better get off to pick Josh up.' He kisses me on the cheek. 'See you soon.'

Once he's gone, I sit in the empty seat opposite my parents and sister, and when I speak, my voice sounds thin and stringy.

'How did Brianna's interview go?' I ask Chloe. 'We need to talk through what they asked and what the girls said, so we have an overview.'

Chloe sobs on Mum's shoulder and I sit there watching them like a spare part.

'Not now, Juliet,' Mum says, sitting back and shaking her head discreetly at me so that Chloe doesn't notice. 'You can see the state your sister's in; she's finding it hard enough to cope as it is without dredging up every detail.'

'We're all in a state, Mum,' I reply. 'But we need to make sure—'

'I'll go and get us some coffees, shall I?' Dad moves towards the door.

'Just sit down, Ray.' Mum touches her temples with her fingers. 'I need you here supporting me. Not running around making drinks left, right and centre.'

Dad sits back down again.

Chloe is inconsolable now, sobbing loudly into Mum's blouse.

'She was always the sensitive one, eh, Ray?' Mum croons, stroking Chloe's hair.

'Aye,' Dad murmurs.

I get up and walk over, placing my hand on my sister's upper back and patting it gently. I can't help feeling I'm somehow lacking because I'm not falling to pieces, on the outside at least. But the truth is, inside I feel hollowed out and weirdly distanced from the whole thing.

'We were unpacking a delivery at the unit,' I hear myself say as I sit down again. 'We thought the girls were safe with you, Mum, until the police came banging on the door.'

'What are you trying to say?' Mum sits back slightly and stares at me, her small eyes glinting like black beads under the fluorescent lights.

My breathing speeds up a little.

Dad shuffles forward on his chair. 'We couldn't have done any more, Juliet.'

'The girls were playing on the street, as far as I knew. I haven't got eyes in the back of my head, you know.' Mum presses her hand to her forehead and squeezes her eyes closed.

'We're run ragged when we've got the kiddies,' Dad says. 'You know that, love. We can't be expected to—'

'I'm not saying you've been negligent!' Mum's mouth tightens, and I soften my tone. 'I'm not saying that at all. It's just…'

For God's sake. I can do without Mum's histrionics today, but there's no escape, stuck here with her in this tiny room. I just want to sit quietly, think the whole mess through. I really need to discuss the interviews with Chloe so we can piece together what the police are asking them.

'Do you know what the girls were doing on Conmore Street, Mum? It's quite a walk from your house.' I have to push for answers, for Maddy's sake.

Mum holds her handkerchief up to her nose and sniffs.

'They didn't even tell us they were going over there, so how would we know what they were doing?' Dad leans over and hugs Mum into his side.

'I didn't realise the girls knew Bessie well,' I remark.

Dad shrugs. 'They've been at ours when Bessie has visited, listened to her stories about the war.'

Mum's hugging Chloe, Dad's hugging Mum, and I'm sitting here saying the wrong thing every time I open my mouth.

We're all startled when there's a tap at the door and DS March enters the room, looking round cautiously at us.

'DI Neary has asked me to let you know there's been a development.' She leans against the small table next to the door and grips the edge behind her back. 'The press haven't been informed yet, and he's asked you don't repeat the information outside of this room for now.'

I blow out air. The immovable weight that settled on my chest when the police came to the lock-up shifts slightly for the first time.

Have they discovered they've made a terrible mistake and our girls are innocent after all? I feel the rigidity in my neck and shoulders soften slightly.

'What's happened?' Chloe asks, her voice strained and tight. She pulls herself away from Mum and sits up straight.

I make a rapid, silent pledge in my head. *Please, please, please, God, make it be OK and I'll never complain about* anything *again.*

'Sadly, we've just heard that Bessie Wilford has died from her injuries in hospital without regaining consciousness.' DS March speaks slowly, enunciating her words with care. 'It's important the girls don't know this for now.'

The room is silent, the air still.

The detective looks at Chloe and me.

'DI Neary thought you might want to get your brief back in here.' She hesitates. 'I'm afraid we're no longer investigating an assault; we're now looking at a possible murder inquiry.'

12

2001

Joan Voce sat back in the raspberry-velvet-upholstered armchair that used to belong to her grandmother and watched her two daughters put on their performance.

They'd been bored to death in the school holidays, and sick of hearing them grumbling, Joan had suggested they choreograph a gymnastic show. They'd been practising for days now in the back garden.

It was the sort of thing she herself had loved to do as a child: walkover into bridge, cartwheels, back bends… to name but a few. She'd had a talent for it, been so flexible and strong.

When she watched Chloe move, Joan could almost whisk herself back to those young, carefree days that seemed so long ago.

Ray had taken three-year-old Corey out bug-hunting for the afternoon. Their youngest child had been a mistake after a rare boozy night out, although Ray hated to hear her say that. The child undoubtedly brought them joy, but he also brought exhaustion on a whole new level for Joan.

At thirty-nine years old when she fell pregnant, she'd been the oldest mother in her antenatal class, and still remembered the humiliation of the younger women sniggering behind their hands. It hadn't done her anxiety much good, and with a fractious young baby to contend with, her peaceful house and stable mood had swiftly become things of the past.

She'd felt constantly bone tired, yet she was unable to sleep at night once she got into bed. She'd lost interest in everything around her, even her beloved reading and baking. Nothing gave her pleasure any more.

The girls and Ray adored the baby, but Joan just couldn't seem to feel a bond with him.

Ray had begged her to make an appointment to see the doctor, but Joan steadfastly refused. The last thing she wanted to be bothered with was having to get ready and go down to the surgery. It was a small village, and the worst gossips worked behind the GP's reception desk.

Then one day Dr Rahman had appeared at the front door. Joan had flown into a fury with Ray and stomped upstairs, but the doctor simply followed her up there and within a few minutes had diagnosed postnatal depression. He'd prescribed powerful antidepressants to help her cope, and Joan had been taking them ever since.

She had rediscovered her love of reading and baking, and had even taken up cross-stitch. They were all pastimes that required peace and quiet, and that wasn't always easy to come by. But thanks to Ray, she had a little time to herself that afternoon, and once the girls had got their silly performance out of the way, she would be heading upstairs to bed to enjoy an hour reading her new Jilly Cooper novel.

She studied the two girls, who'd dressed in bright colours and tied ribbons in their hair for the occasion.

Of the two of them, thirteen-year-old Chloe was clearly the performer, as Joan herself had been. In her youth, she had nurtured a secret dream of competing in professional competitions, performing at national level as a rhythmic gymnast. So many people had said she was good enough to give it a go.

Her chest tightened as she remembered the cruel cackle of her grandmother, Irma, when, aged twelve, she had finally confided in her and asked if she could travel to London for a rare weekend of open auditions for the junior British gymnastics heats.

'You've ideas above your station, my girl,' Irma had snapped, her wrinkly mouth pulled into a tight knot. 'You'll never make anything of yourself. Mark my words.'

But Joan's ambition had burned even brighter at Irma's scathing words. She knew she was special, had always felt it. If her own mother, Tessa, had been alive, she would have supported her dream, she knew.

Now, all these years later, she was loath to admit that Irma's prediction had come to pass. As far as her performing aspirations were concerned, anyhow. The most she had ever done was a short stint on stage during an amateur gym showcase at school.

It was meeting Ray that had put paid to her dreams. He'd promised her the earth and she'd taken her chances and ended up in this ramshackle little ex-mining village where nothing ever happened.

But sitting there watching Chloe cartwheel from one side of the room to the other, well, it brought back the feelings Joan had had herself as a young girl. The freedom, the joy of getting caught up in the beauty of movement... it felt almost as good as the real thing.

She was entranced as her elder daughter skipped and jumped, her slim fingers poised and toes elegantly pointed, enjoying the warmth of her mother's attention.

Her heart beat a little faster when she began to consider just how far Chloe could go with this. Joan had been blocked from achieving her dreams, but maybe, just maybe, it wasn't too late.

Absent-mindedly she rubbed the arms of the chair, her fingertips grazing over the worn, bare patches. It was entirely possible that with her help, Chloe could really excel as a gymnast, and Joan, her devoted mother, would naturally accompany her on the journey.

'Mum!' She was pulled out of her pleasant reverie by her other daughter, Juliet, two years younger than Chloe and forever trying to grab attention for herself. 'Watch this, Mum.' She performed a clumsy balancing posture in front of the mahogany sideboard. She had all the grace of a baby hippo, and Joan was forced to look away to conceal a snigger.

Juliet was academically bright. On the last day of the summer term, she'd come home proudly displaying a sticker on her pullover, given to her by the teacher apparently for coming top of her class in a maths test.

Maths! Joan thought disparagingly. Where was the glamour in *that*?

At the end of the girls' little performance, their mother clapped enthusiastically.

'Bravo!' she called, like the ladies dressed in furs and pearls did in the black-and-white films she enjoyed watching.

'We'll try and get you enrolled in a proper gym class,' she told Chloe when her daughter skipped over and perched next to her on the arm of her chair. 'I can see you performing as a rhythmic gymnast, and I'll be right there in the front row to cheer you on.'

'And me too?' Juliet prompted from the other side of the room.

Joan laughed. 'Not everyone's a natural mover.' She stroked Chloe's silky ponytail. 'You're better off concentrating on your school studies, Juliet.'

Chloe laid her head on Joan's shoulder and watched as her sister's face dropped.

'I don't want to go if Jules can't come, Mum,' she said.

'Don't be silly.' Joan suddenly sat up so Chloe's head slid away from her shoulder. 'If you've got a talent for something, then you go for it, my girl. Don't be weak and don't let anyone get in the way.'

13

The village

As the coach pulled into the school car park, Tom drew up behind the other vehicles that lined the pavement outside the school.

He'd thought he'd left plenty of time for the journey here, but a lane had been blocked by a broken-down car on Annesley Cutting, resulting in a ten-minute delay, and now it was a few minutes past three-thirty and it looked like he was one of the last to arrive.

His heart was heavy from worrying about Maddy. It was a struggle keeping up the optimism in front of Juliet, but it was essential that he did so. He'd seen a decline in her ability to cope as the business had grown, and he'd supported the doctor's decision to put her back on antidepressants. But if the worst happened with Maddy, it could finish her off.

Still, he felt a little brighter at the thought of seeing Josh and hearing all about his trip. He knew that a big part of his job was protecting his son from the fall-out from the situation. It would be a challenge, but he hoped to keep a least a little normality in Josh's life.

Perhaps if he bumped into his best friend Leo's dad, he could arrange for Josh to go there for a sleepover at some point. Just to help him deal with this initial period of utter chaos.

He jumped out and jogged up through the car park to wait with the other parents at the top. The coach was still reversing into its spot and the windows were slightly tinted, so he couldn't spot Josh or Leo amongst the child-sized faces pressing up against the windows.

At the edge of the group of parents he spotted Nick, Leo's dad, who he usually stood with at the boys' after-school football matches.

'How're things, mate?' He pushed his hands into his jeans pockets and nudged the other man. 'Thought I wasn't going to make it on time, but looks like I just pulled it off.'

Nick looked at him coolly. 'Come straight here from the police station, have you?'

Tom swallowed, taken aback at his unfriendly manner.

'Yes, actually. That's exactly where I've been.' He glanced around him, realising that the low hum of voices had ceased. All eyes were on him.

The whooshing sound of the coach's hydraulic brakes broke the silence and people shuffled a little.

Damn. Why hadn't he anticipated this? He'd been too busy thinking about how, in between talking about the forest survival training and catching up with the footie scores, he could best explain to Josh what was happening to his sister.

'Did they do it then?' a woman's voice called from the back of the group. 'Has Maddy admitted murdering Bessie Wilford?'

Murder? Tom bristled at the word.

'Course they did it!' another mocking voice called. 'Old women don't just batter themselves to death. You should be ashamed, showing your face around here.'

The hum of voices started up again and the obvious disapproval and anger wasn't lost on Tom. Maybe these people didn't understand Bessie had been assaulted, not murdered. His phone was in his back pocket but he hadn't checked it while driving. There was no way he'd take it out here in front of everyone, to check any news. This lot would be watching every facial twitch.

'They should lock them both up and throw away the key for what they've done!'

Tom spun around and faced the crowd, trying to identify who'd spoken, but all the faces looked equally hostile.

There was movement to his side as Nick stepped away from him, leaving Tom standing isolated on his own little patch of car park asphalt.

His heart felt like a battering ram against his chest. He wanted to explode at them all, ask them how they'd feel if their own kids had been accused. The situation was bad enough without them exaggerating it to a possible murder charge. But he imagined Juliet's horror if he did. She'd ask him what on earth had possessed him to lose it in front of the very people they had to see every day.

Maintaining a dignified silence took every ounce of his resolve, but somehow he managed it and held his tongue.

The stand-off was broken when the coach doors opened and a stream of pupils poured out. Soon the waiting parents were caught up in a sea of excited children clutching rucksacks and artwork with twigs and plants attached, all competing to be heard.

Tom caught sight of one of the teachers watching him from the back of the crowd.

The stream of kids thinned out and he walked closer to the bus, looking for his son. Finally a lonely figure came slowly down the steps. Josh.

Tom rushed forward and held out his hand to help him down. He didn't have to ask how Josh was; his face told him everything.

The last person off the coach was Mrs Carrington, Josh's class teacher. She paused on the bottom step to regard Tom.

'Let me know if we can support Josh in any way,' she said sympathetically. 'Perhaps a couple of days away from school might do him good, help him adjust to what's happening.'

She was right, he realised. He had to protect Josh from the animosity he himself had just experienced.

Behind him, he heard comments starting up again from the parents, and now kids' voices were joining in too.

'Better get back to the cop shop!'

'Find another school to go to!'

Josh allowed him to slip the rucksack from his back, and they walked quickly through the car park and out onto the main road.

'You missed a good footie game while you were away, champ. I've recorded the highlights.' Tom's voice sounded ridiculously jolly even to himself, but Josh remained silent. 'I want to hear all about the trip. We can go to Annesley Woods and you can show me some survival stuff. How about that?'

Once they were inside the car, Josh looked at Tom, his face pale and fearful.

'Is it true what they're all saying?' he asked in a small voice. 'Is it true that Maddy's a murderer?'

14

The police station

Driving to the police station, Dana purposely chose the long route around the village that would take her past Conmore Road.

Hordes of people were gathered at the end of it, clustered within inches of the blue and white police tape. Villagers, out-of-town rubberneckers, press… they were all represented there. They spilled off the pavement and into the road, causing the passing traffic to take a wide berth around them.

Predictably, the reporters and photographers had staked their positions closest to the tape. Dana spotted one or two local hard-nosed journalists she'd had the misfortune to meet in other high-profile cases she'd worked on with Neary over the years. Both women were the type who'd willingly destroy their own mother's reputation if it meant getting ahead in their career.

Other reporters fiddled with their microphones, and pho-tographers stood around tinkering with their cameras to ensure they were ready should an opportune moment present itself for a snapshot.

Dana's chest tightened as she spotted faces from the village she recognised. Ordinary people with scowls and clenched jaws, huddled together over illuminated phone screens, waiting like coiled springs for updates.

She could sense the unrest even from inside her car, and it bothered her that their vitriol was reserved for two ten-year-olds who at this point in time had not even been charged.

An attack on a defenceless old lady, with children being questioned as suspects, was exactly the kind of story to bring the big boys over from the nationals. The muscle they had in terms of television coverage could be disastrous for the girls and their families.

Dana sighed as she continued her journey, leaving Conmore Street behind.

Rachel March had already given her a call to warn her they'd just heard that Bessie Wilford had died in hospital from her injuries, but she needn't have bothered. The press were already on it, courtesy of Mrs Wilford's family. Dana had scanned social media and caught an emotional video that Bessie's fifteen-year-old great-granddaughter, Rose, had posted from outside the hospital.

The girl's bloated, tear-streaked face had filled the screen as she pleaded with local people to get behind her family 'to make that scum pay'.

Earlier, after she'd finished the phone call with Conor, Dana had spent the best part of an hour reading every last detail she could find about the case online. There was lots of it, and it had told her the extent of what was publicly known at that point.

But now, following Rose's video, she sensed the mood of the posts becoming much darker.

In her capacity as consultant to the case, she had access to police information not yet disclosed to the public. Yet social media was proving very useful in getting a comprehensive angle on the case, particularly on the swiftly transforming mood of the locals.

And it wasn't pretty. To compensate for the absence of police updates, the press had gone ahead and done what they did best: constructing headline-grabbing stories around sparse facts.

Now, with news of Bessie's death leaking out, local news websites competed for attention with inflaming taglines accompanying reports that lacked any real detail or substance.

Local businesswomen's daughters are now murder suspects.

Ten-year-olds suspected of beating local pensioner to death.

Dana noted with concern that the national press were already in on the act, online at least.

Echoes of Bulger killers in sleepy Nottinghamshire village, screamed the *Daily Mail.*

Breaking news: Wilford family demand justice was the *Express*'s take on the case.

The trial of Maddy Fletcher and Brianna Voce was already well under way in numerous online kangaroo courts. And it wasn't looking at all favourable for the two girls.

Dana had closed her laptop at that point, suddenly grateful that she hadn't time to peruse Twitter and Facebook again until later. She dreaded to think what was being said online, unmonitored and closer to home.

She knew only too well from personal experience that the villagers could be brutal and unforgiving when it came to the mistakes of others.

With only the flimsiest of details known about her suspension in the Collette Strang case, she'd received threatening letters and was once spat at on her own street by someone she often used to say good morning to.

She passed the school and manoeuvred the car into the right filter lane to turn just as the light turned green. She did a double take when she spotted a man who was the spitting image of Maddy's dad, Tom, with a young boy of about seven or eight who looked pale and upset.

She'd seen a family photograph of the Fletchers online and knew Maddy had a brother of about that age.

She pushed her musings aside and focused on the journey, arriving in Hucknall ten minutes later and parking on a side street. It took her just five minutes to walk to the police station, a huge concrete structure with blacked-out windows that faced the busy road.

As she entered the building and made her way to the front desk, she noted that the interior was in even greater need of a facelift than when she'd last been there. Flakes of pale green paint littered the edges of the tiled floor, and a thick grimy border ran along the walls level with the backs of the grey plastic tub chairs.

She didn't recognise the desk sergeant as she signed the visitor book to document that she was here to see Neary, then took a seat as he asked. Thankfully, there was nobody else in the waiting area.

Before she got the job working for the academy trust, Dana had been employed by the local authority as a juvenile therapist. She'd worked all across the county of Nottinghamshire, supporting young people in police custody.

It had been a career conducted at the uncomfortable end of life. There had been plenty of times back then when she'd got home very late, too tired to eat, too emotionally drained to sleep. It hadn't been the best foundation for a healthy relationship. Looking back, it couldn't have been easy for Orla either. Dana didn't want to make the same mistake again, even though it was still early days with Lizzie.

When the opportunity at the academy trust had presented itself, she had welcomed the slower pace with open arms.

Her newly painted office, with its comfy upholstered chairs, potted plant and coffee machine, had helped soften the edges of the uncomfortable subjects she often had to raise in there.

Little did she know that it was the place where her professional unravelling would begin, followed swiftly by her personal life.

It was in this job she'd become involved in the case of Collette Strang and the death of her best friend.

An abrupt click, and a door opening to the left of the front desk shook her out of her thoughts. She stood up and smiled as the tall, broad figure of Conor Neary advanced towards her.

'Dana! Am I glad to see you.' He gripped her hand in both of his and squeezed it gratefully. 'Come on through.'

She followed him down a corridor and into an office. He closed the door behind them, gesturing for her to sit the other side of the paper-strewn desk.

'Before we start, I just want to say thanks. For taking the case, I mean.' He pinched the skin between his eyebrows and squeezed his eyes closed momentarily. 'I know you've had it rough yourself and this is going to be a difficult one—'

It was painful, witnessing him walking on eggshells like this. Trying to select the least offensive words. It wasn't his style at all.

'It's fine, Conor. Honestly. I can't remember the last time I've thought about anything apart from that damn inquiry, but since your call, I've been absorbed in researching events so far online. It makes sober reading.'

15

Neary leaned forward, lacing his fingers together and resting his elbows on the desk, and began his brief on where the investigation stood thus far. Dana took out a pad and pen from her handbag to make some brief notes.

'Our only hope is to get the girls talking. When forensics come back it will be all too easy for the powers-that-be to insist we arrest both of them. This really is our last chance to make a breakthrough.' He sighed. 'We've told the parents not to say anything to the girls about Bessie dying for now. It could scupper our chances of getting them to open up.'

Dana tipped her head to the side and studied the detective.

'Interesting,' she murmured.

'What's that supposed to mean?' The colour in his cheeks rose and he assumed a playful tone, but there was a slight edge to it. 'If you've got something to say, Dr Sewell, then say it. Don't go using your special insights on me.'

Dana had known Conor long enough to see that something was bothering him. It was as plain as the nose on his face.

'In all the time I've known you, I can't say you've ever dithered once a case seemed tied up, but despite placing the girls firmly at the scene, establishing they were both covered in Bessie Wilford's blood and now having a reliable witness to boot, here you are giving them one more chance.'

Conor Neary was a fair man, and in Dana's opinion, a good man. He'd told her once that his job boiled down to something quite simple: he had to ensure that justice was done. Namely, that the right person paid for whatever crime had been committed.

The fact that he'd pleaded with her to take this on so soon after the inquiry spoke volumes to Dana about the profile of the case.

But somewhere along the line, he was troubled by the apparent guilt of the girls. That much was obvious.

'I suppose what I'm saying is, how about you tell me what you're *really* thinking?'

A sardonic smile played around Neary's mouth.

'I feel like I just got a timely reminder why I've stuck my neck out to get you in here,' he sighed. 'And I admit I'm guilty as charged. Something doesn't add up, though it's just a gut feeling at the moment. The evidence against them is the only thing the boss is going to be interested in when I meet with her later today.'

He picked up a pen and tapped out a staccato rhythm on the desk before laying it down again.

'We've got to find out from the kids exactly what happened in that house, Dana.' He fixed his red-rimmed eyes on her. 'The super isn't going to let me wait around forever. The press are frenzied, the locals are already baying for blood. I'm not going to be able to shield the girls for much longer.'

She nodded, understanding. He slid two slim brown wallet folders, each with a typed white sticker on it, across the desk to her.

'There's one for each girl. It's everything we've got on them so far, their families too. There are official records in there, and observations provided by the school, plus additional notes from preliminary interviews.'

Dana pressed her lips together and slid the folders back over to him.

'I'll let you know when I need these,' she said.

He frowned. 'Surely you want to avail yourself of—'

'I will read them, but not yet. These folders are filled with other people's thoughts and opinions. I'd rather start by meeting the girls myself, make my own first impression of them.'

As the detective nodded in understanding, Dana silently acknowledged that her intuition had got her into trouble more times than she cared to recall, including that last case, which had brought about her suspension from duty. She also knew that despite there being right and wrong procedures to follow, her powerful gut feeling was rarely wrong.

'Point taken,' Neary said. He gathered up the folders and placed them in a pedestal drawer, out of Dana's sight. 'Let's go and meet the families.'

16

Juliet

DS March's words ricochet around my head.

I'm afraid we're now looking at a murder inquiry.

I don't feel the heat of panic like my sister. I feel cold and detached when I think about how this situation could escalate.

I've seen it so many times on television as I've sat on the sofa with coffee and a biscuit, watching as the family of the accused proclaim their relative's innocence.

They always sound deluded.

Only this morning, I was loading the dishwasher, planning the evening meal, putting on the laundry I should have set going last night.

Now our precious daughters are in danger of being charged with murder. If that happens, they will never shrug off the stigma. Even if it's proven at some stage that they were wrongly charged, things will never be as they were.

It will raise its head again and again their whole lives, through sly nudges, unsuccessful job applications, friends who fade away… I'm trying so hard to process it, but it's proving impossible. The thought that life as we knew it could collapse so completely in a day is utterly crazy.

Ten minutes ago, Dad took Mum over the road to Costa. Chloe isn't in the mood for talking and has been immersed in her phone and I'm just staring at the walls, wondering if Tom has picked up Josh safely. I thought he might have texted me.

The door opens and I sit up straight. Neary walks in, and a tall woman in her early forties enters the room behind him. She's wearing black trousers and a silky green blouse that complements her short copper-coloured hair and pale skin. She smiles pleasantly at us all. I'm the only one who smiles back.

Neary clears his throat. 'Juliet, Chloe, I'd like to introduce you to Dana Sewell, a brilliant family therapist I've known and worked with for many years now.'

Her name sounds familiar but I can't think why.

We all shake hands, and as we sit down, I notice that her face and forearms are heavily patterned with freckles.

'Good to meet you,' she says in a local accent.

'Dana has kindly agreed at short notice to come and speak to Maddy and Brianna,' Neary tells us. 'We're hoping she can break through the girls' silence. It isn't helping either of them. Do you have any questions?'

'What do you think you can do to get through to them that we haven't thought of?' Chloe asks in a belligerent tone. 'If the girls won't even speak to *us*, their own mothers, I don't see why they'll be any different with you.'

'At this stage, I can't promise anything at all.' Dana moves her hands around gently as she speaks. 'I plan to start by meeting the girls and hopefully establishing some sort of initial relationship.'

My fingers loosen their grip on the sides of the chair. Her voice is soothing, somehow. She's the kind of person I think I could trust.

'And that's it?' Chloe gives a disparaging grunt. '*This* is the genius strategy that we're hanging our hopes on?'

'Dana has a bit of a head start in that she's local to the village and has worked at the school your daughters attend,' Neary offers and I realise I must have heard her name mentioned on a school newsletter. 'They may well recognise her as a friendly face, and she's known for her unique ability to quickly form relationships with young people.'

Chloe frowns and peers closer at Dana, as if she's trying to match her face with a picture in her mind. 'You're not that school therapist they had to fire last year, are you?'

Now I remember! Beth, always an expert on local gossip, had told me about a woman who worked at a handful of local schools, including ours. She had overstepped the mark and been struck off, or something similar.

'She sounds quite a maverick,' Beth had remarked at the time.

'I was suspended, not dismissed,' Dana replies calmly. 'And I've now been fully cleared of any wrongdoing.'

'Well I'm sorry, but I don't want her anywhere near Brianna.' Chloe folds her arms and stares stonily at the opposite wall.

Dana's face flushes pink, but she doesn't respond. I cringe inwardly at Chloe's overt rudeness.

'Juliet?' Neary sighs. 'What's your view on this?'

'Why do you think the girls have stopped speaking?' I ask Dana. Nobody has actually given an opinion on it.

'There could be lots of reasons – fear, rebellion, anger – but we feel it's far more constructive simply to get them talking again rather than worry about why they're choosing not to communicate.'

Chloe gives a derisory sniff, frustration seeming to etch deeper the tiny lines around her mouth and eyes.

'I welcome anyone who can help us get the girls home, and I think my husband will feel the same way,' I say honestly. I feel Chloe's searing glance in my direction and turn to look at her. 'If Maddy and Brianna recognise Dana from school, they might just trust her enough to open up to someone independent. Someone who's neither their parent nor a police officer.'

'That's my hope too,' Dana says warmly. 'We've probably got two very frightened and confused little girls who think they'll get into even more trouble if they speak out of turn. Hopefully I can coax them to help themselves.'

'Brianna has already indicated through her silence and tears that she's confused and terrified,' Chloe says icily. 'I doubt she's suddenly going to relax and open up.'

'We'll see about that,' Dana said in a friendly but firm manner. 'Now, I just want to ask you a bit about the girls. What they love, what they dislike… all very easy stuff but could be crucial in the interview.'

After chatting to Dana a bit about the girls, we're led from Room 15A down the corridor into the viewing room. It's a small, windowless space, with one wall made entirely of glass, so we can see everything in the interview suite. 'When the girls are in here, you'll be able to see them and hear everything too. You're entitled to sit in with them during the session, but they're used to Carol now, and we hope you'll agree it may be better initially to keep them focused on the therapist.'

'Fine, but if Brianna gets upset, I want to be with her,' Chloe says in a clipped voice.

'Me too,' I add.

'Of course.' Neary nods. 'I appreciate you both agreeing to this.'

I text Tom to say what's happening and to ask if Josh is OK. I also text Beth to tell her about Dana Sewell's involvement in the case now I remember she's the one who told me the gossip in the first place. Movement through the glass pulls my attention away from my phone. Carol walks into the room holding the girls' hands, one each side of her.

She leads them to a low round table with several chairs set in the middle of the room.

I want to bang on the glass so that Maddy knows I'm here, but instead I close my eyes and offer up a silent prayer that Neary's plan works and our girls finally tell us what happened in Bessie Wilford's house.

17

The police station

Dana entered the comfortable family interview suite from the corridor, where the two girls were waiting in upholstered chairs. Carol sat slightly set back from the interview grouping.

The children were now dressed in their own clothes their grandparents had brought in from their house. The girl on the left, Maddy Fletcher, wore dark pink leggings and a long lemon and pink striped sweater. Her dark hair was gathered in a loose ponytail, framing a pale, slightly chubby face.

Brianna Voce was wearing a floral long-sleeved dress with ankle socks and trainers. Her slim legs were lightly tanned and she had a sportier look about her than her cousin, with her sun-kissed caramel-brown hair pulled back into a high ponytail.

Dana had been told there was just a couple of months between the cousins in age, but Brianna looked older, more poised somehow.

Before he'd taken her to meet Juliet and Chloe, Neary had furnished Dana with more information on the case, including some disturbing photographs of a badly injured Bessie Wilford taken as officers arrived at the crime scene.

The image of the old woman's neat grey hair matted with clumps of blood and brain matter would stay with her a long time.

Looking at the girls now, she knew she must eradicate the gruesome images from her mind. The only way to reach the truth was to start with a clean slate, to form her own crucially untainted opinion.

She had seen some horrific things in the ten years she'd worked with troubled youngsters – violent deeds, family abuse and acts of delinquency at a relatively young age – but her mind struggled to pair these two innocent-looking children with the vicious attack on great-grandmother Bessie.

'Hello, girls.' She sat down in the empty chair she'd asked to be positioned facing Maddy and Brianna across the low round coffee table. It was vital she keep the interaction as low-key and friendly as possible, and to that end she didn't offer a handshake, but smiled at both children instead.

The girls fidgeted in their seats and Maddy glanced briefly at Carol, but neither child returned Dana's greeting.

Still, her entrance had already told her something.

When she'd stepped into the room, Brianna's eyes had widened fractionally and fixed on her just a beat longer than was absolutely necessary. It suggested recognition, possibly from Dana's visits to school, and as far as she was concerned, recognition was a very good start when it came to gaining trust.

'First of all, I want to introduce myself. My name is Dana Sewell and I live in the same village you do. In fact, you may even recognise me, because I sometimes come to your school to talk to children there.'

Brianna's expression remained stony, while Maddy's heel began to bounce lightly on the floor.

These were the jewels that came from studying body language. In seconds, a single gesture or movement could tell a story of a thousand words. It was the reason Dana had asked to see the girls together without their parents present.

With no familiar adults in the room, she hoped to begin to garner an early impression of the relationship between the two young cousins. Irrespective of their backgrounds, when two juveniles carried out a deviant act together, it was highly likely that one of them was influential in the relationship.

She filled the silence with some additional information about herself.

'I want you to know I'm not a police officer or a teacher. I'm not a social worker or a doctor, either. I'm a family therapist, which means I'm here to help you and your parents and grandparents in any way I can.'

She turned her palms upwards and rested her hands on her knees. She was ultra-aware of her own body placement, careful not to cross her arms or legs in a defensive or threatening manner. She had also ensured that the seating area was arranged informally.

It didn't seem like much, but it was important to avoid subconscious barriers that might prevent the girls from opening up. The smallest details could stop them feeling they had the freedom to communicate in a way they had been unable to do so far with the other authority figures, including their own parents. Dana intended calling on every tiny trick in her considerable arsenal of experience to help her build rapport quickly.

'I know you must be feeling scared and confused,' she said gently. 'That's completely natural, but I'm here to help you help yourselves, if that makes sense. We can start to sort all this out, and we can do it together. The three of us. Does that sound OK?'

Maddy twisted her fingers together before stuffing her hands under her thighs. Brianna stared at Dana and blinked rapidly. It wasn't the verbal communication she'd hoped for, but it was a response of sorts and she felt a flicker of hope.

All signs of communication, no matter how tiny, must be logged and considered.

She assumed a pleasant but neutral expression, looking from one girl to the other in a relaxed manner. She wanted to give them space whilst encouraging them to feel safe in her presence. In a strange place, with a police officer still in the room, it wasn't the easiest task.

'A nod is fine,' she said so softly it was almost a whisper. 'Just so I know you both understand what I've said.'

But there was no response from either child.

Dana stood up and walked past Carol, over to the small window.

She lifted a couple of slats in the venetian blind and peered out at the car park with its small green verge and the red-brick housing estate beyond.

It was warm outside, oppressively so. The grey clouds hung heavy and low, and she could feel the heat of the sun trying to beat a path through. A downpour was needed. Something dramatic that could break up the humidity.

Behind her, the girls would be watching, trying to get the measure of her. They were possibly even glancing at each other. Silently communicating in some way.

The detectives in the viewing room would be watching for that, and Dana would be able to review the CCTV tape herself afterwards, which should hopefully offer up further clues.

After all, she had to bear in mind that these were ten-year-old girls, not hardened criminals or expert psychologists. They would make mistakes in ways they weren't even aware of, mistakes that would assist Dana in her quest to find out what had happened at Bessie Wilford's house that morning.

She stood at the window a few moments longer to allow the girls time to absorb just how ordinary she was. The fact Dana wore no uniform or official badges and there was no note-taking or awkward questions.

The message she was sending was a resolute *no threat*.

Thirty seconds later, she released the blind, the crack of the hard plastic slats fracturing the room's eerie silence like a gunshot.

As she walked slowly back to her seat, neither girl met her eyes.

'Fidget and Jasper,' Dana said simply. She sat down and inspected her short, unpolished nails.

Both girls' heads jerked towards her. Finally she had their attention.

18

Dana took her time, allowed a little space so the girls could think about what she'd just said.

'Nice names. Unusual names for pets. When I was your age, I had a cat and her name was Tabby. All the cats seemed to be called Tabby back then.' She grinned. 'I was wondering how you came up with those names?'

Silence, but their eyes remained on her.

'Fidget. I know he's a hamster, but does he belong to you, Maddy? Or perhaps he's your pet, Brianna?'

Juliet Fletcher had told her in the few minutes they chatted in Room 15A that Maddy thought the world of her hamster; that she'd had to forbid her daughter to get up in the middle of the night to talk to him.

'Not that it did any good,' she had added. 'She still does it most nights anyway. Even more so since she's not been sleeping so well.'

Maddy's chest moved faster. Her breathing had clearly sped up. She was keen to hear how her pet was.

'And I know Jasper is a dog. A Staffie, I think. Is he yours, Brianna?' Dana paused, watched as Brianna pressed her lips together as if she was physically preventing words from slipping out of her mouth. 'It's a lovely friendly name, Jasper. I really like it.'

She allowed a few more moments of silence before she put them out of their misery.

'Well, I want you to know that I checked with your families, and Jasper and Fidget are doing fine.' She saw both girls exhale. 'I'm sure they're really missing you and want you back home as soon as possible. That's another reason I want to help you to help the police understand what happened today. I want to get you back home to your pets.'

Maddy's eyes shone, threatening tears, but she blinked until they cleared. Brianna stared down at the floor, her hands laced in front of her, one thumbnail carving into the soft skin at the bottom of her index finger.

'Maddy, Brianna, you're both intelligent girls. I don't need to tell you how serious this situation is. You must understand that saying nothing at all can only make things worse.'

Dana's favoured interview method was short but regular interactions. She now felt she'd reached the potential of this first interview, and despite the girls' continuing silence, she would count it as being a positive start.

There were results to be tallied here. Both children had shown signs of emotion, and they had clearly responded non-verbally when their pets were mentioned. Yet there was nothing at all yet to separate the two of them.

The clock was ticking and Neary's superiors were getting twitchy. But there was still time for a breakthrough.

Patience was key.

When she'd finished writing up her notes following the interview, Dana went to Neary's office to review the visual recording.

A relieved-looking Conor patted her on the back. 'It went well; there are already signs of improvement there. The pet thing was genius. I know that if anyone can get to the truth, you can.'

The hair above his ears stuck out at odd angles, he had a coffee spill on his tie and his eyes were red-rimmed. The last thing Dana wanted was to rain on his parade, but she couldn't shake the feeling. She had to speak up.

'There's something else I want to try.' She hesitated. 'Something's just not sitting right.'

'You want to speak to the girls individually?' He ran his fingers through his hair. 'I think that's a good idea, but you want my honest opinion? You've nearly cracked them, so I think you should apply a bit more pressure. We're fast running out of—'

'That's not it,' Dana interrupted. 'I mean, I do still want to speak to them alone, I think it's important, but before that, I want to talk to the family. All of them, together. I suspect the fact that the girls have been so stubbornly silent is a symptom of something far bigger. In my opinion, this is a family that's holding secrets, operating within invisible boundaries. The answers to our questions about what happened in that house lie there.'

'I'm only interested in what happened to Bessie Wilford.' Neary frowned. 'I've neither the time nor the inclination to get bogged down in family politics.'

'It's not about that.' Dana pressed on. 'Kids pick up so much stuff without us noticing. I suspect we're dealing with a highly dysfunctional family unit here.'

'The family seem perfectly normal to me.' He shook his head dismissively. 'They're bound to be stressed and act a little odd at a time like this.'

'I agree, any family would be stressed given the situation,' Dana said. 'But trust me, Conor, this is not any family. This is a family that's hiding something. I can feel it in the spaces between their words and the odd dynamic between them all. This may be our only chance to find out what.'

Dana had been meaning to start back at the gym regularly for months now but hadn't managed it yet, just the occasional visit.

She was tied in to an eighteen-month contract so had been forced to continue the monthly payments even though she hadn't used the facilities enough to justify the expense. It bugged her every time she checked her bank statement.

There always seemed to be a sound reason not to go as planned: something she wanted to watch on TV, an important task she needed to get done at home like wash the tea towels. She was aware of all the ways her lack of confidence after the job ordeal showed itself but it didn't make it any easier to deal with it.

When she left the police station, she made a snap decision and drove to the gym rather than back home. Her packed workout bag had been in the boot for weeks, a habit Orla had encouraged her to adopt.

It had been over three years since Orla had moved back to Dublin. Dana had been very sad their relationship broke up but in the end, they'd wanted different things and they had both agreed it was for the best.

Strangely, it was the break-up and a rare gym visit that had paved the way for her meeting Lizzie.

She parked up and walked into the large, airy reception of the gym, striding purposefully with her bag, hoping the nervousness didn't show on her face. She waved her membership card at the electronic monitor, a beep sounded, a green light lit up and she walked through the turnstile; it felt like she'd never been away. Her mood lifted as she headed for the smart changing rooms with the piped music.

After she changed and deposited her bag in a locker, she walked to the spinning room and chose a bike on the third row back. The class was nearly full and there was a pleasant buzz which made Dana feel at home, even though she didn't actually speak to anyone.

It reminded her of the day she met Lizzie here.

The music started for the warm-up and Dana had felt exhilarated. She'd done it! Such great strides in one day: there had been a visit to the station to discuss a forthcoming job with Conor Neary, and now the gym. Life had felt good for the first time in a long time.

A woman had entered the class late, selecting the spare bike next to her.

Just as the music ramped up, the woman had slipped, nearly falling off the equipment. Dana had jumped off her own bike and quickly adjusted the seat height and handlebars for her so she was able to complete the class.

'Thanks,' the woman had told her at the end of class. 'That could've been so embarrassing. I'm Lizzie.'

'Dana.' She'd shook her small, warm hand.

The woman was diminutive, with a sad air about her, and she had the most incredible amber-flecked brown eyes that complemented her caramel-coloured hair perfectly. Dana remembered thinking she looked like the kind of person who could do with someone to lean on.

Over lattes and polite conversation in the gym café that Lizzie insisted on buying, Dana had felt herself melt a little inside.

Was it too much to hope that her life was finally back on track?

19

Juliet

All the rooms in this place are faceless, and I sit in one of them now with Chloe, waiting for Carol to bring the girls through to see us.

I didn't recognise Maddy in that interview; Brianna either, for that matter. Our girls are usually so full of energy and life; it's a constant battle to get a word in edgeways when the two of them are together.

And now… now, they won't make a sound, even though at times I can see Maddy battling to swallow down the words.

The only thing that makes sense is that they are traumatised. But how, why…? We think we know our children so well, but is it possible that they are actually capable of such a terrible crime?

I once read a magazine article about how to spot the signs of a killer in childhood. I remember it was in the dentist's surgery, a way of passing ten minutes' waiting time when I got there early. Never for a second did I suspect that such subject matter would ever apply to my family.

Setting fires, hurting small animals, uncontrollable aggression and general callousness were all mentioned amongst other horrible behaviours that I felt relieved my daughter had never displayed.

Maddy is a kind girl. She loves her family, loves animals and has shown no aggressive or dangerous behaviours that could possibly indicate that anything is amiss.

Could I ever imagine her hurting an elderly lady? Never in a million years.

Likewise, I'm certain Brianna has never displayed any such awful tendencies, although in my opinion, she isn't as placid a personality as Maddy. I've seen her swing in the space of a few minutes from acting upset and crying to breaking one of Mum's precious Royal Doulton figurines in the throes of a temper.

Mum and Dad have now gone home to get some rest and feed Jasper. They've texted Chloe to say there are rubberneckers on the street, people from out of the area shouting questions about what has happened. Sounds like they've gathered at both our houses, judging by Beth's earlier text warning of people looking through our windows. I expect Mum may soon be back in bed with a headache if it continues.

I still haven't heard back from Tom but he should have picked up Josh from his school trip by now. I tried calling him but it went through to voicemail.

There are pepperoni pizzas I bought yesterday waiting in the fridge, with Josh's favourite Ben & Jerry's cookie dough ice cream for afters. It was to be his welcome home tea, where he could tell us all about his survival adventure at Hathersage.

We'd have sat together around the kitchen table and learned how to construct a shelter in bad weather, which wild berries and mushrooms were safe to eat and how long it had taken Josh to spark together two sticks to make a fire.

Now our priority has got to be explaining the situation with Maddy in a sensitive but truthful way that Josh can understand. We agreed that Tom will broach the subject on the journey here, and then we'll fill in a few more details together.

It occurs to me that I haven't thought through what I'm going to do with Josh while Maddy is still being questioned. Under the circumstances, I don't feel comfortable letting him go to Mum and Dad's. It might seem unfair, but I can't deny the lack of trust I now have in their ability to keep my children safe.

I look over at my sister. She's a bag of nerves, scratching, fidgeting, blindly leafing through magazines and tossing them down again. She doesn't want to chat, that much is obvious. I can sense one of her brooding moods coming on.

There's so much waiting involved. We're all at the mercy of other people, telling us the next procedure that must be followed, when all we want is for this nightmare to be over.

It's that lack of control I find most difficult to cope with.

I just want to take Maddy home, wrap her up in her favourite fleece blanket and cuddle her close. But I can feel the chances of that fading with every minute that passes.

There's a tap at the door and Dana Sewell comes in.

'I just wanted to say that I think that went well for a first session,' she says. 'There was lots of non-verbal communication.'

'We're not going to find out what happened in that house through *non-verbal* communication, though, are we?' Chloe indicates speech marks in the air.

Dana completely blanks her comment, and I feel a glow of admiration.

'I also came in to offer private therapy sessions to you both. DI Neary has approved this.'

'What do *we* need therapy for?' Chloe huffs. 'The focus should be on the girls.'

Dana thinks for a moment. 'Kids are very good at picking up underlying tensions in families. It might be useful for us to explore that angle.'

'Not interested,' Chloe says shortly. 'It's not therapy I need; it's getting my daughter back home that's important.'

'I wouldn't mind a session,' I say quietly.

'That's great, Juliet. I'll sort out a time with DI Neary.' Dana smiles and leaves the room

When I look up, Chloe is staring at me.

'Mum says Maddy is always dragging Brianna outside to play,' she remarks spitefully, nibbling at a fingernail. 'Never happy just to play in Bree's bedroom or watch stuff on TV these days, she says.'

I look at her blankly. 'I suppose that's understandable given the nice weather, isn't it? Kids like to be outside.'

'Hmm, maybe.' Her voice suddenly sharpens. 'Juliet, are you sure Maddy didn't talk about this Bessie Wilford woman? She's never mentioned her to you at all?'

I pull the corners of my mouth down and shake my head. 'Not to my knowledge. What about Brianna?'

'Oh, I'm certain Bree doesn't know her well. She'd have told me.'

I prickle at the implication that lies beneath her words. Maddy's the one who wanted to play outside, Maddy's the one who knew Bessie Wilford.

'Well, Maddy talks to us about everything too, and she's never mentioned her, but they did both meet her at Mum's. We know that.'

Chloe twists a piece of hair around her finger.

'It's just that… well, Maddy's the quieter one, isn't she? More secretive. Like Mum always says, Brianna can't hold her water; she finds it impossible to keep anything a secret. Remember when she ruined Dad's surprise birthday tea last year because of her obvious excitement? She's always been the same. It's just not in her nature to be silent.'

I know what she's getting at; she's trying to say it must be all Maddy's doing.

I don't want to be drawn into an argument, but neither can I sit and listen to her casting unfounded doubt on my daughter like that.

'Silence doesn't suggest someone is more likely to beat an old lady around the head,' I say icily. 'If we're looking for differences between the girls, then Brianna's temper needs to be flagged up.'

'What are you trying to say?'

'I'm discussing the girls' personalities just like you are,' I say lightly. 'But we can second-guess all day. The only thing that's going to help is to get them talking. We have to know what happened in that house.'

'But what if one of them *did* do it, Juliet?'

'Huh?'

'We know that when the police arrived they were halfway up the street and they both had blood on them. We keep refusing to believe they had anything to do with the attack, but what if one of them did kill Bessie Wilford and the other one is innocent?'

I'm shocked that she can even utter the words.

'It's impossible.' Every fibre of my being rebels against the thought. 'I refuse to believe either of them could be capable of doing such a thing. It must have been some kind of awful accident.'

'We can't dispute they were there.' Chloe's voice drops low.

'Then why don't they just say so?' I counter.

'Juliet, we have to consider that one of them might have killed Bessie Wilford by accident and one of them could be completely blameless. We can't let *both* their lives be ruined because we refuse to face the facts.'

But I know the only fact Chloe would be willing to face is Brianna's innocence. She might not be so keen on Maddy escaping punishment if the opposite scenario proves to be the case.

Punishment… innocence and guilt… My head feels woozy, as if I've been drinking.

'I need some air.' I stand up.

'We need to talk about this stuff, unpleasant though it is,' Chloe says curtly as I take a step forward. 'You can't just keep running away from it.'

I close the door behind me and lean against the cool plaster of the wall in the corridor outside.

I know just how quickly things can escalate when my family want to point the finger of blame. It sounds as if Mum and Chloe have been discussing which of the girls might be responsible for the attack and Maddy has come off worse.

Time in this place drags while we wait continually for the next step, the next scrap of news. But then, in a matter of seconds, it flashes forward so terrifyingly quickly that I feel breathless with the dreadful possibilities of what could happen to Maddy if this ghastly mess isn't sorted out soon.

The corridor is quiet and cool and I feel my breathing begin to return to normal.

I've been a fixer for as long as I can remember. As a child, if anyone in the family had a problem – Mum, Chloe, even Dad – I'd get this clenching ache in my stomach that meant I couldn't rest until I'd figured out how to make it all right again.

Even if it meant taking the blame myself.

Of course, most of the time I just got in the way. I suppose I must have seemed quite the little busybody. But it came from a good place, whatever people might have thought of me.

I find parenting Maddy easy. Most of the time she accepts my guidance, although there have been a few incidents at home in recent months that show she's definitely forming her own opinions.

Tom finds my willingness to advise more irritating. I struggle to find a balance between helpful suggestion and interference, like the day before his interview, when he was deciding what to wear.

'You've got to strike the right balance, Tom.' I eyed the mid-blue Ted Baker suit he'd selected from his wardrobe. 'I think the navy one would be better.'

'But they've got a young leadership team there.' He hesitated, held the suit away from him to study it and then tucked it back into the wardrobe.

I watched as he deflated in front of me, his enthusiasm dissipated by my apparent criticism, which was really only a keenness to help. There was little I could do to stop myself.

Right now, I feel the need to fix things. It's building inside me like a furnace, and there's nowhere for it to go. A door opens further down the corridor and Carol steps out. She looks at me quizzically but I don't explain why I'm standing out here on my own.

'I was just about to come up to see you both,' she says. 'The girls will be interviewed again at five o'clock.

That's in one hour's time. I hope Tom gets back with Josh for then.

20

2003

'For goodness' sake, I can't hear myself think. Get that noisy little sod out from under my feet,' Joan Voce snapped, pinching the top of her nose. 'This headache is never going to go away in this heat if I don't get some peace and quiet.'

'You go and have a lie-down, love,' Ray soothed, steering her to the bottom of the stairs. 'I'll bring you up a cuppa.'

He watched his wife's slim figure as she climbed slowly upstairs. She was a striking woman even when she felt unwell, like today. Raven-black hair and creamy skin, with piercing green eyes.

Ray was under no illusion he was very lucky to have her. He knew he was the envy of all the men he worked with at the factory.

Joan was very nearly perfect, if she could only curb that temper of hers. That would just be the icing on the cake. Still, you couldn't have everything, he supposed.

He walked into the kitchen and across to the sink to fill the kettle. The two girls were sitting quietly at the table. Juliet always had her nose in a book, and if keen gymnast Chloe wasn't bending her body in all manner of strange shapes out in the back garden, she was sketching like she was doing today.

Sometimes Ray privately thought they'd have been better not having children at all. Joan hadn't seemed that fussed after they got married, and Ray admitted it was he who had pushed for them. But he hadn't realised just how much attention his wife needed. How she quickly wilted under pressure and couldn't bear too much noise.

Of course, he'd never said as much to her.

Their two girls were now thirteen and fifteen and were quite grown up. Chloe had been the first, and Ray remembered how happy he'd felt that Joan adored her and bonded immediately.

She had wanted to stick with just the one child but eventually agreed it would be nice for Chloe to have a brother or sister. Ray had been so happy, he'd barely registered that Joan was noticeably less affectionate and maternal towards Juliet. Later, he wondered if it was because she had somehow felt steamrollered into the decision.

And then, out of the blue eight years later, baby Corey had come along. He'd just turned five now and was a little live wire who barely slept a wink. He lived his life in an almost constant state of activity, always doing, never resting… and you could never feed the lad enough, yet he was skinny as a rake.

It was too much for Joan, and she'd all but downed tools when it came to caring for the boy, so Ray and the girls had learned to pick up most of the slack, keeping Corey entertained and out of Joan's hair.

Ray had lost many hours of sleep himself, trying to work out why it had never been like this with either of the girls when they were tiny. Could it be that he and Joan were just so much older and less able to cope now?

Then last year, Dr Rahman had finally diagnosed Corey with ADHD. Ray had felt a tremendous weight lift from his shoulders. At last they were able to explain why nothing seemed to work when it came to calming Corey down.

It wasn't that they were bad parents or incompetent after all.

He and Joan had attended a course for parents of children with ADHD. It had covered the implications and how families might best support their child.

'How long will he be like this?' Joan had asked the nurse who ran the session.

'Probably for the rest of his life,' she had answered.

Ray would never forget the look on Joan's face in that moment. Something had dimmed in her eyes, as if a spark of light had just been extinguished.

But things got better. Corey was prescribed Ritalin, which helped to quieten him down, enabled him to focus more effectively and even to sleep better some nights.

Ray also spoke to the girls, explained that they'd need to take on more responsibility in looking after their brother.

He flicked the kettle on now and frowned as Corey burst into the kitchen making aeroplane noises, with his arms stuck out at right angles.

'I'm a jumbo jet,' he screeched. 'And you're all in my flight path.'

Ray snagged one of his arms as he juddered by in an effort to stop him.

'Hey, quieten down. Mummy's just gone upstairs for a nap.'

Corey shrugged him off and flew on into the living room, engine noise louder than ever.

'Come on, girls,' Ray sighed. 'I need you to take your brother to the park for an hour until it's time for his tea. If he can run off some of that energy, we might even get him to bed on time tonight.'

Everybody suffered when Corey wouldn't give in to his tiredness. It was virtually impossible to watch anything on television with him dashing noisily around in his pyjamas. On those days, Ray usually took him into the kitchen so Joan could watch *Coronation Street* in peace.

Chloe ignored her father's plea, but Juliet sighed and closed her book.

'Get your shoes on, Corey,' she called. 'We're going to the park.' Although she felt exhausted from being awake half the night coughing from a persistent chest infection, the park was only just around the corner and a few breaths of fresh air might help to give her a better night's rest.

Seconds later, her brother scooted back through, still in jumbo jet mode.

'Don't wanna go to the park. I want to make a den.' He circled his father, forcing Ray to pause in pouring boiling water into Joan's mug.

Juliet sighed. 'Fine. We'll go down the warren and make a den, then.'

The warren was a swathe of green-belt land about a twenty-minute walk away, opposite Mutton Hill. It was an oasis of bracken, trees and steep hills with plenty of places for kids to build concealed hideouts. Corey loved it there.

Ray glanced gratefully at Juliet. She'd been quite unwell herself and was still taking the strong cough medicine the doctor had prescribed for the bronchial infection she'd had for nearly two weeks now. She looked pale and tired, and Ray felt a spike of concern. She wasn't one to complain and he made a mental note to keep a watchful eye on her.

'I'll get his shoes.' Juliet left the room and Ray heard her open the under-stairs cupboard where they kept their coats and walking footwear.

He looked at Chloe, who continued sketching quietly as if she hoped nobody might notice she was still there.

'Our Juliet's still quite poorly, love. She shouldn't really be going out on her own; it's sweltering out there and it's quite a walk to the warren and back.'

'But it's all right for me to bake to death in the tropical heat?' Chloe said snarkily. 'Nice.'

'Hardly tropical,' Ray scoffed. It was the beginning of August, and the country was in the iron grip of a heatwave that had broken nearly all records. A hosepipe ban had been imposed and the newspapers were full of advice about how to care for the elderly and pets. It amused Ray that the very same villagers who complained about the snow and freezing temperatures in winter were now moaning non-stop about the heat. 'Take a drink and suncream. It'll be a nice stroll out.'

'He's *your* son, why can't you take him?' Chloe retorted, carefully shading in the trunk of an oak tree she'd drawn on her pad.

'I have to look after your mother,' Ray said, finally pouring boiling water into Joan's delicate china mug.

Chloe didn't reply, but set her drawing pad and pencil aside. They all knew that there'd be hell to pay for days on end if Joan's headache worsened and she was unable to shift it with painkillers and lots of quiet rest.

'Dad says I've got to come with you to take the little monster out,' Chloe grudgingly told Juliet when her sister came back into the kitchen. 'I really wanted to finish my drawing, too. I can't always get back in the creative zone if I'm interrupted.'

'It's OK, Chloe, you don't have to come.' Juliet slathered suncream on her pale arms. 'I'm not going to stay out long anyway.'

'Well, if you're sure…' Chloe relaxed back into her seat and picked up her pencil again.

Ray scowled at her, but she was already immersed in her artwork and didn't even look at him.

'Thanks, love.' Ray smiled fondly at Juliet. 'See you when you get back.'

He smiled to himself as he headed upstairs with Joan's tea. He might have a lie-down himself for half an hour in the cooler back bedroom, enjoy the brief peace and quiet.

Little did he know that it was going to be a long, long night.

The worst night of his entire life, in fact.

21

Juliet

Carol informs us that we're moving to a purpose-built facility on the edge of Mansfield at about seven o'clock, which is in three hours' time.

'You'll be more comfortable there, and although it's a secure unit and the girls won't be able to leave, there's a more relaxed feel to the place. You'll have your own rooms and a private bathroom, so I suggest you use the next couple of hours to get together anything you want to take there with you.'

I shiver and cross my hands in front of me, rubbing my goose-bump-covered upper arms. The harsh reality of our situation has cranked up a notch.

Up until now, I've just about managed to convince myself that the detectives will have some kind of breakthrough and we'll be able to take Maddy home tonight after all.

When I was in the police car earlier, travelling to the station, I truly believed she'd be released within the hour. If someone accuses your child of something so awful and you'd wager your life they are innocent, then waiting for the realisation that the police are wrong doesn't seem so silly.

But in telling us we're moving so they can keep the girls over-night, Carol just shattered all my illusions. She doesn't realise it, but she has broken my heart.

Tom texts me to ask me to meet him outside in the car park, and I go there right away without speaking to anyone else. I need a hug right now, and so will Tom when I tell him they're keeping Maddy until tomorrow.

He's parked over the far side, and as I approach, I spot Josh's little face pressed up against the window. My heart leaps inside me, with joy for once instead of dread. I realise just how much I've wanted to see my son, hold him close, since this nightmare began.

I pull open the door and he almost tumbles out. He squirms a bit as I cuddle him too tightly, too hard. Still, he doesn't complain.

'I've missed you so much; let me take a look at that handsome face.' I hold his shoulders and push him back slightly. The smile fades on my lips. 'Josh… what's wrong?'

His red-rimmed eyes and trembling mouth tell me all I need to know.

'Tom?' I duck down and look into the car. 'I've been texting you, ringing you but your phone was off.'

'Just get in for a few minutes, Jules, while I explain.'

I get in the back seat with Josh so I can continue to hold him close as Tom tells me that Josh already knew all about Maddy before he even returned to school.

'How can that be?' I say faintly.

'A few people had brought their phones on the trip,' Josh sniffs miserably. 'They had to hand them in on the first day for safekeeping, but the teacher gave them back when we got on the bus to come home, and Bradley Macken's mum had sent him a text to say Maddy had been arrested.'

'She hasn't been arrested yet.' I roll my eyes in fury. Parents acting like juveniles, spreading gossip via their own kids! I'd like nothing more than to give Bradley bloody Macken's mother a piece of my mind right now.

It unnerves me, hearing Maddy's name and the word 'arrest' paired together so casually. Other people are peddling inaccuracies that mean nothing to them but have the power to wreck our lives.

I shiver, even though it's stifling in the car.

Josh rests his damp cheek on my shoulder.

'It was horrible, Mum.' His voice is muffled as he speaks into my arm. 'After Bradley got the text, the others who had phones started googling and reading out what had happened. Then someone started a chant about Maddy being sent to prison.'

I feel heat rising through my chest and neck.

'And what the hell were the teachers doing while all this was happening?' Tom fumes.

'Mrs Carrington took their phones back until we got off the bus,' Josh said. 'But it was too late then because everyone knew about it. Leo moved seats.'

A lump rises in my throat and I battle not to throw up. I open my mouth to ask Josh more questions, but there's a disconnect between my thoughts and my voice. Nothing comes out.

'Shall I take him to your mum and dad's?' Tom watches me.

'No!' I snap.

Josh pulls away, a little startled. He looks at Tom and back at me.

'Why? Why can't I go to Gran and Grandad's?'

'Because… it's not convenient right now. They've got a lot on their minds.'

'It's better than him staying at the station though, surely?' Tom dips his chin and looks at me meaningfully.

I doubt there'll be a bed for Josh at the new unit. We've got to try and protect him from all this, but both Tom and I need to be close to Maddy right now.

I'm aware that it's totally unfair of me, but I silently curse Tom's parents for taking their annual holiday at the worst possible time.

'I want to see Maddy,' Josh says quietly. 'Is she in a cell?'

'No, no. It's not like that, Josh,' I try and reassure him. 'They're just asking her and Brianna lots of questions so we can find out exactly what happened.'

'Maddy wouldn't do that, she wouldn't hurt Bessie.'

I look at him. Something about the way he referred to Bessie nearly made my heart stop. I glance at Tom, but I can see it hasn't registered with him.

'Josh, did you know Bessie Wilford?'

His pale face flushes a little.

'Not really,' he says in a small voice. 'I only went with them there once.'

My mouth drops open and Tom's brow furrows. He turns more fully in his seat to face us in the back.

'You've been to Bessie Wilford's house with Maddy and Brianna?' He is struggling to keep his voice level.

Josh swallows hard and his hand grips mine a little tighter.

'You're not in trouble, Josh. It's just very important that your dad and I know every scrap of truth.'

'You're not in trouble at all, champ.' Tom smiles, but it looks more like a grimace. 'But we're a team, you, me, Mum and Maddy, and teams have to work together, right?'

'Right,' Josh whispers.

'So you just went to Bessie's house once with Maddy?'

'Yes, Dad.'

'And Brianna was there too?'

Josh nods.

'Now this next bit is really important,' Tom says. 'Can you remember exactly when it was you went there?'

Josh thinks. 'It was our last school holiday. May half-term, I think, Dad. We were at Grandma and Grandad's for a few days.'

'That's great, buddy. And can you remember why the girls went to see Bessie?'

Josh shrugs. 'I think she asked them to.'

Tom and I look at each other.

'She did?' I say lightly. 'How did she do that? She lives on the outskirts of the village.'

Josh opens his mouth to speak, and then hesitates.

'It's OK, Josh. You and Maddy won't get into trouble for any of this. We just need to know all the facts so we can protect you both. Do you know how Bessie managed to ask the girls to visit her?'

He nods, and I feel his grip on my fingers loosen a little.

'She rang and invited her,' Josh says.

He's not making much sense and I start to wonder if he's over-tired after the trip.

'Maddy hasn't got a phone though, poppet. You know we've always said she has to wait until she goes to senior school.'

'Bessie left a voicemail on her secret phone.' Josh shoots me a sideways glance. 'The one she's hidden in her bedroom.'

22

I kiss Josh on the top of his head.

'You did the right thing telling us all this.' I smile at him. 'Sit here for just a minute; I need to have a word with Dad.'

Tom and I get out of the car, closing the doors behind us.

'Carol just told us we're moving to a juvenile detention centre in Mansfield. It sounds horrible, but it will be better as we get a private bedroom there, so we can stay tonight.'

Tom looks shocked. 'They're keeping them overnight?'

I nod. 'I feel like she's slipping away from us with every hour that passes. But listen, it's not the right place for Josh.' I glance towards the car; our son is pressing his nose to the window, watching us forlornly. 'I'm not happy him going to my parents' house, for obvious reasons, so I'm going to ask Beth to look after him. She's been texting me loads anyway, asking if there's anything she can do.'

Tom nods. 'Sounds like the best option under the circumstances.' He runs his fingers through his hair. 'I can't believe Maddy kept a secret phone from us. What else don't we know about that she got up to?'

'Don't even think that, never mind say it,' I tell him sharply. 'There are enough people out there who want to believe Maddy is guilty of something she can't possibly have done. She doesn't need us turning against her as well.'

He hangs his head guiltily and nods.

'Kids are kids,' I add. 'They do silly things, hide stuff from their parents. It doesn't make Maddy the monster everyone is trying to say she is online.'

Tom blows out a long breath.

'I just... I don't know, I'm *shocked*. I would have bet my life that she wouldn't do anything remotely deceitful.'

'Yes, well, we didn't conceive an angel, Tom. She's always been mischievous, you know that... remember the bathroom flooding incident at the dance school and the prank with Mum's neighbour's cat?' I'm snappy, but it's only to disguise my own shock that my daughter could be capable of flouting what she knows is an important rule to me: no phone until senior school. That somehow she's got hold of one and proceeded to hide it from us.

It makes me go cold just to think about it. But I don't want to get bogged down on this point.

I know she didn't kill Bessie Wilford and that's all that matters.

Tom sighs. 'Listen, I know it's bad timing, but because of the special circumstances, the HR manager has agreed to meet me before she finishes at six. I'm going to need some time off while we get Maddy through all this.'

'OK, but just sit in the car with Josh for now, will you? Just while I call Beth. I'll ask if she can come and get him right away.'

Tom nods, his face as troubled as mine, and I turn away and walk over to the side of the building.

Beth picks up on the second ring, and I just sort of vomit everything out in one sentence: Josh's trip, the bullying comments, the fact that the girls are due to be interviewed again in about an hour by the family therapist.

'And then to top it all, they've just told us they're keeping the girls overnight, so we have to relocate to the juvenile detention centre in Mansfield.'

'So you want me to have Josh until tomorrow? That's no problem at all. I'm not at work until the afternoon.' I hear the rattle of her keys. 'I'm on my way right now.'

That's one of the things I love about Beth: she's so practical. She has this ability to make my problems seem straightforward when I'm inclined to wrap them up in barbed wire until I can't see a way to solve them.

She knows what it's like to lose a brother, the way we lost Corey. Over the years, she has always been there to cushion the guilt arrows from my own family and reassure me that I'm not a bad person.

'I know you'd have laid down your life for him, Jules,' she once told me sadly. 'The way I would've gladly put myself in that car instead of Andrew.'

Beth's brother was travelling home from a weekend break at Butlin's with his best friend's family. They were just three miles from the village on a busy dual carriageway when a car coming the other way hit them head-on. Andrew was the only person who didn't die at the scene.

Mum was still working part-time at King's Mill Hospital when he was brought in by the ambulance crew.

'His injuries were far too severe for him to live,' she told us afterwards. 'He never regained consciousness.'

It almost killed Beth to know he was alive and all alone for two hours after the accident. She blamed herself that she didn't get to see him before he died, but Mum sat down with her, held her hand and tried to set her mind at rest.

'The team did everything they could for him, Beth, love. He didn't suffer.'

It was the first time I realised that Mum was able to transform herself into another person altogether, becoming this caring, sensitive soul who, with a few well-chosen words, was able to really help Beth. I remember wondering why she was never able to show us, her own family, that side of her nature.

Losing our brothers bound Beth and me even tighter together. Much to Chloe's annoyance.

Seeing that each other's guilt was unfounded helped a little, even though we weren't able to forgive ourselves.

Beth arrives ten minutes later. She jumps out of her car and folds both me and Josh into her arms.

'I've been worried sick. I'm so glad you called,' she sniffs, her eyes shining. 'Where's Tom?'

'He's had to go into work, and then he's going to get more clothes and stuff from the house.'

I feel bad not keeping her up to speed with what's been happening.

'I'm sorry, there just seem to have been a thousand things to do,' I tell her. 'But thanks for being here and for offering to look after Josh.'

'Sorry I can't stay with you a while,' she says. 'I've got an online food shop delivery scheduled.' Beth lives in Newstead, a village just a couple of miles away.

'I'm really sorry to muck up your plans,' I apologise. 'Just take your rucksack with you to Beth's, Josh. I can sort out your dirty clothes and stuff tomorrow.'

'I want to stay here with you and Dad.' Josh scowls, folding his arms. 'And I want to see Maddy.'

'You can see her soon, I promise, sweetie.' I kiss the top of his head again.

'But when will she be home?' he demands.

I look at Beth. 'We're not sure yet, Josh. Soon, I hope.'

There's no conviction in my words, and it's painful to hear. Josh looks at me a little fearfully. I think he can sense the emptiness, how things have changed.

Beth holds out her hand to him. 'I've got two words to say to you, Josh Fletcher. Pizza and Netflix. Coming?'

He tries to keep frowning, but his mouth softens and finally he takes her hand.

'Good man.' Beth winks at me. 'Let me know what's happening soon as you hear anything. I've got a spare key to the industrial unit, so I can be there for the delivery in the morning if you need me to be.'

I hit my forehead with the heel of my hand. 'It completely slipped my mind! You're a lifesaver, Beth, thank you.'

My head hurts with the effort of trying to juggle everything that needs to be done. Right now, I can't see even a *glimmer* of light at the end of the tunnel.

23

I look at my watch and see I've got forty-five minutes before the girls are interviewed again. What I need to do will take about half an hour if I get a move on.

I haven't said a word about my plans to anyone else, even Tom. I didn't really even make up my mind to do it until Beth agreed to look after Josh, but now I'm decided.

I'm going back to our house. Alone. I just hope Tom doesn't decide to pop back home and I bump into him there. He wouldn't approve.

Tom has taken the car, so I open my Uber app and order a cab. They estimate a five-minute pick-up time. I don't want to risk bumping into Chloe or the detectives while I wait, so I walk quickly across the car park and out onto the road.

I sit on a low brick wall to wait, and start questioning my decision. What am I hoping to find? The answer to that is easy: Maddy's secret phone.

If I do find it, what will I discover on there? Josh has already said that Bessie left a voicemail message asking Maddy to visit back in May. It's July now, so there might have been more messages since.

If I find the phone, then it is evidence, and if the police decide to arrest the girls, they might well search our houses. Do I seriously want to be in a position where I hide possible evidence from the police? Of course not.

But I don't want there to be any nasty surprises either.

I could cancel the Uber and focus on what's happening here at the police station. Maybe new evidence will come to light and the girls will be released without charge.

I look up as a silver Nissan turns the corner. My cab has arrived.

The journey takes twelve minutes. I use the time to formulate a plan in my head. It covers what I'll say if I bump into anyone – I'll explain politely that I'm not able to discuss anything at this point – and precisely what I'll do when I'm inside the house.

I haven't got much time, so I won't waste time picking up clean clothes; Tom can do that when he gets back and before we go to the new facility in Mansfield.

It's paramount that I'm back in time to sit in on the girls' next session with Dana Sewell.

Increasingly I feel like Tom and I are Maddy's only supporters, with my parents and Chloe slowly moving into Brianna's corner.

'You can drop me off just up here…' My voice fades as I spot an enormous crowd of people right about where the cab is going to pull up. 'Actually, I'll jump out now, thanks.'

'They'll be here for the murder of that old lady.' The driver shakes his head as the car comes to a standstill. 'Terrible business, isn't it? They ought to throw the book at those two girls, kids or not.'

'Have you heard of the saying innocent until proven guilty?' I snap before slipping out of the car and flinging the door shut harder than necessary.

I'm about two hundred and fifty yards from the crowd. They certainly don't look a friendly lot, but this is my house and my daughter has not yet been charged. I'm damned if I'm going to cower from this motley crew.

As I get closer, people begin to turn around and whisper to each other. Suddenly a roar seems to go up and they all rush towards me.

'Mrs Fletcher, has your daughter admitted to killing Bessie Wilford?'

'Will you be accompanying the girls to the juvenile detention centre, Mrs Fletcher?'

We've only just found out ourselves that they're transferring Maddy and Brianna. These people must have a hotline to confidential police information.

Photographers battle their way to the front of the mob, sticking cameras in my face as I walk. I mustn't stop, because they'll surround me and prevent me from moving.

The noise feels like I'm at a football match with Josh. Everyone yelling and shouting different things at the same time. I can't hear myself think.

'No comment,' I say firmly, but my voice is lost amongst the noise. Even though I'm nearly at the front gate, I wonder if I'm going to make it. My legs are shaking and I feel light-headed, but I have to stay strong. For Maddy's sake, I have to do this.

I can barely hear anything coherent now amidst the collective roar. The odd poisonous word or phrase manages to escape and worm its way into my ears. *Killer… murderer… parental neglect.*

I keep my eyes trained on the pavement and forge ahead as microphones are pushed close to my face. I'm making slow progress, but I'm nearly there. I'm very nearly there.

I push open the creaking gate that I've been asking Tom to fix for weeks now and look at the house. A gasp catches in my throat and I stall momentarily.

KILLER! RIP BESSIE W!

The shocking words have been daubed in foot-high black letters on the pristine white garage door we had fitted last year.

People are so close, pushing behind me now. I can hear them breathing and I force myself forward and up the path, turning only to shout as loudly as I can, 'This is private property. Keep out!'

I've made a terrible, terrible mistake coming here. I knew the locals would be buzzing with the awful gossip, but I didn't expect *this*… this lynch mob.

Moisture prickles my forehead and my hands shake as I fish blindly in my handbag for my keys. The shouting continues, structured questions from reporters mixed with insults from locals intending to shock.

I try not to listen, focusing on just getting inside the house.

I push the key at the lock again and again, but for some reason, it isn't going in. I hear mocking laughter from the crowd, and when I peer closer, I see the lock has been encased in a bulbous ball of hardened glue.

I walk around the side of the house without looking back. It's cool here at the back. I wish I could stay here a while to calm down.

I'm mindful that time is ticking on and I have to be back for Maddy's second interview. I *have* to be.

I let out a relieved breath when the back door opens easily. I step inside the kitchen, locking the door again behind me. I leave my bag on the breakfast bar and walk into the hallway.

This morning I stood in exactly the same spot, calling upstairs for Maddy to get a move on.

'What have you been doing up there?' I asked when she appeared at the top of the stairs. 'You've not even brushed your hair yet, madam!'

Now I can't help but wonder if she was listening to a voicemail from Bessie instead of getting ready. Maybe it was all completely innocent, just a lonely old lady who loved the two vibrant young cousins to pop in to brighten her day.

But then why the secrecy? Why didn't Bessie communicate with the girls via Mum or Dad, who she knew well… and who gave Maddy that blasted phone in the first place?

I slump against the side of the polished mahogany banister. I can still hear the muffled noise of the crowd outside.

This morning, there wasn't a soul at the gate. Life was normal, the fabric of our family intact. We were all looking forward to a pizza tea and Josh coming home.

Now, our faces are plastered all over the Internet.

The stairs are opposite the front door, and as I walk forward and turn to climb them, my hand shoots up to cover my nose. There's the most awful stench in here.

Today's mail is scattered on the floor, and… No, it can't be! I step closer, and my worst suspicions are confirmed. Three piles of dog mess have been delivered through the letter box on folded sheets of newspaper.

I dash upstairs, away from the horror of it, pushing the abusive, vile act from my mind before it sends me over the edge. I can't dwell on the thought of how much someone must hate us. I just can't.

I head straight for Maddy's bedroom, standing for a moment in the doorway to look around. I dash in and out of the kids' rooms on a daily basis, usually to pick up dirty washing, replace clean laundry or strategically place stuff they've left downstairs on their beds to be put away in its proper place.

But busy with the everyday demands of life, I never take the time to really *look* at the room my daughter spends so much time in.

Her dressing table is cluttered with all the usual stuff I'd expect to see there. A hairbrush, colourful hair clips and bands, random items she's obviously put down when she's walked into the room: a half-empty glass of cordial, a dog-eared paperback about a lost puppy, and a small teddy she's loved since she was a toddler.

There's a hand towel draped there too, and when I lift it, I see a make-up compact underneath. Not one specifically designed for children, but a proper adult set with a Perspex lid that shows off the collection of dark, sultry eye colours, mascara and eyeliner.

It's odd. I wouldn't buy her anything this adult, and I know for a fact Tom wouldn't either, even if she begged him.

I shake myself. Time is of the essence, and although I have some questions that need answering, it's not going to happen now. I have to find that phone and get back to the police station.

I rifle through her chest of drawers and the one in her bedside table. I drop down and peer under her bed, sweep my arm across the carpet there, but there's nothing apart from the missing side plate I was hunting for yesterday, complete with toast crumbs and smeared jam.

I hoist myself up and take a couple of strides across the room, flinging open the wardrobe doors. I slide my hand along the shelf, which is packed with all manner of rubbish, but I can't feel anything like a phone. I spot a pile of hardback annuals by the side of her bed and carry them over to the floor in front of the wardrobe.

When I stand on them, I can see everything that's on the shelf. I pull it all out, letting the whole lot fall to the floor.

Soft toys, board games, a blanket, screwed-up T-shirts I haven't seen in ages – and there behind it all, a small, old-fashioned silver Nokia phone.

24

The village

A quarter of a mile away from the Fletcher house, Dana found herself with time to kill before she needed to get back to interview the girls again.

She'd driven back to the village to feed her unimpressed cat, Heston, who was particularly keen on regular mealtimes, always appearing from nowhere a minute before the next one was due.

But when she opened the fridge to feed herself, she found it bare save for a tub of spreadable butter and a solitary egg. She vaguely remembered planning on picking up a few items from the supermarket, but that was as far as she'd got.

She decided to take a walk out to the row of shops at the end of the road and get a sandwich from the small general store as the bakery closed at four.

As she turned the corner, the pretty cornflower-blue canopy of Hetty's Café caught her eye and a sudden craving for one of their speciality salmon and cream cheese bagels set her stomach rumbling.

She ordered her sandwich and a latte, and when her coffee was ready, she took it over to a small table tucked away in the corner and sat down, easing her feet out of the new flat pumps she'd bought last week. She hadn't broken them in properly and they'd skinned both her heels.

She felt tired, but it was a good tired. She'd missed the adrenalin of a case that swallowed up the hours in a working day in a flash. She'd missed the total absorption in her work, the feeling of driving as hard as she could towards the truth.

Yet her blossoming relationship with Lizzie was a welcome new addition to her life and so she was mindful of not screwing it up like she'd done with Orla. She had to at least try and strive for that mythical work–life balance thing that filled half of the women's magazines she read.

Still, she'd invited Lizzie round for a takeaway and a movie later, so that was a good start to her plan. And Lizzie had insisted on cooking rather than ordering food in, which Dana had appreciated. They were taking things very slowly, which suited Dana. Although she'd missed having someone special around, she'd also found herself wary of complicated relationships.

She and Lizzie hadn't sat down and robotically dissected their approach on the matter, but they had agreed there was no rush, and were enjoying just getting to know each other, with the odd show of affection, before moving on to the next stage.

While she waited for her order to arrive, she reluctantly took out her phone.

It was essential she keep tabs on the mood of online posts. While Neary and his team did the same thing in an effort to contain local uproar, Dana knew that the girls' families would be affected by what was being said online. This sense of unease and possibly fear and shame could be subconsciously passed on to the girls in the interactions their parents had with them.

Online abuse could be devastating to both the victims and the accused families.

Dana looked up at the sound of a tinkling bell and watched as a middle-aged woman with cropped blonde hair and dark roots entered the café.

There was something about the way she didn't gravitate towards the counter to be served like the other customers that was unnerving. Instead, she looked around, spotted Dana and walked purposefully towards her table, only stopping when she was standing directly in front of her.

'Can I help you?' Dana said in a pleasant voice that belied the creeping sense of dread in her lower abdomen.

She didn't need to be told that the woman standing before her was going through a rough time. She looked dishevelled, with her smudged mascara and creased black trousers, but the Hobbs jacket and the black leather Radley handbag showed that this was someone who usually prided herself on looking smart.

'I'm Helen Bootle,' she said simply, and Dana saw the effort it took for her not to give in to the sea of emotion roiling just under the surface. 'I'm Bessie Wilford's daughter.'

Dana stood up immediately, her chair scraping on the floor in her haste.

'I'm so sorry, I didn't realise. Dana Sewell.' She held out her hand.

Helen ignored it. 'I know who you are.'

Dana pulled out a chair. 'Please, Helen, take a seat. Can I get you a coffee?'

Helen shook her head and hesitated, but then sat down, twisting the strap of her handbag between her fingers.

'I'm so sorry for your loss,' Dana offered limply.

'I… I still can't believe it.' Helen stared vacantly at the tabletop. 'I can't stay long, but someone said you were in the café and so I had to come in. I just had to.'

'I'm glad you did.' Dana pressed her lips together. 'I can't imagine how you must be feeling—'

'Of course you can't. That's why I had to see for myself the woman who's helping those two… *girls*, the so-called children who murdered my mother.' Helen's eyes were trained like lasers on Dana's face, the sadness in her voice now replaced by a brusque harshness.

Dana swallowed. 'Helen, I know how terribly difficult it must be for you right now—'

'I mean, how *could* you?' Helen leaned forward, her words louder now and flying at Dana's face like tiny poisoned arrows. 'How will you sleep at night while you're putting your efforts into helping those little monsters and their families while my loving, gentle mother is lying in the morgue?'

Dana sighed and held up her hands in a placating gesture.

'It's about finding out what really happened, Helen. We have to establish the facts, and to do that, we have to understand the girls' state of mind.'

'Rubbish!' Helen's voice ramped up an octave. The hum of voices in the café faltered slightly and heads began to turn towards them. 'You're trying to get them *off*.' She hesitated for a moment as if thinking better of continuing, but then let rip again, her mouth twisting into an ugly sneer. 'I've already been told all about where your loyalties lie, working with these troubled kids who get excluded from school and commit crimes. You're nothing but an apologist for delinquency!'

Dana shook her head. 'Helen, *please*. Just calm down a moment and let me explain. I'm not a police officer, I'm a family therapist. It's not my job to decide who's guilty or innocent.'

'Exactly. So you make excuses for these families like the Fletchers and the Voces, the ones who raised those… those little beasts.' She spat out the words as if she was glad to be rid of them. 'The two of them looking so innocent, skipping around the village with their ponytails… It's all an act. Can't you see that? Everyone's saying they were known to be up to no good.'

The café was deathly silent now, and Dana looked up to see several people looking at her with the same expression as Bessie's daughter. She felt a twinge in her throat. Maybe it was time to leave.

'It's not just idle gossip,' Helen hissed. 'There's stuff you don't know about that family. Stuff hardly anyone knows.'

The village had become a critical hive mind. Somehow it knew about every development in the case, and judgements were being formed accordingly.

Dana couldn't ask what Helen was alluding to. Not here in the tea shop. She was working with the police, and she couldn't be seen to be gossiping with the victim's daughter in public.

'Helen, I know it must be very—'

'She was fired herself for breaking the rules,' a man sitting at the front called out, breaking Dana's train of thought. 'Middle-class liberals like her, they're nothing but bloody do-gooders sticking their oar in. Discipline is what kids like that need. I say make an example of the two of 'em.'

'Hear, hear,' a woman's voice piped up.

Dana stood up and pulled her handbag strap over her shoulder.

'I'd really like to speak to you, Helen, but not here.'

'What's the point?' The venom had gone from Helen's voice, leaving it sounding flat and hopeless. 'You've got one goal and that's to get them off. That's the truth of the matter and you know it. We all know it.'

It was only a few yards to the door of the café, but to Dana it felt like a country mile.

When she passed the table at the front, she leaned forward and spoke to the man who'd levelled his criticism so publicly at her.

'Just for the record, I wasn't fired. I was suspended pending an investigation that has now cleared me of any wrongdoing. Get your facts right next time.'

It was a mistake to challenge him.

'Suspended, fired, it's all the same,' he roared back. 'You'll bend over backwards to help them that really need banging up to teach them a—'

The rest of his words remained trapped inside the café as Dana stepped out into the fresh air and pulled the door closed behind her.

She'd known tensions were running high in the village, but the altercation had taken her by surprise. Everyone she'd met so far seemed utterly convinced about what had happened in Bessie Wilford's house today.

It was obvious that most of them had already tried and convicted Maddy Fletcher and Brianna Voce.

25

2003

Juliet and Corey walked past the brown, crisping front lawns of the smaller houses of the village and then up Derby Road, where the expansive red roofs of the big detached houses steamed in the heat.

Corey's chatter was a constant backdrop to the walk. He hated silence and would do anything he could to fill it, but Juliet had stopped listening a while back.

When they finally reached the warren, around a mile from home, she was struggling. The soporific effect of the medication, paired with exhaustion from little sleep, had tightened its grip on her, and she was feeling more and more drowsy.

She should have accepted Chloe's grudging offer to accompany them.

'Come on, slowcoach!' Corey sang repeatedly as he skipped effortlessly ahead.

The vast expanse of bracken and wooded areas stretched out before them. Incredibly, given the parched conditions, it was still quite green, although Juliet saw that the curling ends of the bracken had turned brown and the usually lush long grass that bordered the footpaths had a sort of half-baked, bone-dry look about it.

She usually felt a sense of freedom coming here, but today, she was overwhelmed by the distance she'd have to cover to get to the thicker bracken that was essential for den-making.

'Maybe we'll do just a little walk today,' she suggested hopefully, but Corey was having none of it.

'I want to climb Stony Side Hill,' he insisted. 'I want to find my den. I *have* to find it, Juliet. Can we find it? Pleease!'

Last time they'd been here, a couple of weeks earlier, she'd helped Corey make a start on what he proclaimed was his best den yet.

One side of Stony Side – Corey's favourite hill – was rich with bracken and soft slopes; the other side was barren and rocky. They always stayed on the safer green side and during their last visit had located the perfect pitch for a den. It was sheltered from the wind and in a bit of a dip where it couldn't easily be spotted from the ground.

They'd started by constructing the floor, stamping down the clay-rich soil and laying a carpet of bracken so that it wouldn't turn into a sea of mud if it rained. That had been a good afternoon, and Juliet had enjoyed spending time with her brother, but today would be different and she couldn't wait for it to be over.

By the time they reached the top of the hill, she was really flagging. Her back was slick with sweat and she felt weak and light-headed.

'I'll just have to have a little lie-down,' she gasped. 'Have a quick search around and shout me when you find the den.'

She lay back and looked up at the blue sky, scattered with white clouds. The grass tickled the back of her neck and a cool breeze soothed her fevered brow. The sun beat down on the pale skin of her face and she vaguely berated herself for only applying sunscreen to her arms.

She watched the tendrils of wispy white entwine in the vast blue above her, slowly drifting across and out of view… so slowly, so serenely.

She allowed her eyes to gently close.

She'd rest for just for a minute or two. If she could gather her energy a little, she'd surely be good as new, and it would give Corey time to find his den before they began work on it again.

Juliet sat bolt upright. The sun had disappeared behind a thick puff of candyfloss cloud, and she shivered even though it was still very warm.

'Corey!' she yelled, standing up so she could easily spot her brother's bright green Teletubbies T-shirt.

But he was nowhere to be seen. Her own T-shirt felt damp and clammy on her back, and the skin on her face tingled unpleasantly. When she touched her nose and cheeks, she knew immediately that she had burned badly in the sun.

'Corey!' she called again, but there was no answer.

She checked her watch. It was 4.20. She'd been asleep for thirty-five minutes! She *never* napped in the day; that was a habit for old people like her parents. It drove her mad when Mum and Dad slept after Sunday lunch and instructed the three of them not to make a sound for the next hour. Trying to keep Corey quiet was like trying to harness the wind.

'Corey? It's time to go home now,' she called, and began to walk across the brow of the hill to the large rock at the top that acted as a viewing platform.

She climbed onto it and peered over the edge, down the steep side that gave the hill its name. It was dotted with sharp, jutting rocks that all the kids around here had been warned to stay away from.

Suddenly her eyes narrowed in disbelief and horror. Halfway down the slope lay a small, crumpled body, T-shirt glowing neon green as the sun finally managed to break through the cloud again.

26

The village

After the incident with Helen Bootle at the tea shop, Dana had returned to her small terraced house, relieved to be away from the harsh judgement of the locals.

She didn't feel in the least bit hungry, even though she had ended up leaving without her lunch.

She sat quietly in her living room, exploring her own thoughts and feelings. She had come across the attitude Helen had expressed many times before. Lots of people found it difficult to understand how she could support people who had been accused or convicted of serious crimes.

Dana's closest friend at university, Polly, had become a criminal defence lawyer. She frequently dealt with abuse on the street because she willingly took on clients who had committed rape and murder and gave them the best defence she could in court.

'If I don't do my job, then justice can't be done,' was her stock answer, but people didn't understand it and it never won her any points when there was trouble.

But Dana got it completely. It wasn't about getting people off, or helping them get away with criminal acts.

She believed as much as Helen Bootle and the café customers that justice should be seen to be served in each and every case.

The catch was that the only way that could happen was to ensure that all parties had their say. Both defence and prosecution should have a chance to put forward evidence that could then be carefully considered and judged by a lawful legal process.

She could understand Helen Bootle's frustration, of course she could. But equally, she realised there was nothing she could have said to make her feel better. In fact, if Dana had told her what she really thought, she'd have only succeeded in making Helen even angrier.

In the Strang case, everyone had believed that fifteen-year-old Collette was responsible for the death of her best friend. All the evidence had seemed to point that way; Dana had been the lone voice of doubt. But gut feelings didn't carry the same weight as witness statements and forensic detail.

The police had instructed her to back off. Neary hadn't been leading that team, but he knew about it and advised her to let it go. She ignored him. She ignored all of them.

The academy management cautioned her, put her on another case, but still she couldn't ignore the feeling that there was more to it, that Collette was innocent.

So, after another full day of deliberation, she'd taken it upon herself to follow up with the family of the dead girl in her own time, speak to a few people off the record.

But she had found her courage too late. By the time Collette's cousin had broken down and confessed, Collette had already hanged herself in her bedroom.

Her family had sued the police for mismanagement of the case, saying that Dana's off-the-record visits proved that the authorities were squabbling and disagreeing amongst themselves instead of following procedure. The judge agreed, and the family were awarded substantial damages.

There had been nothing spooky about Dana's intuition in the case.

The stuff people told her either added up or it didn't. Simple as. And right now, she felt convinced that the families of the two girls were hiding something.

She could just sense there was something stuck at the back of all their throats like a fish bone. Something they wanted to protect at all costs, whether they consciously realised it or not.

It might be invisible to Neary and the rest of them, but to Dana, it was glaringly obvious. The stilted communication between family members, the clandestine glances and tense body language that some of them displayed and some didn't.

Just like her last case, she wasn't about to ignore it.

27

The police station

It was just before five o'clock and Dana was scheduled to speak to the girls again. DC Carol Hall had given the parents refreshments and had requested, via Neary, that they have no contact with their daughters during the break.

Surprisingly, they had agreed without protest, on the understanding that they could sit in on the next interview. Chloe began to put up an argument based on what Seetal had told her were her legal rights, but with no support from Tom and Juliet, she reluctantly backed down.

When Dana entered the room, she saw that the girls were sitting in the same places as before. Each child had her mother present, sitting on their right-hand side, with the lawyer tucked at the end. Apparently Maddy's father, Tom, had left to attend a work meeting.

There was nothing wrong with the set-up, yet Dana immediately picked up a peculiar prickling tension she hadn't noticed before.

It wasn't something that existed between Maddy and Brianna, but the two mothers.

Chloe Voce sat stock still, staring straight ahead. Her arms were folded, her mouth set in a flat, determined line.

Juliet Fletcher had turned her body slightly towards her daughter. Her hands were folded neatly in her lap and Dana noticed she swallowed frequently, a sure sign of nerves.

Neither woman looked at or spoke to each other. It was as though an invisible force field crackled straight down the middle of the two families.

The girls themselves looked braced to scoot, like frightened rabbits.

Brianna fidgeted in her seat, the nail of her index finger scratching at the side of her thumb. Maddy sat motionless as a statue with her fists balled and her jaw firmly locked.

Dana noted these crucial early observations. The way people actually felt inside compared to the way they wanted to appear externally was always an interesting study to begin with.

'Hello again, girls,' Dana said pleasantly as she sat down in the charcoal-grey upholstered chair. 'I hope you both got something to eat and drink. If you need anything else, you will let me know?'

No reaction.

She addressed only the girls. The mothers had been briefed that they were there only as silent support and they should not contribute or intervene at any point.

Neary had expressed surprise when Dana told him she wanted to interview the girls together again, this time with their mothers present. She'd stipulated the mothers only, adding that Tom Fletcher could observe from the viewing room. She had her reasons for this, although in the event, he was absent anyway.

Family dynamics were fascinating things, and in Dana's experience, they best revealed themselves when there was a balance. The dynamic between the sisters, Juliet and Chloe, was of great interest to her, and would have been skewed if Maddy's father had also been present.

She placed her notes and pen on the low table in front of her and sat back in a relaxed manner.

'I spoke to your teacher, Miss Barr, earlier, and she wanted me to tell you that she's thinking of you both and sends her love and best wishes.'

Both girls stared into the space ahead.

'Miss Barr tells me that during lessons, you are both so good at speaking up. You, Brianna, aren't afraid to put your hand up and have a go at answering when the teacher asks a question. Maddy, you have a quick brain for remembering facts and nearly always get the answer right when asked.'

Chloe Voce tapped a fingernail on the side of her hand.

'So your teacher was quite shocked when I explained that neither of you had said a word yet.'

Dana left a pause, and Juliet Fletcher filled it with a small cough.

'Miss Barr asked me what the reasons behind your silence could be.'

Brianna Voce shot a lightning-fast glance at the viewing window, but it didn't escape Dana. Sitting behind the mirrored glass, the detectives were watching and listening. Both girls had been told this.

'You know, there are lots of reasons why people stop speaking,' Dana continued. She sat back in her chair, looked from one girl to the other. 'Sometimes, when they feel very afraid, it's easiest to say nothing at all, because they think it might make things even worse for themselves... or for others.'

Chloe Voce bit her lip.

'But that's very rarely the case. Talking about a problem often helps, because it provides an outlet for all that stress bottled up inside. Have you ever seen anyone blow up a balloon at a party? If you just keep blowing and blowing and filling up the balloon with air, what do you think happens?' She paused for a moment or two and then carried on as if the girls had reacted anyway. 'That's right, the balloon bursts. All that air will find a way out in the long run, and it's exactly the same with fear and stress. Saying nothing might feel like the answer right now, but in the long run it can just make things so much worse.'

She picked up the water jug from the table and poured herself a glass. The trickle sounded like a thunderclap in the small, airless room.

'Another reason for keeping quiet might be because someone else has told you to—'

'What are you trying to say?' Chloe Voce snapped before pressing her lips together.

Dana completely blanked her interruption.

'Sometimes we do things for other people that we know aren't right. Usually we know it's wrong because we feel it here.' Dana tapped the waistband of her trousers, level with her solar plexus. 'But we do it anyway because we're scared or worried or just confused.'

She stretched her legs out and crossed them at the ankles.

'I'm going to let you into a secret. Last year, I made a mistake in my job. I did something that broke all the rules and I did it because I wanted to help someone who was in serious trouble.'

The girls both looked at her.

'It all went horribly wrong because the person I tried to help died and I found myself in quite a dilemma. I couldn't take back what I'd done and I knew the right thing to do was to tell the truth, even if my bosses didn't understand. But I was afraid of being blamed for the death and I felt so bad for the family of the person who died.'

The girls were actively listening now, interested. Dana took a breath and continued, trying to keep her voice relaxed and praying that neither mother intervened at any point.

'I couldn't sleep properly, I couldn't eat. I didn't want to leave the house, I didn't even want to visit my family and I didn't want to speak to anyone if I could help it. I felt so miserable, as if I'd caught myself in a trap. And then I suddenly thought, *anything is better than this*. I made a decision. It was a brave decision, I think. I decided I would just go to my bosses and tell the truth and let the consequences take care of themselves. And that's exactly what I did. I was truthful, but I also explained exactly what happened and why I did what I did.'

Dana looked at the girls. Maddy Fletcher's chest rose and fell with increasing speed.

'It's called accountability,' Dana explained. 'Facing up to your actions and working hard to try and put things right.'

Brianna suddenly sprang to her feet and kicked the metal leg of her chair, causing the whole thing to skitter back.

'It was Maddy's fault!' Her screeching voice seemed to bounce around the walls as she staggered back towards the door. 'Maddy was the one who hurt Bessie!'

In seconds, the tension dissolved from Brianna's body and the girl seemed to deflate in front of Dana's eyes. Her shoulders slumped and she wrapped her arms around herself as she leaned against the wall, apparently shocked at her own outburst.

Chloe leapt up and rushed over to her daughter, wrapping her in her arms. Seetal shifted in her seat but didn't say anything.

The room fell silent again. Dana held her breath and looked at Maddy, who had barely moved. Juliet had grasped her daughter's hand, her expression a mask of pure dread.

'Maddy?' Dana said gently. 'Have you got anything you want to say?'

The girl's face looked pale and haunted, her eyes like dark sunken pools of navy blue. Juliet had turned pale and her hands began to shake.

Dana held her breath. Waited.

'It's true.' Maddy spoke so quietly that Dana had to lean forward in her chair to catch her words. 'I'm the one who hurt Bessie.'

28

As soon as the words left Brianna's mouth, Chloe felt her shoulders drop. The tension that had kept her face, neck and chest rigid and almost painful to the touch for most of the interview seemed to seep away in seconds.

'Good girl,' she muttered under her breath. '*Good girl.*'

Juliet's head jerked towards her, and Chloe saw disbelief and denial changing the very fabric of her sister's face, distorting her pale features. She was looking to Chloe to make it better, just like she used to do when they were kids. But that was a long time ago now. Things had changed and they were on a different playing field altogether.

There was nothing Chloe could say or do to help her. Her loyalty had to be to Brianna alone.

It had taken so much courage for Bree to speak up like that. There were times in the last few hours when Chloe had worried she didn't have it in her to do so. But her daughter had come through in the end, and she was so proud of her.

She felt sad for Juliet and Tom. But they were their own worst enemies; they'd never been able to see Maddy's faults. The flaws that were so glaringly evident to the rest of the family.

Like her solitary nature and unwillingness to compromise. A few months earlier, Brianna had got friendly with another girl in their class and invited her over to the house to play during the school holidays. The girl had gone home in tears early, before tea, refusing to say why.

Later, her father had called Chloe and told her that when Brianna went to the bathroom, Maddy told the girl that her cousin had put spiders and insects in her sandwiches and she'd have to eat them otherwise the adults would get very angry.

Chloe had a word with Juliet about it, but Maddy denied everything. She put on a pretty good show, too, a proper little actress.

That kid could be very dark. There was no doubt about it. And now the truth was out at last.

Once they got Brianna safely home, Chloe would do her level best to support her sister and niece. Of course she would. Despite everything, she was fond of Maddy. She'd always believed Brianna was innocent, but she was shocked that Maddy had proved to be such a monster. It chilled her to think what might have happened if the girl had turned her vitriol on her cousin.

The feeling of relief was fantastic. It was a good sign. Hopefully now Chloe could start to resolve the other problems she had.

Dana looked at her. 'Chloe, if you'd like to leave the room now with Brianna and Carol, I can chat a bit longer here with Juliet and Maddy.'

Chloe stood up and took Brianna's hand and Carol held open the door. Juliet didn't look at her or say anything at all.

She placed a well-meaning hand on her sister's shoulder as they left the interview room, but Juliet shrugged it off.

29

Dana could see that Juliet Fletcher's breathing had become erratic. Her chest was rising and falling and she was pulling in too much air and in danger of hyperventilating.

'Just relax, Juliet.' Dana told her. 'Nothing is going to happen immediately because of what Brianna just said. I'm hoping Maddy can shed a bit more light on what happened in Bessie's house.'

Maddy looked at her mother and back down at her hands.

'Maddy?' Juliet said gently, touching her arm. 'You have to tell the truth and help yourself now in any way you can. Do you understand?'

Maddy gave a faint nod.

'Anything you can tell us will help us to help *you*,' Dana added.

Maddy began to tap the heel of her foot on the floor.

'Your mum said you've not been sleeping well for a few weeks, Maddy. Is that right?'

Maddy shrugged then nodded.

When they'd had their brief chat in Room 15A, Juliet had explained about hearing Maddy walking around her bedroom in the early hours and how she'd started going downstairs and sitting in the armchair, alone in the dark. Juliet had also said Maddy seemed to have a bit of an attitude lately, answering back and refusing to do some tasks like her homework. Apparently this was out of character.

'Do you know why you've felt more restless? Why you can't seem to relax at night?' Dana pressed her gently.

Juliet nodded at her daughter to encourage her to speak.

Dana allowed a few moments' pause. Just as she was about to ask another open-ended question, Maddy spoke up.

'I just wake up for no reason and then I can't get back to sleep.'

'Horrible, isn't it?' Dana pulled a face. 'That sometimes happens to me, too. Mostly when I have stuff on my mind, stuff I'm worried about that comes up in my dreams.'

Maddy nodded.

'It's not easy, I know, but I want you to think back to before you went to Bessie's house. Can you remember if you were worried about something then?'

Maddy thought for a moment. She glanced at Dana and looked quickly at her mum.

'It's OK, sweetie,' Juliet reassured her. 'I promise you won't get into trouble, whatever you say in here.'

Juliet was so helpful in this process. She seemed to know just what to say to support Maddy in the best possible way.

'I… I'd been having bad dreams.' Maddy wriggled a bit in her chair. 'That someone was telling me to do something bad.'

Juliet looked uncomfortable but to Dana's relief, she stayed quiet.

'That must have been upsetting,' Dana said. 'Was it someone you know?'

Maddy nodded.

'Was it Brianna?' Juliet said and then bit back. 'Sorry, Dana.'

'Can you remember what the person was asking you to do?' Dana continued, ignoring the interruption.

Maddy pressed her lips together, tapped the knuckles of her thumbs against each other.

'Anything you can remember might be useful,' Dana said softly.

She was almost certain by Maddy's body language that the child could remember exactly who had tried to control her and what they'd asked her to do. But it was important Maddy felt safe enough to believe she had the upper hand.

'They told me I had to do bad things otherwise awful things would happen.' Maddy glanced at her mother's stricken face. 'It was just a dream, Mummy.'

'Yes,' Juliet said faintly.

'And do you know who the person in your dreams was, Maddy?' Dana asked her. 'The person who wanted you to do bad things?'

'I'm not sure,' she said quickly. 'I think I knew them but…'

'That's OK.' Dana smiled. 'Can you remember what they asked you to do?'

'They wanted me to wake Bessie up by shouting in her ear,' Maddy said. 'They said I had to stay silent to stop the bad things happening.'

30

Chloe sat alone in Room 15A.

Carol had said Brianna and Maddy's interview was still ongoing. What a turn-up for the books when Brianna had spoken up. Chloe felt so proud of and relieved for her daughter.

Her peace was shattered when Ray and Joan burst in, her mother's eyes bloodshot and puffy.

'Mum? What's wrong?'

'People back at the house.' Ray frowned, rubbing Joan's back as he helped her into a chair. 'Onlookers. Press, asking bloody questions and upsetting your mother. The sooner this nightmare ends the better.'

Ray shook his head and sat down next to Joan with a sigh.

'It might be ending sooner than you think, Dad.' Chloe blew out air. 'Bree found the courage to speak up finally and Maddy just admitted she was the one who hurt Bessie.'

Ray's face dropped. 'Oh no, not Maddy!'

'Would you rather Brianna had kept her mouth shut and taken the rap for something she didn't do?' Chloe scowled. 'The girls don't know yet but that old lady is dead, Dad. *Dead!* Of course I'm gutted Maddy is capable of that but I'm so relieved Brianna is in the clear.'

'Have they said that?' Joan looked up. 'Have they said Brianna is in the clear?'

'Not in so many words but she's got to be, right? Maddy has admitted it.'

'Hmm.' Joan didn't elaborate and Chloe ignored her.

'What do you think, Dad? Do you think Brianna should take the blame for something she had nothing to do with?'

'Don't ask him, he knows nothing about how the law operates,' Joan sneered.

'Of course I don't want Brianna to take the blame! It's just… she was there and the police may need more than just a confession from Maddy.' Ray gave a heavy sigh. 'I don't know what I expected, to be honest, but it wasn't *this*.'

She looked at her father. His hair seemed greyer, his wrinkles deeper since this morning. But after Maddy's admission, Chloe felt lighter inside than she had done for days. Even before this terrible incident, she'd felt incapacitated by worry.

The family had been fractured by what the girls were going through here, and it would be fractured again when Chloe had a heart-to-heart with her sister and came clean. She didn't know if the family unit would survive it.

She knew that stuff hadn't gone away in terms of Brianna's involvement, far from it. But she had a right to feel relief for a short time.

Chloe looked down when her phone suddenly illuminated.

She had turned it on to silent mode during the interview, so when the screen lit up with an anonymous incoming call, she simply pressed a button to end it. But then the answerphone icon popped up, and a creeping uneasy feeling started in the pit of her stomach. Making an excuse, she stepped outside to listen to the message.

Turned out it was the call she'd been dreading. She listened to it twice, trying in vain to extract clues from the tone, the inflections of the voice on the other end of the line.

It took her a few minutes to pull herself together enough that she could go back inside without her legs giving way beneath her.

She craned her neck around the door.

'I've just got to pop back to the house,' she told her parents, aware that her voice sounded thinner and higher than usual. 'I'm going to insist Seetal gets Bree out of here today and I need to make sure everything is ready at home.'

'I can sort that for you, love.' Ray spoke up. 'If you tell me what you—'

'It's OK, Dad. I'll go, if you don't mind lending me the car. The break will do me good.'

'You'll have to brave the mob outside the house. At least let me come with you then,' Ray insisted.

'I'll be fine,' she said, irritated now.

Joan looked over and studied Chloe through narrowed eyes, but Ray pulled the car keys from his pocket and handed them to her. 'I've parked just around the back of the station, on Hudson Road. Don't say I didn't warn you.'

'Thanks, Dad. Won't be long.'

Chloe stepped into the corridor and breathed a sigh of relief at finally getting away from the enquiring eyes of her mother. She swallowed hard, battling the feeling of nausea that rose in her throat, then walked briskly through the security door and across the foyer without looking at the receptionist. DI Neary had said they must sign in and out of the premises, but she didn't care about their stupid protocols. She had more important things to worry about.

There was a couple in reception dressed in grubby tracksuits and whispering to each other behind their hands. She swept by them with ill-disguised disdain.

This morning when she'd woken, she had a life, and now… now it felt as though the sky was about three inches from falling in on her head. She just needed to get away from this place. That would surely help.

Outside, she dragged in air like a drowning woman. Once she stopped feeling sick, she pulled out her phone and sent a text.

She'd promised herself she wouldn't, but now she felt like she had no choice.

Walking around the back of the station, she found Ray's dark blue Toyota. She adjusted the driver's seat to accommodate her shorter legs and sat for a few moments before starting the engine. She could detect a very faint smell of smoke inside the car. Seemed like her father was up to his old smoking tricks, despite Joan demanding he give up his twenty-a-day habit following last year's health scare when he'd had breathing problems after a bad cold.

Smokers didn't seem to realise that to a non-smoker, even one cigarette was pervasive. Its odour lodged itself almost instantly in soft furnishings and clothing, lingering there for hours.

Chloe gave a sardonic smile. Her father's secret was safe with her. After all, they could all hang each other with everything else they knew.

31

'Thanks for agreeing to see me, Juliet. I know this must be a very difficult time for you,' Dana said when the two women sat down in Neary's small office. She chose one of the comfy upholstered chairs rather than the detective's rather intimidating leather swivel chair behind his desk.

'Thank you for suggesting it,' Juliet replied. 'If I don't talk to someone about Maddy soon, I think I'll implode. Tom's still not back yet, so it's the ideal time.'

Dana nodded and set down her notepad and pen on the small table to her side.

'I've asked you in here because although Maddy has confessed to hurting Bessie, both DI Neary and I are keen to explore this a little further before events run away with us.'

Dana had thought long and hard about how to approach the session with Juliet. She could hardly say that both she and Conor Neary were of the impression that something didn't feel right about the whole thing, or that she suspected there were issues within the family that might have a bearing on matters.

'I'm so grateful.' Juliet let out a long breath. 'Everyone else seems to be quite happy to accept a ten-year-old's accusation and then Maddy's hasty admission and run with it. I *know* she didn't hurt that old lady, Dana. I just know it, and yet I feel like everyone, my parents and my sister, are more than willing to accept the possibility.'

Dana didn't correct Juliet when she used the word 'hurt' instead of 'kill'. She could see it was simply a coping tool for her. Juliet was working hard to control her facial expressions, but her fidgeting hands and grey skin told a different story altogether.

Dana wanted to be completely transparent with her. Juliet deserved that much at least.

'You're probably wondering what I want to talk to you about.' Juliet gave a faint nod.

'I thought this might be a good time to take pause for a therapy session, as you agreed. You see, it's my experience that often when children commit crime – and I just want to point out that despite her apparent confession, I'm not saying that Maddy has done so – the most useful clues in uncovering the truth often come not from an external source, but from within the family unit itself.'

'Okaaay.' Juliet lengthened the word cautiously.

'I've only met your family briefly, but the dynamics within it are… interesting. I'm keen to find out a little about your own childhood and upbringing. It might help me approach Maddy from a better position of understanding. I'll then be able to offer her more support.'

'I see.' Juliet sat up a little straighter and pressed her lips together. 'Well, I can't say I enjoy speaking about my childhood. It wasn't the best time, if I'm honest.'

Dana noted the new pinched look that had appeared on Juliet's face, the way her hands had gravitated together and locked tightly in front of her stomach like an immovable barrier.

'No rush, we can take it as slowly as you want to.' She imagined Neary objecting to her relaxed approach, given his pressing timeline. 'If you're comfortable doing so, I'd like to continue.' She eyed her notepad but left it where it was. 'Rest assured our chat will be subject to the same confidentiality as an ordinary private therapy session unrelated to this case.'

When Juliet said she was happy to continue, Dana made a start.

'Why don't you tell me a little bit about your childhood? I'm interested in what life was like at home for you.'

Juliet thought for a moment.

'I mean, it was OK. Mum likes to say it was a lot better than some kids have, and she's right. We lived in the village in a decent, clean house with a garden, same one Mum and Dad still live in now. We were well fed, we had new clothes and shoes when we needed them. Nothing really to complain about.'

Dana gave her an encouraging nod, but silently dissected the language she'd chosen to use. *Decent, clean, well fed…* No mention of happiness, love or closeness. Given the opportunity to speak about anything at all, Juliet had chosen to outline only the basic needs that her parents had provided. She'd made no reference to Chloe, her sister; to shared happy family times, or to feeling loved.

Juliet was silent for a few moments, as though she expected to be asked another question. But Dana did not speak. Before long, Juliet began talking again.

'Dad worked in the same place for thirty years, a small engineering factory that made injection-moulded packaging. Mum was a nurse when she met Dad and dropped to part time, but she gave it up in the end because she found it too stressful to cope with when her anxiety became worse.'

'So when your mum finally gave up work, she was at home?' Dana asked.

'She was home… but not always present.' Juliet allowed herself a sad little smile. 'For as long as I can remember, she's suffered from bad anxiety. That's why she gave up nursing in the first place, but being at home didn't solve it. If anything, having more time to dwell on stuff made it worse.'

'And how did that show itself, to you and your sister, I mean, as children? How did you know your mum was feeling bad?'

'Well, on her worst days, she couldn't even get out of bed. I'd do what I could to keep things running in the house, but Dad worked long hours at the factory and… it wasn't always easy.'

Dana had been involved with many families over the years where a parent was incapacitated through illness, depression and anxiety, or sometimes from being an addict of one type or another. Often the kids would take the full hit, be required to act like adults and assume responsibilities way beyond their years. She wondered if life had been like that for Juliet and Chloe growing up in the Voce household.

'Chloe is older than you; did she help you around the house when your mum took to her bed?'

'Not really.' Juliet chewed on her lip. 'I mean, she struggled to deal with Mum's episodes. Chloe's kind of sensitive, and if too much pressure is put on her, she spirals down very quickly. Mum's always said she's like her in that respect.'

'And you didn't mind taking on adult duties like that? It didn't affect your friendships or your social life?'

Juliet hesitated. 'I never really thought about it; I just got on with it. Someone had to do it, and it wasn't Mum's fault. I'd just turn invitations down without thinking.'

'There were just the two of you? No other siblings?'

Juliet coughed. She crossed her legs and then uncrossed them again.

'I was the middle child. Chloe's two years older than me, and then… We did have a much younger brother, Corey.' She took a breath. 'But there was a tragedy in the family when I was thirteen. It was a terrible time for all of us. I don't… I can't really talk about it.'

There was a sudden marked change in Juliet's demeanour. Her darting eyes settled on Dana's face. The colour rose in her cheeks a little and her fingers unlocked, balling into soft fists on her thighs.

Dana recognised the signs. Juliet was challenging her to ask something… possibly to accuse her of something? She wasn't sure, but it was significant, showing that unresolved issues still loomed large in Juliet's psyche.

Again, though, Dana remained silent.

'Things were never the same after Corey. Everything changed.' Juliet's eyes grew dull. 'Mum got worse. Dad had an accident at work and lost a finger when his hand became trapped inside a machine at the factory. They made him redundant and he couldn't get another job. He'd travel up to Scotland two or three times a year for a couple of days to do labouring jobs for a guy he used to work with but that was it. Chloe ran away and they had to call the police out to find her.' Juliet sighed. 'It was like our world fell apart in lots of different ways… and it was all my fault.'

'*Your* fault? Is that what your family told you?'

'Not in so many words, but… well, it happened because of me, because I failed to take care of my brother. So it was my fault.'

'It was a long time ago now, and yet it seems to me you still haven't forgiven yourself.'

'I never will. I've tried all my life to make amends, but I never feel any closer to getting there. You can't make amends for something when it's so terrible.'

No redemption. Another value that the young Juliet had picked up from somewhere.

Dana allowed a pause before speaking.

'It was probably hard on everyone.'

Juliet nodded. 'Mum took it worst. She couldn't bear to look at me for months. Corey and I had exactly the same colour eyes, you see.' She stared into the middle distance, remembering.

'Can you tell me about your brother?' Dana asked gently. 'What happened?'

Juliet took a breath and looked at Dana again.

'I'd like to leave it there for today, if that's OK.'

32

2003

Juliet froze above the rocky ledge. She felt rooted to the spot, couldn't scream, cry for help. All she could do was stare at the crumpled figure of her brother.

None of it seemed real. It felt as though she'd been drugged, like she was moving and thinking in slow motion. This couldn't really be happening, could it?

'Juliet?'

The familiar voice snapped her out of her trance-like state. She turned and saw Chloe waving at her in slow motion from the bottom of the grassy side of the hill, away from the rocks. She watched as her sister started to climb towards her. She felt dizzy, as if she'd been spinning around and around and had just stopped still in the middle of it.

She forced herself to peer back over the side of the hill. She'd have to get down there somehow. Corey might be OK, just dazed. It was possible, if he'd managed to avoid the rocks on the way down.

Last month, a St John Ambulance team had been into their school and demonstrated how to check if someone was breathing, how to position them correctly and administer the kiss of life. Juliet had dissolved into giggles when Beverley Jones had said she would try it out on the school heartthrob, Danny Boreham, at break. How she wished she'd paid more attention now.

She took two or three crab-like steps down the uneven slope.

'Don't do it!' Chloe quipped a little breathlessly as she clambered up the final steep grassy brow and collapsed in a dramatic heap at the top. 'Seriously, Jules, get back up here, that drop is lethal.'

Juliet, feeling out of kilter, dropped her hands to the floor and clambered back up on all fours.

'I wanted to make sure you were OK,' Chloe said. 'We might just make the start of *Grange Hill* if we get off home now.'

Juliet was still trying to catch her breath, and couldn't speak.

'Why aren't you saying anything? Where's Corey?' Chloe looked around, frowning. 'You haven't let him wander off on his own to make a den, have you?'

Juliet opened her mouth but still couldn't summon words that would convey the horror that lay directly behind where she was standing. She lifted her hand towards Chloe.

'What's wrong? Why are you…' Chloe suddenly seemed to register her grey complexion, the look of pure dread on her face. She rushed over to her. 'Jules, what's happened? Where's Corey?'

Juliet pointed to the drop. 'I must have fallen asleep,' she whispered. 'I… I can't remember anything after getting up here.'

Chloe dashed to her side and peered down the steep drop.

'Shit! Oh no.' She sat down and swung herself over the edge. 'Wait here.'

'Chloe, no!' Juliet cried. 'There's no sense in you injuring yourself too. We should just get help.'

'You go and get someone. Hurry up. I'll be fine.'

But she couldn't do that. If Chloe ended up hurt too, Juliet would never forgive herself. No, she was better staying put and helping as much as she could.

She watched as Chloe expertly descended the hillside, clinging on to tough clumps of fescue grass and testing protruding rocks and clumps of earth before committing her weight to each step.

She'd always been sportier than Juliet, always had a natural affinity with movement, and her gymnastics kept her supple. If only Juliet had accepted her offer to come up here with them in the first place.

She could hear Chloe grunting and panting with the exertion of the treacherous descent. She felt so useless, so stupid. Her head was clearing now, and it was all becoming horribly real.

Chloe passed easily over the lethal jagged edges of the large slate-coloured rocks that jutted out at regular intervals. Finally she reached the grassy ledge underneath the rock where Corey had come to a natural stop.

'Is he OK?' Juliet called down, her voice shrill and desperate. 'Is he breathing?'

Chloe looked up, her expression blank. Juliet swallowed down the bilious feeling that rose quickly from her chest.

'Run to the nearest house, Jules,' Chloe called urgently. 'Ask them to call an ambulance, and then ring Dad and tell him what's happened.'

33

The village

Out on the side street, Chloe started Ray's car, opening the window a touch and checking in her mirror before steering the Toyota out onto the road.

Her armpits were damp and her heart was racing. She'd imagined every possible nightmare scenario over the last month, but soon the waiting would be over. A sort of acceptance of the inevitable had began to settle over her like a layer of thick, cloying dust.

She'd seen Juliet popping her antidepressants, ever eager to keep herself in the nice, safe medicated bubble she existed in. Not for her the grim side of life; she'd surrounded herself with her loving husband and an interfering best friend, both keeping watch over her like a couple of Rottweilers, looking out for anyone who might upset her.

Juliet had been living in a fantasy world that was about to well and truly crash down around her ears. Around *all* of their ears.

And there was even worse to come.

Everything Chloe had tried so hard to keep hidden was stirring in her guts now like a coiled eel. They would not be quietened any longer.

Regardless of the terrible timing, she knew she had to tell her sister. She had no choice. It was too late to make amends, and in some ways, she couldn't wait to bring everything out into the open. She was so tired of wrestling with the shame and deceit.

On a whim, she took a sharp left turn at the Badger Box pub at the bottom of Derby Road and drove up Forest Road so she'd pass Juliet and Tom's place.

She could see the motley crowd of people spilling out across the pavement and into the road way before she even got close to the house. She couldn't slow down for fear of drawing attention to herself. The car was familiar around these parts, after all. Ray had owned it for five years or more, and she'd already spotted a couple of villagers her parents knew well.

The reporters and photographers stood apart from the locals, and Chloe was shocked at the sheer volume of people. She'd seen from the online headlines and local press that the story was swiftly drawing attention, but it hadn't even been a day yet and there were some serious players here. She saw flashes of the colourful logos of Sky News and the *Daily Mail.*

Had they already found out about Maddy's admission?

A single policeman stood outside the front door of the house, keeping a watchful eye on the fractious group of villagers milling around next to the press.

In the seconds it took to pass the property, Chloe took in the graffiti daubed on the garage and the ugly mood of the onlookers. Their sneering faces, the movement of their mouths spitting out unfounded opinions like rotten morsels they couldn't bear to chew on any longer.

As one woman turned and stepped away from the wooden fence, Chloe caught sight of a home-made banner attached there, the words *JUSTICE FOR BESSIE WILFORD* daubed in thick black letters on a torn piece of grubby white sheeting.

She breathed a sigh of relief as she passed the scene and it shrank in her rear-view mirror. It seemed the villagers were too caught up in their dismal protest to spot her father's car.

She felt even more relieved that Brianna was nearly free of the whole sorry mess.

She pressed her foot a little more firmly on the accelerator, eager to put some distance between herself and Juliet's house. But her respite was short-lived. Five minutes later, the car approached her parents' house, and she took a sharp breath. The sight that confronted her was stark… shocking.

She forced herself to keep driving, past a much smaller group of locals, who seemed to have gathered for a chat outside the front gate. She'd expected more people, after her parents' description of the 'mob' but the crowd outside Juliet and Tom's place was much bigger. Still, what had happened here was more distressing and unexpected.

Again, the onlookers were too immersed in their conversations to notice her passing. Only when she had rounded the bend at the bottom of the road and was safely out of sight did she pull over and allow herself a minute to process what she'd seen.

The living room window had been completely smashed. She had clearly seen the cream leather sofa with her mother's red fleece blanket folded over the arm. Without the filter of the glass, the framed photograph of Brianna on the wall was there for all to gawp at.

So many times she had read in news reports about people getting a brick through the window. It didn't sound that bad when it was happening to someone else, but in reality it felt utterly violent and intrusive.

This was an act designed to expose their family shame to everyone. It encroached on their privacy and violated the safe space that was their home.

Billy from next door had been inspecting the damage with his builder son Kev as Chloe had driven past. He was a practical man, and she felt grateful that he'd be there to help put the mess right, probably even before her parents returned home later.

It seemed the locals had already held an unofficial trial and found the entire Voce and Fletcher families guilty. Maddy's confession should set them straight, convince them that Brianna and Chloe were free of any blame. But these things didn't always play out logically.

It had been unnerving to see how rapidly friends could become enemies. But could they turn back again… from enemies to friends?

Chloe wasn't sure.

Her chest felt crushed with the realisation that things were probably never going to be the same around here for any of them. Chloe, her parents and Brianna were still Maddy's extended family, and would be labelled accordingly by the other villagers.

People around here rarely forgave, never forgot. Old men were still getting abuse on the streets for breaking the 1984 miners' strike in order to feed their families.

Something had to be done before it was too late for all of them. Maddy had confessed, and yet Brianna was still being held by the police. Once Chloe got back, she'd put more pressure on Seetal to get working on her release.

She glanced at her phone on the passenger seat to see if her WhatsApp message had been read yet. Sure enough, two little blue ticks had appeared, showing that it had been delivered and read.

That was something at least.

She continued her journey to Sutton-in-Ashfield and turned off at the reservoir, the tyres crunching over the gravelled car park. This had become their safe place for meeting. Squirrelled away from sight of the main road.

There were only four or five other vehicles parked up, their occupants probably running around the reservoir or walking their dogs, but Chloe took no chances and manoeuvred the Toyota over to the far side to wait.

It wasn't long before another car turned into the car park, and she saw with relief that it was the familiar silver VW Golf.

She checked her face in the mirror and tucked lank wisps of hair back behind her ears. The passenger door opened and closed again, and the car filled with the soapy, clean smell of him.

Chloe felt her neck and shoulders relax a little.

'Hi, Tom,' she breathed as she reached for her brother-in-law's hand.

34

Juliet

We're transported to the new facility in a small minibus – me, Mum and Dad, the girls and DC Carol Hall.

Chloe has taken Dad's car to go back to the house and when Tom got back from his meeting and I filled him in on Maddy's confession, he abruptly made some excuse about needing time to get his head around it, and left again. The gulf between us seems wider than ever.

It's all getting to Tom, I could see that as he left. He looks a shadow of his former self, wearing the worry about Maddy like a mask for all to see. I feel like I can't touch him emotionally at the very time we should be pulling closer together.

During the journey, Maddy presses close to me and we hold hands. Brianna sits behind us next to Mum and Dad, so although I constantly whisper reassurances to Maddy, I don't discuss her interview with Dana. There's enough pressure on her right now, and I'm sure the detectives understand her confession was a knee-jerk reaction.

The stuff she said about someone pressuring her to do 'bad things' is bothering me but I try to remind myself it was just dreams. It didn't happen in real life and there's a big difference.

Maddy doesn't say much, but she *is* talking. They both are. So I'm praying we'll soon get the whole truth out of them and it will be proven that Maddy did nothing wrong after all.

When we first climbed into the minibus, I tried to catch Mum's eye a couple of times. Whatever our girls say, there's no point in us falling out about it. That won't change or resolve anything.

But Mum makes a distinct effort not to look my way at all. There is this sort of distracted air about her, as if she hasn't even got her mind on her granddaughters.

If I had to hazard a guess, I'd say there's something else bothering her.

But what could be more important than all this?

The new facility is a single-storey prefab-type building on the outskirts of Mansfield. There are electric gates, and Maddy's eyes widen as they swing open and a security guard waves us through.

'Is this a prison?' she whispers, and my heart leaps at the sound of her voice. Earlier today, I'd begun to think she might never speak again.

'No, sweetie, it's not a prison. It's going to be much more comfortable here for us all while we sort out this mess with the police.'

I hear Mum say something to Brianna, but I can't catch the words.

Inside the centre, we kiss the girls. 'We're off to get something nice to eat,' Carol tells them. 'You'll see your mums again soon, OK?'

Brianna pulls away and tries to hang onto Dad's arm, but Maddy just looks at me sadly and turns away.

'I'll see you in a little while, Brianna,' Mum says tightly. 'Come on, remember what I said. Be a brave girl and this will soon be over.'

As the girls walk away with Carol, I glare at my mum.

'What's the matter with you?' She frowns back.

'We're far from home and dry,' I say. 'Brianna is obviously as confused as Maddy; they're just reacting differently.'

'Is that so?' Mum says smugly. 'Have you considered that Brianna might be telling the truth rather than just trying to save her own skin?'

'Funnily enough, no!' I snap. 'I haven't considered that because it would mean Maddy is cruel and violent, and as you know, Mum, that's simply not true.'

An attendant shows me my room, a small but adequate space not unlike a private hospital room, with an adjoining bathroom, then leads me to the family room to wait for Tom. Mum and Dad are already in there. They're both staring down at newspapers strewn over the floor.

Neither of them looks up when I walk in and close the door behind me.

I am invisible. I am on the outside looking in. My chat with Dana has opened up a chink in my coping defence and I have an overwhelming desire to be alone.

I have my handbag on my shoulder. Inside it is the phone I found in Maddy's wardrobe. I need to turn it on and see what's on there, but I've not been able to bring myself to do it. If there is anything incriminating – and according to Josh, there might well be – I'll put myself in a very tricky situation with the police.

'It's going to be all over the papers tomorrow, Juliet,' Dad says eventually. 'The nationals have got hold of the story good and proper now on their online websites.'

So this is how they want to play it. The elephant in the room: Brianna's accusation, Maddy's admission. Never to be mentioned.

Nothing gets talked about in this family. Nothing.

Opinions and judgements are made by my mother, and then the rest of us carry them like a torch. Questioning Mum's reasoning has never been an option.

That's how families work, isn't it? Nobody actually sits down and says, 'These are the family rules.' We receive them subconsciously, we follow the example of others. Learning from childhood to turn a blind eye to the comments of a bigoted uncle because 'that's just the way he is' and overlooking constant rudeness from a grumpy 'but loveable' aunt.

We willingly accept different standards of behaviour from different people and before we know it, the brainwashing is complete. We never think to question it when we become adults.

'Are you all right, love?' Dad narrows his eyes to get a better look at me. 'You look a bit peaky.' If the situation wasn't so dire, I'd probably laugh at his comment.

'Funnily enough, I feel terrible.' I turn my gaze to look at Mum and Dad. 'Seriously, think about it. I don't hear you rushing to my daughter's defence. If you think Maddy killed an old lady all on her own, that means Brianna was there and had nothing whatsoever to do with it. Does that make sense to you?'

The looks on their faces say it all: *You are breaking the family rules, confronting us like this.*

Mum's hand flies to her throat. 'What are you trying to say, Juliet? That Bree is *lying*?'

If the cap fits…

'I'm asking you what you think of Brianna's accusation and Maddy's admission. I'm not trying to start an argument.'

'Good, because there's no point in us falling out,' says Dad, eyeing Mum. 'We have to stay strong for each other.' He stands up and guides me to the chair next to Mum. 'Sit yourself down there, lass.'

My thoughts feel indistinct, like I can't quite grasp them. This room is so stuffy, I can't bear it. But I don't sit down.

'This is my daughter's life we're talking about here. I'm not going to stand by and watch her be vilified on the strength of an accusation from her ten-year-old cousin, who may well be trying to save her own skin.'

Mum and Dad glance at each other, but nobody speaks.

DS March puts her head around the door and asks a little awkwardly if we can get everyone together as soon as possible.

'DI Neary has some important news for you.'

Mum's jaw sets and Dad pats her hand.

I feel heartened that they might have new evidence, or that they don't believe Maddy's confession.

'I'll try and contact Tom,' I say. 'I don't know where he's got to.'

'Much appreciated.' March nods and sweeps out of the room with an air of urgency.

Mum turns on me.

'Tom should have stayed put.' She fixes her dark eyes on me. 'We're all struggling to cope but we can't just run off with our heads in our hands.'

'Everybody has their own way of coping, Mum.' I tell her. 'If the business collapses and Tom loses his job, our problems will double overnight. We could lose the house and be declared bankrupt. It's a heavy load to bear. And Chloe isn't here either, don't forget.'

'Chloe's daughter hasn't done anything wrong.' Mum can be so effortlessly cruel.

I feel a sudden urge to run out of the room. Anywhere that's away from them.

'Your mum's just worried, love.' Dad sees my face, immediately defaulting to his smoothing-over mode.

'That's always been the case though, hasn't it, Dad? Mum's worried so we're all expected to keep our mouths shut and our opinions to ourselves.'

I turn away from her and call Tom, but it goes straight to voicemail.

'He must have got delayed,' I murmur, waiting for the beep so I can leave him a message. 'Tom, it's me. DI Neary needs to speak to us all. Can you come back here as soon as possible? Thanks.'

After ten minutes of sitting with my parents in near silence, DI Neary appears at the door. 'No Tom or Chloe yet?'

'Sorry. I've left Tom a message, but he's not back yet,' I say.

'OK, well I've waited as long as I can, so I'll just tell you and you can pass it on when he gets here. There's been a development.' He sounds a little breathless. 'We've had a witness come forward.'

35

Chloe is the first to arrive at the juvenile detention centre. She is pale and shocked.

When I try to speak to her about Brianna's accusation, she shrugs me off. 'I need to speak to Mum and Dad about damage to their house first.'

I go back to my room. I don't want to sit among them knowing they all support Brianna's accusation.

Eventually Tom gets to the juvenile detention centre around ten minutes later. He texts me to say he's in the lounge area with Chloe and our parents as he doesn't know where my room is.

'Where the hell have you *been*? I've been trying to get hold of you.' I rush over to him and then take in his expression. 'What's wrong?'

He looks at each of us in turn, as if he's assessing the situation.

'Have you got a moment, Juliet?'

Chloe sort of half gets up out of her chair as if she's about to say something, and then changes her mind and sits back down again.

I walk out with Tom without saying another word to the others and close the door behind us.

'Jeez, what's the mood like in there? The atmosphere's toxic.'

'You don't want to know,' I murmur. 'Just another dose of Voce family back-stabbing.'

In the brighter light of the corridor, I see that Tom's face is grey. It's scaring me, the way his mouth is turned downwards, his eyes bloodshot and troubled.

'There's been an incident, Juliet.' He grasps at my arm as if I might run away. 'A fire at the clothing unit.'

'What? Is there much damage?' An icy finger traces up the length of my spine and pincers the back of my neck.

'Everything in there has been destroyed. All your existing stock, equipment, everything… It's just a shell.'

I slump against the wall of the corridor. If the stock has gone, it means we can't fulfil our existing orders.

'The fire brigade are still there, but the fire is out now,' Tom adds. 'They've started investigating.'

'But what happened? Was it a faulty cable or something?' My mouth is dry, my mind racing through what we must have lost.

Tom looks down at the floor and shakes his head. 'I'm sorry, Jules, they think… it might be arson.'

'*What?*' I whisper.

The poisonous graffiti on the garage door, the dog mess posted through the letter box, everything that's being said online… I should've recognised the danger. Considered that it might escalate.

'They don't know for certain yet,' Tom adds. 'But the senior fire officer said there were possible signs of accelerant use. I'm so sorry. You've worked so hard at the business.'

Shit, shit, shit. And we just signed the massive new contract with Van Dyke's. Thank goodness their clothes order hasn't arrived yet though. It could have been worse.

My thoughts and words won't seem to link up.

'I don't think Chloe will cope, Tom. She's putting on a brave face, but there's something wrong. She's been acting weird for weeks now.'

He's struggling himself, I can tell. His face darkens and I can't bear to look at him. I feel so tired and have so many worries in my head, I just can't seem to think straight.

He touches my cheek.

'We'll get through this, Jules, we will. But we can't support Maddy and help the rest of the family if we fall apart.' His tone is kind, but the words are spiked with the unthinkable. 'Our needs take priority, remember that. We have to keep strong through everything that comes our way. Chloe will have to find a way of coping.'

My phone pings with a text from Beth.

Just heard about the fire. I'm worried about you. Tell me what I can do to help, pls call asap. B xx

When we signed the contract with Van Dyke, we put in a twelve-week order for all the stock to be made to our specifications. We paid a fifty per cent deposit via a temporary overdraft agreed with the bank on the strength of the contract.

Fulfilling orders with our other suppliers was going to go a long way to funding the remaining balance that's outstanding… but now we have nothing left to sell because our existing stock has been destroyed.

'We're talking thousands of pounds, Tom. This could bankrupt us.'

I feel like I could cry for a week. Cry for my beautiful daughter, caught up in this terrible nightmare that won't go away. Cry for the eighteen months of seventy-hour weeks I have put into the business to secure the future of my family.

I call Beth.

'Anything I can do, just tell me, Juliet,' she says urgently.

'Can you meet me outside the juvenile centre in Mansfield?' I ask. 'I can get Tom to pick up the paperwork I have at home, and my memory stick. We may have lost everything else in the fire.'

'Just let me have what you can, including your insurance company details, and I'll start to piece things together. I'll make a list of anything I need to ask you. The main thing is to fulfil that order according to the contract you signed. If we can do that, there might just be a way forward. I'll be in touch later.'

'Is Josh OK?' I ask.

'He's absolutely fine. Glued to the TV I'm afraid, but I figure it won't do him any harm, keeping his mind off stuff. He's staying away from the Internet as people are saying some pretty rotten stuff.'

At home we've always strictly limited his television time, but Beth is right. It's an effective diversionary measure right now.

When she rings off, I just stand there, looking at Tom.

If we lose the business, we lose everything we own.

36

2003

The ambulance didn't take long to arrive, but each minute seemed like an hour to Juliet, all sorts of awful scenarios running through her head as she waited.

She had raced down the hill and up to the top road that traced around the boundary of the warren, running faster than she'd ever moved in her life.

A small bungalow, perched close to the edge of the warren, was the first house she got to. A lady answered when she knocked at the door and immediately called the emergency services.

She introduced herself as Anne and kindly allowed Juliet to use her telephone to call home. She listened to the ring and through the kitchen window, watched a small boy on a toy tractor, trundling up and down the path of the long back garden.

'Dad?' she said breathlessly when he finally answered. 'Come quick as you can to the warren. Corey's had an accident on Stony Side Hill.'

'What kind of an accident?'

She couldn't answer.

'Juliet?'

'He… he fell. Just come quick, Dad, *please.*'

Her father continued to bark questions at her, demanding to know exactly what had happened, but she quietly said goodbye and replaced the receiver.

She couldn't handle facing her own incompetence so starkly, not at this moment and not in front of a stranger.

Anne gave her a glass of water and thankfully left her alone to wait for the ambulance on the front step. A golden retriever nuzzled her hand for attention and Juliet lay her face against the warmth of his head for a moment.

The ambulance arrived and the paramedics immediately pulled portable medical kits from the back and followed Juliet to the entrance to the warren. When she pointed to Stony Side Hill and explained where Corey had landed, the two men upped their pace. They soon moved well in front of her, jogging towards the foot of the hill. She followed as swiftly as she could with hope in her heart.

She imagined Corey sitting up, rubbing the back of his head. Chloe would be comforting him and joking about his misadventure in that way she had that could sometimes make you feel better about stuff you'd done wrong.

But Dad would be on his way now, and Mum… well, Mum was a different story altogether. Juliet could barely face the thought of facing Joan, telling her she'd somehow fallen asleep and left Corey to his own devices. It was enough to turn her blood to ice.

Her fingernails begin to flex against her hand as she walked, squeezing the soft flesh of her palm a little harder with each step.

After her initial flare of adrenalin, she was flagging again, but still she focused on keeping up her pace, trying to forge through the exhaustion.

By the time she'd reached the bottom of the hill, the paramedics were halfway up it.

Please, please let Corey be OK, she chanted to herself like a mantra, in time with her laboured strides.

There was no denying that Corey was a little live wire, and he got on *all* their nerves at times, but Juliet adored him. She would never willingly do anything to put her brother at risk.

She had heard her mother say some awful things to Ray: that she had never wanted a third child, that Corey was hyperactive and out of control and she was sick to death of the sight of him. But that was just her mum. Underneath all the showboating, Juliet knew she loved him. She loved them all, didn't she?

It was just that she struggled to cope with life itself sometimes. But if anything happened to Corey, her mother would be devastated.

They all would.

37

Tom suggests I make a list of the things I need. 'I'll go back to the house and pick everything up you need for Beth,' he says. 'You're best staying here in case Maddy needs you.'

I realise there's something I need to tell him.

'It's crazy at the house. I've been back there, just before Dana spoke to the girls the second time. There are press there. Lots of them outside the gate and…' I sniff. 'There are locals hanging around. Unfriendly ones, shouting abusive stuff. When I left, I had to sneak out of the back across another garden to call a cab to come to the road behind ours.'

He's incredulous. 'Why on earth did you go there alone?'

'I had to look for the secret phone Josh told us about, and I knew you'd try and put me off if I told you what I had in mind. The people outside the house… they said awful things I don't want to repeat. I just don't understand how they get to know everything that's happening. I thought this stuff was supposed to be confidential.'

Tom's shoulders shoot up to his ears. 'Word gets around; you know what the village grapevine is like, it's more effective than any newspaper. Neighbours will have seen the girls being taken away from the house, heard that the old lady had been attacked.' His voice drops low. 'Did you… find the phone?'

I nod and pat my handbag. 'It's in here, but I haven't looked at it yet. If I'm honest, I'm scared to.'

'Give it to me,' he says gently. 'I'll take it to the car and look through it so there's no chance of anyone seeing.'

I clamp my jaw closed, sparking with the injustice of us having to behave this way because of people we don't even know judging our daughter.

'Tom, it wasn't just the horrible stuff they were shouting; there's some really vile graffiti sprayed across the garage door. The front door lock has been blocked with glue and someone' – I wince – 'has posted dog mess through our letter box. The whole place stinks of it.'

Tom sighs and touches my arm.

'Give me the phone, Jules,' he says, and holds out his hand.

When Tom has gone, I stand on my own for a few minutes in the corridor. One or two members of staff walk by and eye me cautiously. DS March strides past and stops to ask if I'm OK.

There's nowhere to reflect here, nowhere to sit and gather my thoughts. Reluctantly I return to the family waiting room.

'What was all that about?' Chloe narrows her eyes as if she's trying to get the measure of me. 'What did Tom want to talk about?'

I take a breath. 'There's been a fire at the lock-up unit. We've lost everything.'

'What?' Chloe frowns. 'Maybe you should remind Tom I'm a director in the business too. I don't appreciate being cut out of that conversation.'

I feel too weak and worried to argue. 'The fire officer said it's looking like it might be arson.'

Chloe picks up her phone and taps on it.

'There are online news reports coming through about it now,' she murmurs. 'Bessie's death is trending on Twitter. People are being… vile. That's the only word.'

She holds out her phone and I take it and look at the screen.

She has found a thread on Facebook from a woman called Marcia Parminter. I've never heard of her, but she posted a public status just two hours ago.

Beware: our village is not safe with these two little evil cows still in it.

She attached an unofficial online article reporting on Bessie's death, and the comments of other people underneath the status are far from flattering.

I was at school with Juliet Fletcher. She's snooty, thinks she's better than everyone else.

The kids' mothers are obsessed with their clothing business, have a lock-up storage place on Ashfield Industrial Park. Sounds like the kids had to sort themselves out a lot of the time.

Maddy Fletcher is the quiet one and they say that sort are the worst.

I heard Brianna Voce is sly.

I know Brianna's mum, Chloe. Her husband dumped her while she was still pregnant.

Shame if Chloe gets tarred with the same brush as her stuck-up sister.

'Dumped me while I was pregnant? I don't remember that! Full of inaccuracies and lies.' Chloe's face is puce. 'I'm not sitting back and letting them say stuff about me and Bree any longer. I'm sorry, Jules, but the press need to know Maddy has confessed.' She looks at me. 'It's only right.'

The phone slips from my fingers and clatters to the floor.

'Careful!' Chloe tuts and scoots forward to retrieve the device before looking at me.

'We shouldn't dignify this crap by reacting,' I remark, looking at them all in turn. 'We need to keep a united front. Stick together.'

'Course,' Chloe says pointedly. 'I'm sure you'd stick by *us* if it was Brianna who'd confessed.'

My blood feels like it's boiling in my veins. 'We are all in this together, whether you like it or not. Both our daughters were at

Bessie Wilford's house. We still don't know exactly what happened there. It's not enough that Brianna has accused Maddy.'

'Things have changed now.' Chloe's voice assumes a cold edge. 'Maddy has admitted to attacking Bessie. You can't expect Brianna to take the rap for it.'

I glare at my parents. 'Maddy is your granddaughter too, but I don't hear either of you defending her. You *know* she's not capable of doing anything bad.'

Mum and Chloe glance at each other, and then Chloe clears her throat.

'Chloe…' Dad says in a warning tone.

'No, Dad! She needs to know. She thinks the sun shines out of that kid's backside. It's time she heard the truth.' Chloe looks at me, her mouth a mean tight line. 'You should know that last week Maddy stole some money from Mum's purse.'

I pull in air. 'What?'

'She's been acting differently for a few weeks, Juliet, you must've noticed that.'

'Differently how?'

'Just her general behaviour. I asked you if she was OK once or twice, but you just brushed it off, said she must be tired.'

I think about Maddy's insomnia and her quiet spells when she seems to be deep in thought. Kids go through these phases, everyone knows that.

'Tell me what happened with the money.'

'I had a folded ten-pound note and a few coins in my purse,' Mum says, picking at a thread on her skirt. 'When the milkman came, I realised I'd calculated his bill wrong and needed a bit more cash. But when I went to my purse, the tenner had gone.'

'And what's that got to do with Maddy?'

'Joan, love, we agreed. This is not the time.' Dad's cheeks flush with colour as fast as I feel the blood drain from my own.

'Can you just stop talking around it and get to the point?' I look at them both in turn.

The edges of Mum's mouth droop downwards. 'I asked the girls if either of them had taken it and they both said no, but Maddy went very quiet and I thought she looked guilty. When they were playing outside, I found it tucked in the front zip of her little rucksack.'

'And you didn't think to tell me?'

The two crimson patches on Mum's cheeks intensify.

'She started to cry when I asked her about it.' She looks at Dad.

'She begged us not to tell you,' Dad says apologetically. 'She said she was frightened you'd get really angry.'

Chloe folds her arms, a smug expression on her face. It's all I can do not to wipe it off.

I glare accusingly at her. 'You've seen me every day at work but never mentioned it.'

'Not my place to.' She shrugs. 'Mum and Dad didn't want to worry you because… well, you've found life hard enough to cope with lately, haven't you?'

The three of them against me. That old familiar battle ploy.

But Maddy… my bright, joyful Maddy, involved in such a dishonest incident? Another one I didn't know about.

My skin feels like it's crawling with bugs. I scratch at the back of my neck, the inside of my elbows.

'We just didn't want to upset you, love,' Dad says pleadingly. 'What with you taking the antidepressants and all, and Chloe said how stressed you've been at work lately. We thought—'

'Well you thought wrong. You can't just go making decisions like that. She's *my* daughter.'

I'm seething. I can't look at them. Any of them.

My parents and sister, discussing my child and making decisions about what I should and shouldn't know!

I stand up and then sit down again.

'Tom will go crazy when I tell him. You can't go keeping important stuff like this from us. You just can't!'

Mum folds her arms. 'He already knows. He was the one we went to to sort it all out.'

'It was Tom who asked us not to mention it to you,' Dad says gently.

38

The village

It was after 7.30 p.m. when Dana got home. Used to letting herself into an empty house, it was a treat to walk in to the comforting smell of delicious food on the go.

Yesterday when Lizzie had offered to cook dinner, Dana had jumped at it and handed over her door key for the first time. Neither of them said anything, but it felt significant in their developing relationship.

Dana hoped Lizzie would invite her over to her own place soon. She'd already explained it was poky and not where she wanted to be, but still, Dana would appreciate the gesture.

'Risotto,' she said over Lizzie's shoulder as she stood at the hob, stirring. 'My favourite!'

Lizzie ordered her out of the kitchen and into the lounge. Minutes later, she came through carrying two large glasses of red wine.

'Hey, why the long face?' She handed Dana a glass and frowned. 'Not thinking about work, I hope.'

'Guilty as charged, I'm afraid.' Dana took a sip of the velvety Merlot. 'I'm just wondering how those girls and their families will cope this evening in the juvenile detention centre. I don't think there'll be much sleep happening; it'll be a long, long night. But forget me – tell me about your day.'

'My day has been boring and routine, and if you want to offload, I'm offering you the chance now. Once the food is on the table, it's a strictly no-shop-talk zone.'

'Get it out of the way, you mean?' Dana grinned and took another sip of her wine, relaxing back into the soft cushions behind her. 'It's just this case; it's getting to me when it should be fairly straightforward.'

'Getting to you how exactly? Worrying about the girls, you mean?'

'Hmm. There's something not right about it all. It's like there's a piece of the jigsaw missing, but I've no evidence. It's just a feeling.'

Lizzie laughed and made a spooky noise. She put her wine glass down on a coaster by her feet before speaking.

'Could it be it's because the case is so troubling? Two ten-year-olds carrying out such a horrible attack is enough to mess with anyone's head. It might just be that you feel uncomfortable about it.'

Dana nodded thoughtfully. It felt so good to come home and let everything out instead of having it churning around in her head like an out-of-control washing machine.

'I don't need to tell you that sometimes pretty horrible stuff does happen in this world,' Lizzie continued gently. 'None of us want to believe it in this case: two young girls from what appear to be decent families. But could it be possible that in a moment of madness, they attacked that poor old lady and turned temporarily mute with the shock and denial? Thinking about the most famous child murderer cases, their awful deeds are hardly ever planned. Maybe your compassionate mind is just trying to make sense of it all.'

Dana nodded again but said nothing. She knew only too well that bad stuff happened. It still didn't change the stubborn feeling in her gut.

'What do the detectives think?' Lizzie said.

'Neary thinks there's probably more to it, but he's under pressure to follow the evidence and get a conviction. Tension is building in the village by the hour, and the investigation has come to the same conclusion: that the girls did it.'

Lizzie placed her hand on Dana's and pressed down to reassure her.

'It's not in your job description to save everyone, you know,' she said. 'You're allowed to follow the evidence too, and you're allowed to come home and relax at the end of the day. Now, I'll check on the risotto and you make a deal with yourself to take a break.'

She took her wine with her, and a few seconds later, Dana heard plates and cutlery clinking in the kitchen. Lizzie wanted the best for her, that much was obvious.

Dana knew her own faults; she knew she'd often become over-involved in complex cases in the past, and eventually that had been her downfall. Now it was starting to happen again.

But this time she felt another feeling deep in her bones that refused to be ignored, and that was this new chance of happiness in her own life. Her blossoming relationship with Lizzie was like a small flame that needed to be nurtured and given the time and space to grow.

There wasn't time to save the world as well.

Lizzie was right, she thought, picking up her wine and heading for the kitchen. Maybe it was finally time to put herself first.

39

Juliet

I finally collapse exhausted into my temporary bed at the centre around 9 p.m.

Soon as I'm horizontal, my exhaustion disappears and my brain starts to zing with a thousand awful thoughts.

I'm too warm, tossing and turning this way and that. At least I have the small double bed to myself. Tom decided to take the business information over to Beth and then stay in a cheap Premier Inn near home and the lock-up. He couldn't possibly stay in the house with everything that was happening there.

'I can keep an eye on what's happening and speak to the chief fire officer and the police. Plus I can call in at Beth's in the morning and check up on Josh too,' he said.

It makes perfect sense really, but I can't help feeling there's something he's battling with on his own.

'I've looked at Maddy's phone and there are a few text messages on there that don't really make any sense to me. I've called the number they came from and there's just a recorded message saying the call cannot be put through. There's nothing on there the police need to know, anyway.'

I feel relieved at this news but I'm so angry about the incident with the missing money from Mum's purse. Why wouldn't Tom share that with me? He might think he's doing me a favour, but the way it's come out has caused far more distress in the long run.

I will confront him about it, but I want to do that face to face. Speaking on the phone is too ambiguous. I need to see his expression, hear his voice when he responds.

Tom emailed the school, and the head replied out of hours. She has agreed it's probably best if Josh stays away until things quieten down a little. Tomorrow they're going to provide him with some work to do at home, to keep him occupied and to ensure he won't fall behind the rest of his class. I don't want to think about how he's going to feel going back there, not after how the other kids, including those he counted as mates, taunted him so cruelly on the coach.

Before he left to get the stuff for Beth, Tom lifted my chin gently with his hand and kissed my nose.

'We will get through this, you know,' he said. I nodded to make him feel better, but he looked at me even more intensely. 'It's really important you hear what I'm saying, Jules. I mean really *hear* me. Whatever challenges are ahead, we can get through them together. I want you to remember that and hold onto it, no matter what happens.'

I lowered my eyes and took a step back. His words seemed loaded with something unsaid, and the feeling it gave me made me want to turn and run.

Thinking about all this has got the negative stuff churning away in my guts again. The rising panic, the building dread, it's all there in my solar plexus, gathering strength and getting ready to make a break for it.

Anxiety.

Despite going back on the tablets, I can feel I'm really in trouble this time, and I don't know how long I can keep pushing the feeling away.

I'm overwhelmed but trying to put on a brave face so I'm no trouble to anyone around me. I look up at the clean white ceiling and try to breathe deeply. I wonder how many other mothers have lain here, looking up and dreading the dawn of the next day, unsure what will happen to their child.

I can't get Maddy's pleading face out of my head. They let us kiss the girls goodnight but said it wasn't possible for us to stay in the same room. She had on her own pyjamas that my parents brought from their house. She keeps the red and white Christmas ones there, insisting on wearing them all year round.

Someone had neatly combed her hair and she looked so vulnerable… so innocent.

Carol said, 'Kiss your mum and then we can read your book together before bed.'

Maddy held onto me tightly, quietly sobbing, her hair becoming damp and messy around her hollow face.

'I don't want to go, Mummy, I want to stay with you.'

I pulled her close and we locked ourselves together until I finally had to let her go.

Now I'm lying here trying to imagine what life will be like if we can't take Maddy home again, if our family is broken into tiny pieces that can never be put back together.

The physical pain in my chest is unbearable; the thought of losing my daughter is an ache like no other.

When Corey died, I found out at thirteen years old that the pain of a broken heart is as real as any physical injury. Over time, it lessened, but the ache never went away, and now I might have a fresh gaping wound to add to it.

I feel myself begin to drift off to sleep, and then suddenly I'm sitting bolt upright, my heart pounding like a jackhammer in my chest. For a moment I think I can smell smoke, and I jump up and grab my dressing gown, but there's nothing, no smouldering, no fire.

I slide open the sash window, which only opens a couple of inches, and crouch down to drag in the cool, fresh air.

The business is all but ruined and we'll probably lose the house now. Getting over that fire feels insurmountable, even though we still have the orders.

A sharp pain in my hand causes me to look down, and I see I've broken the skin on my thumb with my fingernail. I can see the dark blood against my pale skin in the light of a nearby car park lantern that casts everything in a sort of sepia filter, as if it isn't quite real.

But this is very real. Only twenty-four hours ago, I was at home, in bed. Tom was finishing watching a film downstairs, Josh was safely away on his school trip and Maddy was fast asleep in her bedroom. I had a successful business, and I remember I couldn't even focus on reading my book because I was too busy running through everything I had to do the following day. All those terribly important tasks that just couldn't wait had now dissolved into thin air.

Now that life has been all but decimated, and the forced helplessness is the worst thing of all as I wait and wait in this sterile box until we learn our fate.

I have nurtured and protected my daughter for ten whole years, and now she's slipping away from me like sand through my fingers and there's nothing I can do about it.

Nothing at all.

40

2003

Halfway up the hill, Juliet was forced to slow her climbing pace right down. She felt hot and breathless and had to take regular rests. It was all she could do to plod the rest of the way up the hill one step at a time without keeling over.

About ten minutes later when she eventually reached the top, dizzy and disoriented, she saw that between them, Chloe and the paramedics had managed to haul Corey back up to the top of the rocky slope.

The little boy looked pale and lifeless. Something dark and indefinable had Juliet by the throat, sucking the very air out of her lungs.

One of the paramedics looked up and jumped to his feet.

'Sit down, take a breath.' He pressed her shoulders gently and Juliet sank to her knees on the grass. 'You're having a panic attack. Close your eyes and breathe. In… one, two. Out… one, two. That's right, just carry on like that for a bit.'

She felt the tightness in her throat give a little, and opened her eyes.

Chloe walked over to her. 'Calm down, Juliet. The paramedics need to keep their attention on Corey.' Her voice was sharp, but she laid a hand on Juliet's arm. 'Come on, they think he'll be all right.'

'He looks…' Juliet couldn't manage to speak and breathe at the same time.

'He looks bad because he knocked himself unconscious, but he's awake now. They've told him he has to keep as still as possible and not go to sleep.' Chloe sighed. 'He's taken a nasty bump to the head and broken his leg, and they need to get him to hospital to do some scans and X-rays.'

Thank you, God. Thank you for sparing him.

Juliet's breathing eased a little more and she got to her feet. She took a few steps forward and saw Corey's eyelids flutter, and her heart squeezed in on itself.

She walked over and crouched down beside her brother's head.

'I'm so sorry I let you down, Corey,' she whispered, stroking his cheek. 'I'll make it up to you, I promise.'

His face seemed so pasty, and he looked skinny and frail just lying there listlessly as the paramedic placed an oxygen mask over his face.

She would explain to her parents what had happened: that she hadn't wilfully neglected her brother but had been unwell herself.

Hopefully they would understand.

'What on earth were you thinking, you stupid little bitch!' Juliet ducked as her mother aimed a teacup at her head. 'You were asked to do one thing… *one measly thing* to help! And now your brother's in hospital with all that *that* entails.'

The cup hit the kitchen cupboard next to Juliet and smashed into pieces, showering the linoleum with tiny shards of floral china.

'Come on, love, calm down,' Ray chided. 'You've only just got rid of that migraine.'

'Yes, and I shall have another one twice as bad at this rate.' Joan glared at Juliet, then leaned back against the worktop, suddenly breathless. 'Why have they got to keep him in? Two or three days, they said.'

'It's the concussion; they think he might have a little bleed on his brain,' Ray told her.

'Bleed on the brain' sounded so awful. Corey was only five, Juliet thought sadly. He shouldn't have to go through this. Her entire skull was pounding and she willed it to get worse. She hated herself for what she'd done. It could so easily have been avoided.

'What were you thinking, Juliet?' Ray shook his head and sighed. 'Falling asleep like that when you were supposed to be looking after the lad!'

'I didn't do it on purpose, Dad. I just felt so tired. I couldn't keep my eyes open.'

'Thank God Chloe had the sense to come looking for you, that's all I can say,' Joan snapped.

'I know you hardly slept last night, and you'd never knowingly put our Corey at risk, but—'

'Oh stop pandering to her, Ray,' Joan snapped. 'It's her fault Corey slipped and there'll be a suitable punishment coming as soon as I can get my thoughts in order.'

Juliet gulped. The worst punishment she'd ever had from her mother was when she'd failed to tidy up her side of the bedroom she shared with Chloe.

While she was at school, Joan had gathered up her stuff, which included a letter from her late grandma, Ray's mother, to whom she'd been close, and a selection of poems Juliet had written and painstakingly made into an illustrated booklet that had won top prize in the school's young poet competition.

When she got home, her precious belongings were reduced to a small pile of ash in the corner of the yard. She'd felt raw for months afterwards. Violated.

'I don't know how I'm going to get to and from that hospital, Ray, what with this sciatica in my leg.' Joan rubbed the top of her thigh.

'You don't have to, love. I can see to him while he's in there. He'll be home soon, anyhow.'

Joan opened the cupboard under the sink and plucked out the dustpan and brush, sliding it across the floor.

'Get that cleaned up.' She indicated the smashed crockery around Juliet's feet.

'I'll come and visit Corey with you, Dad,' Juliet said.

'No chance. You're grounded, and that includes going to the hospital.' Joan's mouth puckered into a tight knot. 'You've done enough harm to your brother as it is. Stay away from him.'

A couple of days later, Juliet peered through the crack in the door and saw her mum and dad sitting close together on the sofa. Joan laid her head on Ray's shoulder, dabbing at her eyes with a tissue.

There was something curious about the scenario, something Juliet didn't quite understand.

Since the accident, she had felt a relentless ache deep in her guts. There was no respite from it. She badly needed Corey to come home, to see him running around screeching in that boisterous way of his that used to drive her mad when she was trying to read.

But standing there watching the quiet misery of her parents, the ache had developed into a snaking sense of dread.

Something was wrong. She could feel it.

She crept upstairs and sat on her bed facing Chloe, who was sitting up against her headboard idly sketching on her drawing pad.

'I'm worried about Corey,' she whispered, keeping one ear alert for footsteps on the stairs. 'It's been three days and there's no sign of him coming home yet. Mum and Dad are being weird together downstairs. I was wondering…'

'Wondering what?' Chloe looked up from her drawing.

'Maybe we could secretly visit him. I hate not knowing how he is.'

'Mum would crucify you if she found out.' Chloe frowned. 'He'll be fine. Besides, it's really peaceful here without him.'

'Chloe!' Juliet stood up, shocked.

'Can't you take a joke any more?' Chloe wiggled her back further into her pillow. 'It's no good getting ratty with *me*. This is all your fault, remember?'

Juliet said nothing. Silence cloaked the room and Chloe went back to her drawing.

Her sister was right: this *was* all Juliet's fault. But everybody made mistakes, didn't they?

The awful truth suddenly hit her between the eyes.

Even when Corey was well again and back home, her family would never let her forget what had happened on Stony Side Hill.

DAY TWO

41

Juliet

I don't know how, but somehow I manage to drop off into a fractured sleep, in which my nightmares from the past struggle to compete with the awful reality of what's waiting for me in the morning.

When I wake, it's not one of those instances where for a wonderful moment I think I'm still at home and everything is fine. No, I know from the second I open my eyes that today is judgement day. The day Maddy will be charged or, by some miracle, will be able to come home.

I reach for my phone and see I have a text from Beth.

I need to speak to you RIGHT NOW. Are you awake?? B x

It was sent twenty minutes ago, at 5.52.

Yes! What's wrong? Can talk now. Shall I call?

I press the send button and throw the phone on the bed while I visit the small bathroom. The phone starts to ring while I'm still in there.

I rush out, hastily pulling up my pyjama bottoms, and snatch up the phone.

'Juliet?' Beth's voice sounds frantic.

My heartbeat begins to gallop. 'Is everything OK? Is Josh all right?'

'Josh is fine.' She pauses. 'Look, I know today is shit for you before it's even started, but I've found something and I have to tell you. I hope I'm wrong… but I don't think I am.'

I close my eyes and press close to the wall. I want to throw up, but there's nothing in my stomach.

'Just say it, Beth.' Despite the panic I feel inside, my voice comes out totally flat. I've nothing left to give.

'I spoke to the insurance company. I had to pretend to be you otherwise they won't talk due to data protection. I had to give them all the business details and they were non-committal, said they'd look into it and get back to me.' She's babbling, playing for time. 'I woke up to a voicemail from them. Juliet, I'm so sorry, I can't—'

'Just tell me,' I whisper. 'Please, Beth. Just say it.'

'They're saying the policy has lapsed. It expired two weeks ago and it hasn't been renewed.' Beth's voice catches. 'You can't claim a penny for the contents destroyed by the fire and you've automatically breached your lock-up rental lease too by letting it lapse.'

'What? But Chloe said…' My voice tails off. Chloe gave me her word everything was up to date with the admin. Why did she lie? What is so complicated in her life that she couldn't make one phone call to renew the insurance?

'I'm sorry, Jules. I don't know what to say and… there's something else.'

I can't speak. I slide down the wall and clamp the phone to my ear, hugging my bent knees close to me.

'Jules? Are you there?'

'Yes,' I croak.

'The lifesaver in a situation like this is the regular back-up program you need to run each evening so all your information is on a zip file.'

'Chloe does that.' My heart blips with hope. 'That's one of her jobs.'

Hesitation on the end of the phone. 'I've checked your back-up files and nothing has been updated in the last five weeks, Juliet.'

I let out a little cry. My hand is shaking so hard I think I might drop the phone.

Beth's voice is back. 'Listen to me, Jules. You have to focus on Maddy right now. Josh is fine, so don't worry about him, and let me know the second you hear anything, OK?'

I hear myself croak again, and then I end the call. I close my eyes and breathe.

It's not exactly fresh in here. The window is open, and I can smell exhaust fumes from the busy road that runs along the boundary of the property.

The conversation I had with Chloe only yesterday about the admin replays in my mind.

I'm on top of my responsibilities, thanks for asking.

That same stock reply. She's been distracted, sort of distant for the last couple of months. I've sensed something isn't right, but she has fended off every attempt to get her to open up to me.

I've never been able to reach her, not really. There's always been something invisible there, standing in the way of us enjoying a closer relationship. I've always known it, always just accepted that's the way things are between us.

I guess I've always assumed, deep down, that she can't quite forgive me for Corey.

I hear voices outside in the corridor as the centre begins to crank into life.

I've had it with pussy-footing around Chloe. She needs to face up to what she's done and as my sky has already fallen in, what have I got to lose?

I take a quick shower and get dressed. I don't bother washing my hair, just opt for clipping it up into a rough and ready twist and use a face wipe to get rid of yesterday's mascara.

The thought of applying make-up to my puffy, sleep-deprived face is just ridiculous, and so I don't.

I text Tom and ask him to come to the centre right away. His reply pings back in seconds.

Already on my way x

I pack my few meagre belongings in my overnight bag and set it down by the bed so I can be ready to go at a moment's notice if necessary. Then I lie back, close my eyes and try to breathe deeply to settle the churning sensation in my stomach.

Ten minutes later, I open the door and nod to two members of staff who are walking past wearing ID lanyards and serious expressions. I head to the family room, push open the door and step inside. Mum, Dad, Tom and Chloe are sitting in there together, talking.

Why do I feel I'm on the outside looking in… and why didn't Tom come to my room first?

He looks up.

'Juliet! I was just about to come and find you.'

I frown. He doesn't look like he was on his way anywhere.

'I need to speak to Chloe,' I say. I'm trying to keep my voice clear and level, but I sound groggy and disorientated.

Chloe touches her chest with her fingertips. 'Just me?'

I nod, noticing that she's styled her hair and applied a pale pink lipstick. 'There's an empty office next door.'

For a second or two, she actually looks nervous.

'Do you need me to come too?' Tom stands up and brushes the creases from his shirt. 'We've just been discussing the implications of the fire.'

I bite down on my back teeth. Why would he talk to Chloe about that instead of me? Who does the business belong to?

I want to stay calm and reasoned, but my head feels heavy and weighed down. It's a strange feeling, like a slow-build anger is stoking inside me.

'I'll have a quick word with you first, Tom,' I say gruffly, and shuffle out without speaking to my parents, who are sitting there like waxworks.

42

'Why have we got to come in here to talk?' Tom says, shaking his head. I close the office door behind him. 'What's wrong?'

I take a breath and it all rushes out. 'You're not going to believe this, but Beth just called to say the business insurance policy has lapsed. We're not covered for any losses caused by the fire.'

I watch his face as he realises the crushing implications.

'You mean…' He can't bring himself to say it.

I nod. 'We've lost everything. And as if things couldn't get any worse, there hasn't been a back-up done for any of our files for weeks.'

'Shit! How did that happen?'

'*Chloe* is how it happened. It was her responsibility to renew the insurance policy, her responsibility to run the back-up. I asked her yesterday morning if she was on top of the admin, and she assured me she was.'

I grit my teeth. Each time I think it or say it, the more angry I feel. It's not even the act of letting an important policy lapse that's getting to me. It's her constant denial, the way she doggedly pushes away my concern.

'I think we should look at the details together, Jules. Make absolutely sure we've got this right before you go ahead and accuse her.' He pauses, and seems to turn a little paler.

'I'm done tiptoeing around her, Tom. I've got to speak to her now.'

'It's not worth falling out over this.' He stuffs his hands into the pockets of his jeans.

'Are you serious?' I let out a harsh laugh. 'She's been unbelievably negligent. She'd be fired on the spot in a normal company. I'm sick of watching my step around her when I know something's wrong. She's been detached from me *and* her job for months now, and it's time we discussed it.'

'But your family needs to gel at a time like this, not start a fight about something else.'

The grinding pressure in my head is increasing by the second. I can't believe that Tom, who has been the first to criticise Chloe in the past over her lax attitude, now seems to be trying to protect her. It doesn't make sense.

He holds his hand up in a stop sign. 'I'm just trying to cool things off a little.'

'I know that, and it's out of character.' I narrow my eyes. 'You seem to have suddenly found a great deal of empathy for my sister.'

He hesitates. 'You don't want to make yourself feel worse than you do already.'

'I might be on antidepressants,' I say, 'but right now, I feel like I'm the only one in the family who's got my head screwed on.'

'I know, but I just think—' Tom stammers.

'You think *what*, exactly? Is this why you've been lying to me, keeping stuff from me?'

His face drains of colour. 'What?'

'How could you keep something like that from me? You had no right!' My own words pound in my ears; they sound muffled, like I'm underwater.

His face seems to crumple. 'I'm so sorry, Juliet. Please understand I had no choice. I couldn't just come out and tell you. I was waiting for the right moment.'

'I've a right to know if there are problems with our daughter, Tom. I don't believe she stole that money from Mum's purse; she's just not a dishonest girl. Remember when she found twenty pounds on the floor at the Tesco checkout? She handed it in without a second thought.'

I look at him, and the strangest thing happens. The tension slides from his face and he actually smiles.

Ridiculously, I have to fight the impulse to hammer on his chest with my fists. Tom and I have never lifted a finger against each other, but this… this has really pressed my buttons.

'Calm down, Juliet.' His voice sounds infuriatingly reasonable. 'This is not the worst thing that has happened.'

The fury dissipates as quickly as it came, and now I just feel empty inside. 'I'm her *mother*, for goodness' sake. I had a right to know.'

He clenches his jaw, and it looks so square and angular, it could be made of stone.

'I had to make a judgement call, had to decide if the incident with Maddy was serious enough to risk the pressure it would put on you.' He looks at my tear-streaked face and his expression softens a touch. 'I don't think you're aware of how much stress you put yourself under, Jules. Working every hour God sends on the business and then pushing yourself to do even more at weekends. You've been so… so *tense* and snappy since getting that big order. I thought telling you about this might tip you over the edge.'

I get ready to retaliate, but there are no comeback words there when I reach for them.

It's true I've been worried about the big order. These last few weeks have been crucial. Getting the details finalised and contracts signed… anything could have gone wrong.

Nothing else seemed to matter. Nothing. And now look what's happened… Maddy is being accused of a terrible crime and the business is virtually destroyed anyway.

But Tom is laying it on thick. *Every hour God sends?* An exaggeration, surely. I've made it a priority to pick Maddy and Josh up from Mum's house no later than six each day, and we're always home around ten minutes later. I thought that was enough to qualify me as a good mother, a parent who is there for her children.

Yet I feel a niggle deep down that tells me he's right.

Once I get through the door each evening, I simply set my laptop up on the kitchen counter and carry on working. I often cook the children's tea around updating the InsideOut4Kids website.

The reality is, I'm there… but I'm *not really* there. Not all of me.

For the first time, I consider the echoes of my own childhood, when Mum spent so much time in her bedroom.

I can't remember the last time we all sat down and ate together, or watched TV as a family. We often stay in different rooms until it's time for bed. And the outings to the park or the cinema we used to plan and enjoy at weekends? I seriously can't remember the last time we did that.

I thought I was being Superwoman, and it turns out I'm struggling to tick all the boxes like any other mere mortal.

The realisation renders me speechless, and it doesn't take Tom long to capitalise on it.

'Don't feel bad, Jules. I know you haven't registered the extent of it until now. We used to talk about everything.' He pauses. 'I don't know what happened to us.'

While I work most of the evening in the kitchen, Maddy and Josh watch television in the living room and Tom sits in there with them, often doing puzzles on his iPad.

When we go to bed, I'm usually answering emails or looking at trade brochures. Tom puts in his earbuds and listens to a chapter or two of his current audiobook, usually falling asleep well before I turn my lamp out.

The days of lying snuggled up together while we talk about our day have been over for a long time now, and we haven't made love for months.

'You could've said something,' I offer faintly. 'If it's bothered you so much, you should have said so. We could have tried a bit harder.'

A look of incredulity settles over his features.

'I've lost count of the times I've tried to discuss it with you, Jules. You always agree we should try harder, but that's not the problem.' He smiles sadly. 'The problem is in following through and making it happen.'

He's right, I know he is, but I'm getting that old familiar feeling that all our shortcomings are being firmly placed on my shoulders.

'I was building the business for *us*,' I say slowly so my voice doesn't break. 'For our future. The four of us.'

'I know that,' Tom says quietly. 'I'm so proud of what you've achieved, but… I never realised you would become so immersed in it. I didn't know it would take so much of you.'

A sense of loss settles over me. Everything I've worked for has gone up in smoke. Literally. The business has been a drug to me. Even though Chloe is a director, she hasn't got the same passion, the same all-consuming drive as me. I shudder to think what else Beth might unearth that my sister has let slip.

'It's sad, what we've become,' Tom says softly. 'So busy with our lives we've no time to reflect on what we've got. What we had.'

A chill prickles the tiny hairs on my forearms. He's talking as though we've already lost that special spark we had together, that nothing can be salvaged.

I think about all his recent work meetings, and how he regularly pops out for work commitments at weekends too. I only ever half listen to what he says, so I can't even recall the reasons he gives.

He'll often have a shower as soon as he gets in, and yet he hasn't been to the gym for the last six months or so.

'If there's stuff I haven't told you, it's for your own good, Juliet,' he says, the corners of his mouth drooping. 'I just want what's best for you. I hope you'll remember that.'

For a second I think he's going to tell me something else, and I hold my breath ready for the blow, but he just pinches the skin between his eyebrows and sighs.

For the first time, unlikely as it seems, I turn and look at Tom and question if it could be remotely possible that my husband is having an affair.

43

The door opens without a knock.

'You'd better make your chat a short one,' Mum says brusquely. 'They're talking about interviewing the girls again.'

I feel relief that they haven't given up on Maddy, aren't ready to throw the book at her without a bit more digging.

Chloe stands behind Mum, and I see her swallow hard and glance questioningly at Tom as he leaves the room. What is it with those two? Maybe they're worried I haven't taken today's tablets and am about to have a full-scale meltdown. Well I'll let them fret. A meltdown feels pretty close right now.

'So what's this about?' Chloe says boldly when the others have gone, already recovered from her apparent nervousness.

'Tom says you've been talking about the fire this morning,' I say.

'Yes… and?' The old attitude is back with a vengeance now. 'It's terrible news, but I think you'll agree there are other things to worry about here.'

'Cast your mind back to yesterday morning, when I asked you if you were on top of the admin.'

She frowns. 'I told you I was.'

'And you blatantly lied.' I take a step towards her, struggling to keep a lid on my fury. 'We're not covered for the fire. No cover in place for any contents – computers, stock, furniture – because *you* failed to renew the insurance policy.'

'What? No I didn't!' Her fingers tap around the bottom of her neck. 'I mean, we've had the reminder, but it's not due until…'

Her mouth is still moving but the words are failing her now. She looks so scraggy and washed out.

'I didn't realise… Oh God, no.'

'Everything in there has literally gone up in smoke. It will probably totally ruin us.'

'The new Van Dyke order,' she says faintly.

'Thank goodness the Van Dyke merchandise hasn't arrived yet, so wasn't destroyed. Beth's going to try and rescue the order for us, and she's going to carry out an assessment of where we stand and what we've lost as soon as the senior fire officer gives her the all-clear.'

'Beth!' Chloe's mouth twists. 'She always manages to worm her way in.'

'*Thank God* for Beth,' I say curtly. 'Because we've nobody else to help us.'

Chloe doesn't answer. She hasn't even apologised for her seismic error yet, but she does look wretched.

'Look, Chloe, I've been asking you for weeks, months even, what's wrong. I know *something* is, so don't bother denying it. I've known you long enough to tell when you're distracted.'

I'm taken aback when her eyes suddenly swim with tears. She opens her mouth, and a strange little gasp escapes. She tries again and gets the same sound, as if she's trying to form a word that won't quite emerge.

'For goodness' sake, what is it?' Even though I could throttle her for making such an utter balls-up, I soften my tone a little. 'Just spit it out. Tell me now.'

A desperate look crosses her face that makes me fear what she's about to say, and then, just as quickly as it appeared, it evaporates and her forehead creases up with undisguised scorn.

'It's nothing.' She turns quickly and pulls open the door. 'Instead of worrying about me, maybe you should focus on what's going to happen to your daughter.'

And suddenly I find myself alone in the room as Chloe returns to the family fold next door.

44

The police station

Dana tapped on Neary's office door and he beckoned her in.

'Thanks for coming in early,' he told her, shuffling through papers on his desk. 'The witness is on his way.'

'Expecting to find out anything we don't already know?'

Conor frowned and consulted a note on his desk. 'A Mr Peter Brewer, who lives in the house opposite Bessie Wilford's, called the appeal number last night. He said that as he opened his front door yesterday lunchtime to leave for a work trip, he spotted the girls skipping down the street and entering via the property's gate. He watched them disappear down the side of the house before he walked to his car parked on the street.'

So now they had a witness to say the girls had entered the property together.

'Sounds pretty conclusive to me,' Dana murmured, replaying the facts in her mind. 'Sadly, though, only the girls themselves know exactly what happened once they were inside the house, and they've still not told us everything.'

'Well that's just it. Apparently he has some other information he thinks we'll be interested in, but he was a bit unclear in what he said, which is why the officer taking the call asked him to come to the station as soon as possible. We expect him to arrive within the next fifteen minutes.'

Dana grabbed herself a coffee and sat outside underneath the enormous canopy of an old oak tree.

She thought about her first disagreement with Lizzie last night, after she'd cooked dinner for the two of them. It had all started off quite innocently.

'I feel bad that we spend so much time at your place,' Lizzie had said.

Dana pulled a face. 'It doesn't matter to me. I like having you here. It sounds like you're best out of your place for the time being anyway.'

Lizzie nodded gratefully. 'You're not wrong. I hate going back there. I'd willingly leave everything and put it behind me forever, but I'll have to go through Mum's stuff at some time.'

She had told Dana a little about the nightmare she was going through after the recent death of her mother.

'The hospital were negligent,' she'd said, her face patterned with grief. 'I've got two witnesses to say they didn't do anything to help her after her heart failure. It was as though they'd just written her off because of her age and condition.'

'Sounds terrible,' Dana said sympathetically. 'Your poor mum.'

'It's one of those things that's difficult to prove but I know in my heart of hearts they could probably have done something. If they had, Mum might still be here.'

Lizzie was such a caring person; she had a big heart.

It was ridiculously early days to even be thinking it but secretly, Dana enjoyed telling herself that Lizzie might just be the one she'd settle down with.

But maybe it wasn't as daft as it sounded; after all, they weren't naïve nineteen-year-olds in the flush of a first relationship. Dana was forty-two and Lizzie had just turned thirty a few weeks ago. They both knew what they wanted from a partner.

'What are you smiling at?' Lizzie said shortly, and Dana realised she'd let the thought of settling down with Lizzie affect her expression.

'Oh nothing, just this and that,' she said. 'Another gin?'

'No thanks.' Lizzie stood up. 'In fact I've decided I ought to go home after all. I said I'd babysit for a friend who's stuck for help. I'll call you tomorrow.'

And two minutes later she was gone, leaving Dana berating herself, although she wasn't sure exactly what it was she'd done wrong.

What was it with her and relationships?

45

Juliet

Both Tom and Beth have warned me against looking at my work emails.

'I'll handle everything,' Beth assured me when I gave her the passwords to the business sales and client accounts. 'There's absolutely no need for you to give it any more thought. Maddy is your only priority right now.'

She's right, I know it. But with the rest of my life in tatters, the temptation to dip in to see what is happening with the business proves too much to fight.

After five seconds of glancing down the email inbox, I wish I could un-see some of the subject lines.

Order cancellation

Retraction of contract

Please remove us from your communications

When I see the subject line of an email from Van Dyke's, I lean against the wall to keep my legs from buckling.

Contract UK4167915: cancellation clause activation

This is the contract we've already spent thousands on, commissioning our garment suppliers to make the clothing. The contract Tom and I remortgaged our house to fulfil.

I'd hoped – I'd *really* hoped – that because so much of our business is done online via the website, it might just be possible to recover from the fire.

Our existing stock has been destroyed, but we've had an unbelievable stroke of luck because the Van Dyke clothing order has not yet been delivered and so wasn't in the lock-up when it was burned out.

Despite all this, it seems that lots of our clients have somehow heard about our involvement in the investigation into Bessie Wilford's death, and I'm not sure how that can be.

Yes, we do a great deal of business in the local area and it's highly possible that word has reached those customers. But the bigger contracts are with companies much further afield, some of them in Europe.

None of the newspaper reports I've seen so far have flagged InsideOut4Kids as being our business. Have I underestimated the power of the Internet… or could there something more sinister at play here?

Beth hasn't informed me about any of these worrying emails, which have all been opened. I know she's screening stuff she thinks I'm going to find upsetting, but it's made me feel even worse discovering it like this. And I can't just forget it.

Instead of turning off my phone like I know I should do, I open Safari and go to my list of bookmarks for websites that are important to our reputation. A lot of these are review sites like Trustpilot, where customers can leave testimonials about how they found our service and the quality of the products.

New companies we approach, who don't know our outstanding reputation, often refer to review sites to give them the overview on how we treat our customers and judge whether orders are promptly fulfilled.

I tap the business name into the search bar and immediately see that our rating has suffered a catastrophic plunge from 4.6 to

2.9 in less than two days. When I click on the link, I count eight one-star reviews in the most recent posts. One star is the lowest rating it's possible to give.

The anonymous reviews all start with a scathing opinion on our clothes, and then mention Bessie Wilford's death complete with links to news articles. If the same person has posted all of them – and the reviews do look suspiciously similar – it's someone who knows how important positive feedback is to us.

Chloe's face flashes in my mind again, her distant, evasive behaviour the last couple of months: having the odd day or two off, forgetting to renew the insurance policy.

What would she gain by ruining me?

Then I catch myself. We may have our differences but we are *sisters*. The business provides Chloe with a living too.

I pick up my phone and call Beth. She answers on the second ring and I blurt everything out to her.

'So despite promising to leave the business stuff to me, you went and had a good look anyway?' She sighs. 'Juliet, I know it looks bad, and it *is* bad. But even something as terrible as what happened to Bessie Wilford will be fish and chip paper soon. You just have to give it time to blow over. Trust me.'

'But it's worse now, Beth. Maddy has confessed to hurting Bessie and they're interviewing the two of them again. If she doesn't speak up and tell them everything, they could well charge her.'

'Surely they wouldn't charge her with such scant details? The truth has got to come out soon and I can't believe either of the girls did anything wrong.'

Something closes in my throat like a fist. I take a breath and swallow down the wave of nausea spreading rapidly through my chest.

'She's going to get the blame for it, Beth. I just know it.'

'That's ridiculous! She's a child, for goodness' sake. She didn't do it… Maddy *can't* have done something like that.'

'*We* know that, but they don't.'

'Look, the one thing you can do for yourself is to put the business right out of your head. I'll do my very best for you, you know that. You're causing yourself undue distress by dipping in and out like this.'

'I know, and I'm so grateful for all you're doing, Beth. It might sound silly but I really feel like Mum and Dad are siding with Chloe and Brianna now, and Tom's all over the place at the minute. He just doesn't seem like himself at all.'

'To be fair, under the circumstances…'

'Yes, I know. But I need his support and I'm not feeling it. I've put so much into the business for so long, it keeps pulling me back. It's something I might just be able to control, in the middle of my life falling to pieces. That was until I saw how dire things are.'

'I'm trying to warn you off taking an interest, so I shouldn't tell you this, but I've spoken to Van Dyke's and the big order is definitely going through. The goods have cleared Customs and should be dispatched by road very soon.'

Relief washes over me like a healing balm. The cancelled contracts are tiny compared to the Van Dyke order. That contract alone is big enough to keep the balance sheet looking healthy for the next twelve months.

'Oh, thank God!' I fight back tears of gratitude. 'Beth, I can't thank you enough. I—'

'No thanks required. I'll get this contract fulfilled even if I have to sell my soul in the process.'

'Thanks for telling me,' I say sheepishly. 'I promise I'll stop peeking at the emails, now.'

'Good. You've got enough on your plate. Just concentrate on getting Maddy home. And Juliet?'

'Yes?'

'Look after yourself, too.'

'Thanks, Beth. I can't tell you how much I appreciate you looking after Josh. He's had a bit of a hard time on the coach trip home.'

'Just focus on yourself and your family,' she says. 'That's what's really important.'

I hesitate, wondering whether to articulate my wild suspicions about my own sister. I decide against it and push the thought away, for now. Beth, like Tom, already thinks I'm flaky and finding it hard to cope.

46

The police station

Neary asked Dana to sit in on the witness interview back at the police station.

'It will be interesting to hear his take on how the girls were acting when he saw them,' he added.

She nodded, pleased. Any detail, no matter how small and seemingly insignificant, might help shed a little light on the case.

Peter Brewer was a short, stocky man in his mid forties with wiry salt-and-pepper hair. He wore dark brown trousers and a checked shirt and carried a battered brown leather satchel.

Dana watched as the kitchen salesman wiped his forehead with the back of his hand. He was obviously uncomfortable being summoned to the police station.

'Sorry.' He tugged at the collar of his creased shirt. 'Haven't had a chance to get changed yet. I came straight over here soon as I got back from my work trip.'

'And we're very grateful you did, Mr Brewer.' Neary nodded. 'So, if you could start by telling us exactly what happened yesterday, please.'

'I usually have at least one night away from home during the week,' Peter began. 'This week it was Newcastle. I worked from home during the morning and set off about midday. I had a client meeting at teatime and then dinner with our biggest supplier last night.'

Neary nodded while March made notes.

'I came out of the house initially to put my case and some door samples in the car, and that's when the movement across the street caught my eye.'

'When you say movement, are you referring to the two girls?'

'No, actually. There was no sign of the kids at that point.'

Neary leaned forward. 'So where did the movement come from?'

'Someone was in Mrs Wilford's front garden. They had their back to me and they were just sort of standing there.'

'Can you describe this person? Adult? Male or female?'

'Adult and possibly male. I… I'm not sure. Sorry.' Peter looked sheepish. 'I just sort of glanced in the direction of the movement and then thought nothing more of it.'

'Did it not bother you that someone was lurking in an elderly woman's garden?'

'No, not really.' Peter looked flushed. 'I mean, some of the older people on the street have a gardener for a couple of hours a week, that sort of thing. There's never any trouble on our road.'

Neary frowned at the irony but didn't comment.

Peter opened his mouth and closed it again. Waited.

'Can you recall what the person was wearing? Was it dark or light clothing?' Neary tried again to glean any possible shred of detail.

'A dark T-shirt, I think, maybe long-sleeved, and a baseball cap… Yes, a dark baseball cap.' Peter looked pained. 'Bessie's hedges are a bit overgrown. I could only see the upper part of the person. But as I said, I didn't really take anything in. I wish I had.'

'So you took the stuff out to the car and spotted someone in Bessie's front garden,' DS March recapped. 'Then what?'

'I went back inside to do a last-minute check that I'd turned everything off in the house. I grabbed my satchel and keys, and then I left. Locked the front door and opened the driver's-side door, and that's when I saw the two girls skipping down the street.'

'And the person standing in Bessie's garden… were they still there?' DS March asked.

'Sorry, I didn't notice.'

'The girls, then?' Neary prompted.

'They looked quite happy, I could hear them chanting or singing and they were holding hands as they skipped along. I remember thinking how bright and sunny they looked… their clothes, I mean. Dressed for the nice weather.'

Dana replayed his words in her mind. Singing… skipping along, holding hands. The same two girls who had then abruptly stopped speaking and turned against each other.

'Did you speak to them?' March asked.

Peter shook his head. 'You can't say hello to kids you don't know these days unless you want to look like a pervert.' Neary raised an eyebrow. 'Sorry, it's true, though. They were still skipping towards Bessie's house as I got into the car. When I turned the car around at the end of the street, they were standing at the gate. I think one of the girls had her hand on it. After that, I set off and never gave it another thought.'

'Just to confirm, you didn't notice if there was still a person in the front garden at that point?'

'No.' He shook his head. 'I only saw the two girls.'

Was it possible, Dana wondered, that someone else had seen the girls enter the house at the time of Bessie Wilford's attack? If so, why hadn't they come forward yet?

47

The village

Dana hadn't been back in the village long after leaving the station when she got the call.

She and Lizzie were just about to enter the small brasserie when Dana sighed as she glanced at the screen.

'I'm not answering that.'

'Go on, you might as well.' Lizzie nudged her. 'Otherwise you'll be wondering all through brunch.'

It was true. Dana had met this wonderful woman just two weeks earlier and she already seemed to understand her perfectly.

Lizzie tipped her head to one side and watched with amusement, a wry smile playing on her lips, as Dana answered the call and conducted her one-way conversation.

'Hello, Conor. Right now?… I can't, I'm just about to have food. Hang on.'

She took the phone away from her ear and pressed the mute button.

'It's Neary. He said he wouldn't need me until later this morning but he's asking if I can get over to the detention centre in half an hour.' She bit down on her back teeth. Getting some time with Lizzie was proving to be quite the challenge.

'That's OK.'

'It's not really OK. We've had this table booked for over a week. It'll be another week before we can arrange the time again, and I really wanted to—'

'Dana. It's fine.' Lizzie smiled and laid her hand on Dana's upper arm. 'Really. We can do this any time, it's not a problem.' She stood on tiptoe and kissed her on the cheek. 'Go!'

Dana pressed the button and lifted the phone to her ear again.

'I'm on my way,' she said, before adding, 'You owe me, Neary.'

Lizzie asked to be dropped off at the shopping mall on the way.

'I'll only be there an hour,' Dana told her. 'You could come with me, grab a coffee or something, and then we can go for something to eat afterwards.'

Lizzie grinned. 'Tempting as the offer to visit the detention centre is, I'll pass. Has Neary got a problem for you to sort out?'

'He wants to interview the girls again, separately this time.'

'But it's clear-cut now, isn't it? One of them confessed.'

'Maddy Fletcher.' Dana nodded. 'Yes, it should be straightforward if the forensics back it up, but one kid's accusation against another isn't enough. There's something just a bit off about the whole thing, the family vibe. There's something that we're not seeing. Neary agrees we need more information before he makes the final charge.'

Lizzie glanced at her as they walked. 'A bit off? Like what?'

'I'm not sure. Just a feeling that they're keeping something from us.'

'But the girl has confessed. Period. The sooner Neary lets the law take its course, the sooner you can get on with your life.'

The voice of reason she'd been missing in her life. Dana pulled her keys from her bag and unlocked the car. She could understand Lizzie's frustration completely.

'If only it were that easy,' she said wearily.

*

Dana signed in at the centre's reception and Neary appeared from his office, taking long strides up the corridor to meet her.

'We'll speak to Maddy Fletcher first,' he said. 'Then Brianna Voce. But if her mother starts being difficult like last time, I'm going to ask her to leave the room.'

His jaw was set, his eyes slightly glazed over and Dana recognised the signs. He was keenly focused, desperate to make the right call in respect of Maddy's confession and Brianna's accusation.

In a side office, he indicated for her to sit before slumping down himself in a chair.

'OK, so here's where we're at. March and I have spoken to the super and she's given us one last chance to talk to the girls.' He picked up a ballpoint pen and studied the nib intently. 'If we can't get anything else and the kid is still confessing, the super's adamant we charge her with manslaughter.'

Dana sighed. She shared Neary's misgivings about issuing a charge at this point.

'I know, I know. But I can see the super's side of things too. The locals and the press are baying for blood. We don't want to charge the wrong kid, but we can't be seen to be dragging our feet either. We're expecting comprehensive forensics back within the hour.'

'If Maddy had kept quiet, you'd have been forced to release them after thirty-six hours,' Dana pointed out.

'If the forensics didn't support our case, yes. But Bessie Wilford was a much-loved member of the community and we can't appear to be showing leniency when things seem so straightforward, on the surface at least. Thank God the press don't know about Maddy's confession.'

Dana nodded.

'So in terms of these final interviews, I want to go in quite hard. That OK with you?'

She pulled the corners of her mouth down and shrugged. 'I don't see why not.'

'It's for their own good; the only way we stand any chance of getting to the truth.' He let the pen drop from his fingers. 'In your opinion, are they capable of withstanding tougher questioning?'

'I've not noted any signs to the contrary,' Dana replied. 'They both seem fairly well adjusted and competent.'

'Exactly. Not the sort of girls to batter an old lady to death, eh?'

She raised an eyebrow in acknowledgement of the irony and stood up.

Together they made their way to the centre's interview room.

48

The juvenile centre

Brianna Voce sat with her mother on the low upholstered seats. DC Carol Hall sat a little further back from them.

Dana met Chloe's belligerent stare and gifted her most compassionate smile. Nobody wanted their child to be disbelieved or made to feel uncomfortable, but this was one of those occasions when Neary and his team really had no choice.

Maddy Fletcher was Chloe's niece, after all. Surely Chloe was concerned that she should get a fair hearing? Or maybe not. This was a strange family, and Dana clearly hadn't got to the bottom of it yet.

Neary began.

'We're going to ask you some questions, Brianna, and it's very important that you tell us the truth. If you don't know something, say so. If you do, give us as much detail as you can. Is that clear?'

Brianna nodded.

Dana saw Chloe's obvious bristling at the detective's formal, no-nonsense tone. This was already a precarious situation and she prayed that Brianna wouldn't revert to her earlier silence.

The same thing was obviously on Neary's mind.

'Do you understand, Brianna?'

'Yes,' she replied in a small voice.

It was a relief, not that Dana or Neary showed it. It was important not to give anything away now. Both Brianna and her mother needed to know they'd reached the end of the line as far as Brianna giving her side of the story was concerned.

Neary started recording.

'Brianna, yesterday evening you stated that Maddy Fletcher attacked Bessie Wilford, is that correct?'

'Yes,' Brianna said in a surprisingly bold voice.

'Can you tell us how you knew Bessie Wilford?'

She thought for a moment. 'We just *did*. She'd been to Grandma's house before and one day when she left to go home, she asked me and Maddy and Josh in for lemonade in the school holidays.'

'Which school holiday was that?' Neary asked.

'It would be the last one,' Brianna said. 'May half-term week.'

'Had you been to her house before that?'

Brianna shook her head.

'Answer out loud, please.'

'No!' she said curtly, and for a second, Dana caught a glimpse of her mother's fire.

'So you and Maddy weren't worried about going to her house alone?'

Brianna laughed. 'She's an *old lady*! She isn't like a dangerous stranger. A man.'

She looked at her mother, who gave a tiny nod. Brianna was talking about Bessie in the present tense and Dana realised the girls still hadn't been told that Bessie had died from her injuries.

'Can you tell me exactly what happened from when you left your grandma's house yesterday?' Neary said.

'We went for a little walk up the road and then we had a dare to run down to the shops and back again,' Brianna said clearly. 'But when we got to the shops, we decided to go a bit further. To Bessie's street. It was all Maddy's idea.'

'So you got to Bessie's street,' DS March said. 'And what happened next?'

'We just skipped along to her house. It's right at the end of the street. We went in the gate and round the back because that's the door Bessie uses.'

'I see. And did you knock?'

Brianna hesitated. 'We… just walked in. Bessie can't hear you knock unless she's in the kitchen, because she's deaf.'

'And did you call out to tell her you were in the house?'

'She's *deaf*,' Brianna repeated as if Neary suffered from the same condition. 'We went through to the living room and she was asleep.'

'Did you wake her up?' Neary asked.

Brianna's face paled. She looked at her mother, then down at her hands.

'Brianna? What did you do when you saw Bessie was asleep?'

Dana watched as the girl twisted her fingers together and shifted in her seat.

'I can't remember.'

'I think you *can* remember and I need you to tell us what happened next.'

'I can't remember, Mum.' Brianna looked up at Chloe with wide, brimming eyes.

'Think, Bree,' Chloe urged her. 'When you saw Bessie was asleep, what did you do next? What did Maddy do?'

'She shouted loudly in her ear and Bessie woke up and fell out of the chair,' Brianna said in one long breath.

'And what did *you* do?' March prompted.

'I didn't do anything wrong! I stood near the door and then I went to the bathroom.'

'Did you help Bessie get up from the floor?' Neary asked.

'It wasn't me! I didn't do anything wrong. It was Maddy. She was the one who hurt Bessie and she was the one who stole her ring.'

49

2003

Ray stood at the bottom of the stairs and leaned heavily against the faded banister.

He could hear both his daughters moving around in their bedroom and he listened for a few more moments. They didn't know it yet, but what he had to tell them would colour their lives forever. Juliet's especially.

It was all he could do not to walk away and grant them a few more hours of peace.

But it had to be done. He couldn't put it off any longer.

He shouted for them to come downstairs. Seconds later, he heard their door open and footsteps padded along the landing.

He walked back into the living room and sat next to Joan. She held a tissue up to her face, but he knew that underneath it, her eyes were bone dry.

Sometimes he really struggled to understand how the woman he loved was put together, even after all the years they'd been a couple. He knew she loved him, but she could turn instantly cold if he put a foot wrong.

And she ruled the kids with a rod of iron. There were times the girls crept around her as if they were treading on eggshells.

Little Corey never did, though. Joan's moods went straight over his head.

The lad might have been a handful, but Ray's heart squeezed when he thought of his young son's *joie de vivre*, his constant curiosity and enthusiasm. Often for the most ordinary of things.

'What's up, Dad?' Chloe was first through the door, followed by Juliet.

'Sit down,' Ray said quietly. 'We've something to tell you both.'

Juliet looked cautiously at Joan. 'You OK, Mum?'

Joan glared from behind her tissue. She never looked at her daughter any other way now since the accident, but Juliet couldn't leave it there. The heaviness on her chest wouldn't let her.

'This isn't... it's not about Corey, is it?'

'Of course it's about Corey, you idiot child,' Joan screeched, dropping her tissue and pressing both her temples. 'It's *all* been about Corey ever since you mucked everything up.'

'Joan.' Ray held his hands up. 'We agreed I'd tell them.'

'Tell us what?' Juliet said faintly.

'Get on with it then,' Joan growled, snatching up her tissue again.

'There's no easy way to say this, so I'm just going to jump in with both feet.' Ray paused, his bottom lip trembling. 'I'm sorry, girls... your brother died in hospital this morning.'

'No!' Juliet wailed and stood up, raking her hands through her hair.

'The bleed on his brain, the aneurysm, it got bigger and he fell into a coma.' Ray looked at his hands. In this moment, he felt as if he were a hundred years old. 'There was nothing they could do for him.'

He looked at Juliet and saw she was motionless now and staring into space. He'd seen shock before and it looked just like this.

'Chloe, fetch your sister a glass of water, love.'

'But this is all her fault,' Chloe snarled, halfway between tears and fury. 'She should never have taken him to the warren if she wasn't feeling well.'

'Precisely,' Joan said under her breath.

'This isn't the time for pointing fingers,' Ray chided gently. 'We've all got to stick together. We've got to *keep* it together. Me and your mother have talked about this at length, and I tell you now, what happened to Corey must not be discussed outside this house. Is that understood?'

'It's not to be discussed *inside* the house either, after today,' Joan remarked. 'I've got to try somehow and put my poor boy's death behind me.'

Ray turned and looked at his wife. Her chafing fingers, her lined, baggy face. She might not be sobbing but she was suffering, he could see that.

'But the paramedics, they said he'd be OK,' Juliet cried.

'They said he *should* be OK,' Chloe remarked. 'They said he *should* recover.'

'They can't give any guarantees when it comes to head injuries,' Ray said, tears clouding his own vision.

'The main thing is that he's at rest now.' Joan sniffed and dabbed at her dry eyes. Then, in a rare moment of compassion, she looked at Juliet. 'I know you didn't mean to fall asleep. It was a terrible accident and now somehow we've got to try and put it behind us.'

Ray nodded and squeezed his eyes shut. He'd really loved that boy.

They all had.

50

Juliet

While I'm waiting to see Maddy, I think about my therapy session with Dana.

I've thought through everything we talked about. Some of what Dana said to me felt like a powerful spotlight suddenly shining on me after years of sitting in a darkened room.

Could it be possible that I've set my ten-year-old daughter the perfect example of how to take on others' blame and take on the role of the person who always puts things right?

Josh is a healthily mischievous boy. He dodges bedtime, homework and the odd household chore regularly if he can get away with it. Every time Tom or I chastise him, Maddy is there at his side defending him.

'He was helping me with my art homework,' or 'I said I'd sweep up the leaves in the yard for him.'

I've never given it any thought before, but now it seems so relevant, resonating with me at a deep level.

Could it really be that my family have subconsciously cast Maddy in the same role they set aside for me all those years before?

Things have been this way for so long, I truly believe that my mother, father and sister are completely unaware of our dysfunctional arrangement – as I was until I met Dana. I'm certain all of them would refute it, even if presented with the evidence.

It's all so messy and has gone on for so long, it's hard to know what's real and what isn't.

One thing I'm now certain of is that our mother is a narcissist. She constantly craves the attention of her husband, children and now grandchildren in order to feel valued. She labels us according to her own needs, and none of us has been permitted to grow up fully as ourselves. Including my own daughter.

Looking at it now as Dana has helped me to do, with all the crap and family politics neatly brushed away, I feel an aching sense of shame and regret that I didn't work it out for myself before my daughter got pulled into the monstrous machine that is my family.

And Dad? Dad is like a satellite that orbits around Mum, making excuses for her behaviour, smoothing her path and absolving her of any responsibility or blame.

Dad is lovely and hard to get angry with, but he's enabled Mum to act the way she has without challenge for so long.

Being around my family, I always felt uncomfortable, an outsider. But I never knew why.

Dana has helped me to see things clearly at last.

She helped me to see that Chloe has been a victim as much as I have. Although she's always been Mum's favourite, she is neurotic and needy because of it. She thinks everyone is out to get her. Worst of all, although she appears bossy and entitled, she doesn't feel she has any power in her own life at all.

I don't want my daughter to end up like that... like me. I refuse to let Maddy join the treadmill the rest of us are chained to in this family any more. It's not too late to help her redefine herself.

Brianna is being interviewed and Maddy is next in there.

Somehow I have to make her understand that she can speak up and tell the truth.

She doesn't have to bear the weight of other people's shortcomings all on her own.

Like I have for all these years.

51

DS March puts her head around the door as I sit waiting.

'Just to let you know we've interviewed Brianna now. Won't be long until Maddy's turn.'

'Is my sister coming back in here?' I ask.

'She had to pop out, apparently. Brianna is having a drink and a bit of quiet time.' March shrugs and disappears again.

What could be so important that Chloe needs to leave the centre when Brianna obviously needs her support? My niece might have told lies about Maddy but I don't like to think of her abandoned by her mother.

I push my irritation away. If I don't think about something other than what's happening in this place, I'm going to lose it.

Finding out the truth about what happened to Bessie Wilford is one thing, but should a miracle occur, I need to a life to take Maddy back to. If we lose the house, the business, everything we have, we'll be starting again with a whole new set of problems.

If Beth needs any more information about the Van Dyke contract, I want her to feel she can ask me but I know she won't. She's said so many times I'm not to fret about it.

Yet I worked so many hours on the damn thing, I've committed most of the details to memory, and I have a notepad at home full of pencilled scrawls, including costings.

Tom has always scoffed at my preference for a pad and pen when it comes to recording information, but this time it's proved its worth against fallible technology.

Despite everything I said to Beth earlier, I reach for my phone and open up the business emails, just to see if there's any more updates about the Van Dyke clothing that's due to be delivered soon.

I gasp out loud when the screen loads.

I can see immediately that the densely packed main inbox I viewed earlier is now virtually empty, just a few unopened spam-type messages left in there.

Like most people, I don't maintain the housekeeping I should on my emails. I mostly just open them and then leave them in the inbox, apart from the odd few I might delete upon reading, so there should be at least eighteen months' worth in there.

I know I promised Beth I wouldn't meddle, but it's a bit much for her to actually go ahead and make the decision to delete everything. So far as I remember, she's quite a nervous IT user, and I can't quite believe she's had the confidence to do that.

More likely is the possibility that it's some kind of virus that has wiped the communications.

I feel sick. All my suppliers' contacts were on there, and thanks to Chloe's staggering negligence, we have no back-up files. Surely Beth realises that? She's the one who uncovered it, after all.

A sinking feeling in my abdomen drowns the sparks of hope I had that the final stages of the Van Dyke contract might have progressed.

My finger is sliding across the screen to close the email window when a lifeline comes to mind. About a year ago, I deleted an important email by mistake. I panicked and Tom came to the rescue, showing me how easily it could be reinstated via the digital trash bin.

I hardly dare to hope. But if Beth has somehow deleted this stuff by mistake, she might be worried sick about telling me for fear of adding to my problems.

A few simple clicks and I might be able to help her out. Help *myself* out.

I open the trash box and immediately breathe a sigh of relief. It is full to the brim with emails, including, as far as I can see, all the ones I saw there yesterday.

I'm finding it increasingly hard to focus with everything that's happening with Maddy, and I don't want to make a mistake transferring all the messages back, so I decide to text Tom and ask him to sort it out.

But before I can do so, a particular email catches my eye. It's new and from Fenna at Van Dyke clothing. The subject line reads: *Confirmation*, which sounds like everything is going to plan. I open the email and read the contents.

Dear Juliet,

I'm so sorry to hear you've been forced to close InsideOut4Kids. I had no idea about the troubles with your daughter but I appreciate your honesty in letting us know that you're unable to fulfil the contract.

I wanted to let you know that we have been lucky enough to secure our clothing requirements for the next thirty-six months from another quality supplier, so your worries that you have somehow let us down are unfounded.

Everyone at Van Dyke's wishes you the very best in what must be a difficult situation.

It has been a pleasure working with you.

Kind regards,

Fenna Jansen

Head of European Sales

I clutch my throat and sit back. Read the email again and think through what its crazy contents mean.

Obviously *I* haven't contacted Fenna and told her I've had to close the business, so who the hell has?

Then I remember the phone hacking scandal of a few years ago, and it becomes obvious. Some journalists will stop at nothing to get their story, and the press are *very* interested in Maddy and Brianna at the moment. Someone must have hacked into our email system and meddled with the suppliers' communications to cause more excitement around the case.

I snatch up my phone again. It's imperative Beth is made aware of this before she sends out any more sensitive information. Then I'll try and figure out how to change the password on the account.

It might not be too late to rescue the situation. Beth can call Fenna to explain that the email about InsideOut4Kids closing down was a hoax. It's our only chance.

Infuriatingly, my call goes straight through to voicemail.

'Beth,' I say breathlessly. 'Listen. It's possible that someone has hacked into the business account and sent a fake email to Fenna at Van Dyke's saying that the company has been closed. Ring me as soon as you get this; it doesn't matter what time it is.'

I call Tom next, but there's no answer. Where the hell *is* everyone?

I have this sense of trying to herd up a thousand sheep without any escaping. It's an impossible task to stop the suppliers finding out what's happening in my personal life. All Fenna has to do is google my name and it's all there… scant facts tangled up in all the awful hype about the case.

There are voices approaching outside, and I feel a knot of dread at the thought of having to put a face on in front of Mum and Dad. My head feels like it's about to implode.

I snatch up my bag and rush to the door, almost colliding with Dana Sewell, who is on her way in.

'Juliet, are you rushing off? I wondered if you had time for another short therapy session before Maddy's interview.'

'I can't, not right now. Sorry.' I slide past her and rush down the corridor towards the foyer, my head spinning.

Figures fly through my mind. The thousands of pounds that have already been paid to the overseas suppliers for the Van Dyke order. The clothes we've commissioned are specific to their company, brightly coloured with their distinctive logo on pockets and lapels. We've no chance of selling them on to other customers if Van Dyke bail.

If the situation can't be rescued, InsideOut4Kids is finished.

I barrel clumsily towards the main doors. I need air. Space. I need... Tom. Need to tell him everything so that he in turn can find Beth and sort it all out before we lose another minute.

Soon it will be time for Maddy's interview and I need to bring my focus back to that.

A group of people are standing outside, a little way from the reception area, and I spot DS March among them.

She's laughing, joking with her colleagues, and I remember with a jolt that this is just her job. She goes home at the end of the day and thinks about things like what to have for dinner, or what to watch on television.

Instead of walking past the group to the small patch of grass with a wooden seat on it, I turn right and stand behind a short row of conifers: judging by the cigarette ends littering the floor, it's the preferred smokers' spot. I'll wait here, shielded from prying eyes, until they've gone back inside.

A silver car reversing into a parking space catches my eye, and I realise with a start that it's Tom.

Relieved that he's back at last, I step forward out of the shadow of the conifers, ready to rush over to him and blurt out my nightmare hacking discovery. But as the car stops and I glance at the passenger window, my feet root themselves to the spot.

I literally can't move. Every part of me freezes as my brain struggles to make the necessary connections.

Tom twists around in his seat and I see that his face is distorted with temper. He's jabbing with his index finger and baring his teeth as he spits out words like they'll choke him if he doesn't get rid of them.

My gaze turns back to his passenger, and I stare for a moment, trying to make sense of what I'm seeing.

But my eyes aren't deceiving me. The passenger is Chloe.

My husband and my sister are having what looks remarkably like a lovers' tiff.

52

I turn on my heel and scuttle back towards the building. My quick movement catches DS March's eye and she calls out to me.

'Juliet? Is everything all right?'

I ignore her and keep going, issuing an urgent gesture to the busy receptionist to buzz me through. She frowns at the intrusion to her phone call, but does so anyway.

I pull frantically at the door and it opens just in time for me to bump into Dana again, this time literally. She rubs her shoulder, takes a step back and studies me.

'Is everything OK, Juliet?'

'No, it's not.' I swallow, stepping forward and letting the door swing shut behind me. 'Everything is really shit, actually. Sorry, I…'

I inch past her and scurry towards the bathroom at the far end of the corridor.

'Juliet, wait!'

I hear Dana's heels clipping on the hardwood floor behind me. I squeeze my eyes shut and steel myself before turning to face her.

'Sorry, Dana, I just need a minute. I've had a bit of a shock. And I'm racking my brains to think how I can help Maddy, but… Is there any way you can help me? Find out who went to Bessie's house regularly… anything?'

'I think the police have already looked into that, Juliet.' Dana pulls a sympathetic face.

'An old lady has to have some help: a carer or a gardener... Someone must know something. Someone must have *seen* something,' I say.

To my horror, the tears begin to flow.

'Come on. In here.' She takes my arm gently and steers me into an office on the left. I stiffen, starting to resist, but the relief of having a quiet, private space seems to open my emotional floodgates.

I feel Dana's firm hands on my shoulders, pressing me into a seat, and I sink heavily into a low comfy chair. I accept the tissue she hands me, allow my handbag to be set aside. I feel like there's no fight left in me.

Through the tissue I'm holding up to my face, I see a glass of water materialise on the low table. Then Dana's crossed lower legs appear as she takes a seat opposite.

Someone else with an ordinary, normal life. A life I used to have, that I used to despair of at times, sick of the banality of my routine.

It's getting embarrassing now. The tears just won't seem to stop. I've been doing so well, swallowing it all down, and now...

'Let yourself be helped, Juliet,' Dana says softly. 'You can let go in this safe space. Just you and me; nobody else knows we're here.'

She seems to get it so well.

'I'm in no rush. If you want to, you can just let it all out, in your own time. Nobody will judge you, but if you keep blocking yourself like this, you're going to make yourself ill. I think you must feel that's true.'

I do feel it, feel the madness. Like I'm teetering on the edge of a sheer cliff.

But instead of feeling fear, there's a huge part of me right now that wants to just jump and make it all go away.

I open my mouth and everything comes pouring out. Not just my fears about Maddy, but about my husband, too.

*

'And this all happened just now?' Dana says gently once I've finished. 'In the car park?'

I nod, blowing my nose. 'They're probably already inside the building, ignoring each other again, pretending they have no connection at all.'

That's the rub. My husband and sister have never been the best of friends, communicating mostly via me or because of me. But the last few weeks I've had the distinct feeling they've almost been avoiding each other. Like in the family room when Chloe didn't even look up when Tom came in.

Yet it seems they've been seeing each other, or else why would they be in our car together?

Tom has always seemed to give Chloe distance, nothing much to say to her. But he had an awful lot to say just now in the car. The emotion looked very heated. Too heated to be a simple disagreement. It had a history behind it, if that makes sense.

Chloe's lack of focus and interest in the business is suddenly making more sense. She's had her head turned in other ways.

'Juliet. Have you considered facing up to this?' I hear Dana say. 'Tom and Chloe are both here. Why not speak your mind, for once? Instead of dismissing your feelings, air them. Feel the difference it makes to accept that you're angry and upset instead of trying to pretend everything is all right.'

Something about what she has just said prompts the most awful, terrifying thought to cross my mind. What if... No. I can't even articulate it. But the idea lingers in my mind like poisonous gas.

What if Tom and Chloe have conspired to ruin me? Between them they know everything there is to know; enough to ruin the business and send me crashing. So they can be together.

As soon as I give the idea air, I can't stop the rush.

'I don't know how long this has been going on.' I look at Dana. 'I haven't a clue how long they've been having an affair. It could be weeks, months, even years. I've been so absorbed in the business, it would have been the easiest thing in the world for Tom to have an affair. Maybe he's had several; I wouldn't know.'

I couldn't bring myself to spare time to check on my husband and my daughter when there were InsideOut4Kids adverts to place, stock to unpack, emails to answer.

I've probably been happier the last couple of years than I've been in my life, building the all-consuming business that means I haven't the time or inclination to think about anything uncomfortable.

I haven't read Maddy or Josh a bedtime story for months; Tom and I haven't had a dress-up date night for the best part of a year. I've avoided so many people on a social basis: the mums at school, my sister, my parents. It's just been so easy to immerse myself in work as if it's the only thing that really matters.

Dana is still watching me as the cogs in my head race around, waiting patiently for me to continue.

'What if Tom and Chloe have tried to ruin the business to send me over the edge?' I say. 'I haven't noticed how stressed I am, but Tom has. He knows the business is everything to me.'

'Why would he want to send you over the edge?' Dana reflects my own words back at me, and I hear how melodramatic they sound.

'So they can be together! Chloe is the only person other than me and Beth who knows the password to the business email account. I can't believe it's never occurred to me before.' I laugh bitterly at my own naïvety. 'Letting the insurance policy lapse, failing to run a regular back-up of our computerised systems. It all makes perfect sense if you want to ruin someone, doesn't it?'

I sit back and wait for Dana's response, daring her to deny the evidence. I find it irritating how she always seems to reach for a more palatable explanation, even when the facts are so glaringly obvious.

The realisation that everything I've just said fits together feels as satisfying as it does devastating. I've finally worked it out.

'Now that you've come to this conclusion, what are you going to do about it?' she asks.

The fury drains from me and is replaced with an empty feeling, a buzzing in my head.

There's a tap at the door and we both glance up as it opens.

'There you are, Jules! We've been looking everywhere for you,' Tom says.

Chloe stands behind him, tapping away on her phone.

Dana gets up and walks over to the door.

'I'll give you all a few minutes' privacy,' she says, and looks at me meaningfully.

I take a breath, sit a little straighter and fix my gaze on my husband. He's pale and handsome, and I've only just noticed that he's lost weight in his face.

'I need to speak to you both,' I say. 'Right now.'

53

The juvenile centre

Dana Sewell glanced at Chloe as she passed, but she didn't say a word.

Chloe would dearly have liked to wipe the smug, self-satisfied look from the interfering woman's sly, freckle-filled face. Dana seemed to think she knew what was best for everyone here, particularly Juliet, who she'd clearly taken a shine to.

Well, Juliet might have fallen for her therapist's claptrap, but *she* certainly hadn't.

Chloe was too immersed in the real world, had been plunged into it without warning and it had been like being dunked suddenly in ice-cold water. Her problems were too entrenched to be solved by a shallow heart-to-heart with Dana Sewell.

It had been Tom's idea to come straight inside from the car park and tell Juliet the truth. Especially since her mum and dad knew everything now.

Chloe herself had actually thought long and hard about coming clean to Juliet for a few months now, and never more so than over the last couple of days. But now the moment had arrived, she couldn't help thinking they were far better leaving it until after this mess with the police was sorted out.

Her sister seemed fragile, distracted for obvious reasons. Chloe's own daughter was in this mess too, but Chloe took comfort from the support around her. Juliet seemed push people away, to retreat into herself and shun any efforts to bring her into the fold.

Chloe sat opposite her sister and made her best attempt at a smile, but Juliet stared right through her. She looked like a spooked cat ready to dart at the first opportunity. Tom shut the door and sat down next to his wife.

Juliet folded her arms. Her foot jiggled and she chewed at the inside of her cheek. She'd done that since being a little kid, Chloe remembered. It was her way of trying to settle her nerves when something was on her mind.

Well, she wasn't the only one who felt sick with nerves at what was about to come out.

Tom coughed and reached for Juliet's hand, but she snatched it away.

'Juliet, I know you want to talk to us, but there's something we need to tell you,' Tom said gently. 'Please know this isn't easy. We've been waiting for the right time, but... well, I've finally realised there *is* no right time.'

'Have you both considered that perhaps I already know?' Juliet's punchy retort surprised Chloe. She glared at them both in turn. 'Maybe I know all about what's been happening. Maybe there's just a slight chance I'm not quite as stupid and blind as you both obviously think I am.'

Tom shot Chloe a look and Juliet saw it.

'No use batting your eyes at her now, Tom. She can't help you wriggle out of this.' She unfolded her arms and squeezed her hands into fists. 'I saw you both. Out there in the car park together. I—'

'Juliet, you've got this all wrong.' Tom shook his head.

Chloe sighed. 'We haven't—'

'Shut your mouth!' Her screech was shocking in the small space. It reverberated around the room.

Chloe fell silent. This was not going to plan.

'You'll both listen to me whether you like it or not,' Juliet continued. 'I saw you arguing with her in the car, Tom. It was quite obviously an intimate falling-out, a lovers' tiff. And do you know what? It was almost a relief to witness it, because suddenly everything that's been baffling me now makes perfect sense!'

She threw back her head and gave a hard, hacking laugh that sounded manic in the confined space.

'You with your supposed after-work meetings,' she said scornfully before turning to Chloe. 'And *you*, always on your phone texting, always something more important to do than your actual job.'

Nobody spoke.

'So you see, you don't really need to tell me anything at all. I worked it out for myself.' Her eyes watered.

'Juliet,' Tom said quietly. 'You've had your say, and now you need to listen.'

'I don't *need* to do anything.' Juliet stood up. 'At this precise moment, the only thing I need is not to breathe the same air as you two.'

She stepped forward and Tom rose, blocking her path.

'Juliet, you're mistaken. Chloe and I are not having an affair. I swear it on Maddy's life.'

'Don't you dare bring our daughter into this!' She raised her fists and Tom grabbed her forearms as she moved to hammer at him.

The door flew open and Joan walked into the room, Ray at her shoulder.

54

'Maybe you should go and get yourself a coffee or something,' Joan suggested to Chloe. Her voice had assumed the warning tone they all knew so well. The warning tone that translated within their family as: *Make yourself scarce, I'll deal with this.*

'I don't want a coffee,' Chloe snapped.

'It's no use you getting yourself all upset over something that can't be changed,' her mother said firmly. 'If Juliet continues to insist on discussing it, then let us sort it out.'

Tom slapped his hand over his eyes.

'What the hell are you talking about?' Juliet's face was pale and furious. 'Am I going mad or are you all keeping something from me?'

Joan's face hardened.

'If we are, then it's for your own good. There are more important things to worry about than family secrets. Your daughter is close to being charged with manslaughter.'

'We all need to talk, Mum,' Chloe said quietly.

'*Somebody* needs to start talking, I know that much,' Juliet snapped. 'Tom? Chloe? Anybody!'

Joan turned on her. 'What do I need to talk to *you* for? Corey would have been twenty-one now. Do you ever think about that?'

Juliet looked down at her hands.

'I think about it most days, Mum. If I could go back in time, I'd do anything to save my brother. I loved him so much. But people make mistakes. Sometimes really bad ones.'

'She's right, Mum.' Chloe sat a little straighter. 'People do make mistakes, but that doesn't mean they deserve to be vilified all their lives by their own family.'

'I think you've said enough.' Joan glared at her.

'Dad?' Chloe looked at Ray.

'Joan, I adore you and I always will, you know that. But we've not always done right by our girls. You have to admit that's true now.'

'For the love of God, just tell me!' Juliet hissed behind bared teeth.

Joan made a small sound in her throat, like a tiny suppressed cry.

But Ray continued.

'I'd like to get to a place where we can finally be honest. See things straight. What do you say, love?'

Joan's pale face contrasted starkly with her dyed black hair. She cleared her throat and assumed a harsh, guttural tone. 'Don't you dare, Ray. Don't say something you might regret.'

'Look where that attitude has got us, eh?' He reached for her hand. 'Don't be afraid, love, we can sort this out. We can. It's not too late.'

'What?' Juliet demanded. 'What's not too late?'

'Ray… I'm warning you.' Joan looked wild, feral even. She flexed her fingers wide then screwed her hands into tight fists. 'You're out of order. I want to go home right now.'

Tom finally spoke up. 'If someone doesn't tell Juliet, I'm going to tell her myself right now.'

Chloe shifted to the edge of her chair and looked hard at her sister. It was time.

'Juliet, it wasn't you who was responsible for Corey's accident. It was me.'

The words bobbed in a sea of silence and seemed to sit there for a moment, for them all to finally hear, to feel, to touch.

Juliet stared at her sister. The room swam before her eyes. Nothing felt real.

Chloe's face looked strained but she looked at Tom and he nodded for her to carry on.

'I'd followed you to the warren because Dad came back downstairs to moan at me for leaving you to take Corey up there alone.' She took a breath. 'When I got to the top of the hill, you were already asleep, so I lay in the sun for a bit. Corey started whining; he was bored because he couldn't find his den. I chased him around for a while, but he was looking behind him as he was running and he... he just tumbled over the edge.'

He voice faded out.

Nobody said a word. After a few moments, Juliet spoke.

'But when I woke up, you were at the bottom of the hill.' Her voice sounded weak. 'You shouted up, told me you'd just got there. You even asked me where Corey was.'

Chloe hung her head. 'I'm sorry. I'm so sorry. I panicked when he went over... I didn't know what to do. I ran back down.'

'You watched our brother go over the edge and you ran away rather than get help?' Juliet was breathless. 'He might've survived if the ambulance had got there sooner.' She glared at Ray and Joan. 'And you two... you've let her get away with this all these years?'

'She didn't tell us until after Corey had died, love,' Ray said quietly. 'We decided it was best to leave things as they were; no sense in upsetting everyone all over again. The coroner had documented his death as misadventure, and we didn't want the police sticking their oar in if our story suddenly changed.'

Juliet turned to Tom. 'You knew this? You've always known?'

'No!' Tom's expression cracked. 'I only found out recently. I asked Chloe to wait for the right time to tell you because I was worried about your state of mind. That's what we were arguing about in the car. You have to believe me, Juliet.'

Juliet's face seemed to turn to stone. She stopped blinking, seemed to stop breathing. She turned away from Tom.

'Why? Why, after all this time?' She whispered.

Chloe's face darkened.

'It… it was just time to say something,' she stammered. 'It's really got to me lately.'

Chloe remembered the neighbours' whispers and nudges after Corey's accident.

There's the girl who fell asleep while she was supposed to be looking after her little brother.

Juliet used to say that that was what they were all thinking, even though they never heard them say it exactly. Chloe would console her; it was easy. By that time, she had managed to entirely convince herself of the alternative truth.

After all, if Juliet hadn't fallen asleep, she and Chloe could have helped Corey build his den together. He wouldn't have got bored and Chloe wouldn't have ended up chasing him.

Her parents had insisted on holding a private funeral for him, and Joan had declared she would not allow the girls to attend.

'I can't bear to look at you while my little boy lies dead in his coffin,' she had told Juliet, and the two girls were sent to stay with Beth and her father for a couple of days.

Chloe had felt secretly glad. That way, she didn't have to force herself to look at her brother's coffin and face her own awful truth.

'You left me to deal with the guilt and the blame for the rest of my life,' Juliet whispered. 'And now our girls have taken over that legacy.'

55

Juliet

When Carol interrupts us to tell me I can finally see my daughter, I'm glad of the diversion, glad to get away from them all.

I walk out of the room. Somebody calls my name, but I don't look back.

Maddy is waiting for me, looking pale and weak, like there's no fight left in her.

'I'll give you a couple of minutes,' Carol says before leaving.

I put my arms out and Maddy sits down close to me, leaning her cheek on my shoulder. I can feel her shaking. It's breaking my heart just to look at her.

I stroke her hair.

'I want you to know that your dad and I love you so very much. We will always love you.' She turns her face a little and looks up at me. 'It doesn't matter what you have or haven't done. We love you. Do you understand?'

'Yes,' she whispers and gives the tiniest nod.

It's so wonderful to hear her voice again, even if my heart is fractured.

Now that I know the truth about Corey, I understand that no matter what Brianna tells her mother or her grandparents about what happened in Bessie Wilford's house, I will never get to know the truth, because they will all keep it from me and twist it into a story *they* can live with.

If I let them, they will lie to me and deceive me, just as they've done for the last fifteen years. They will let my daughter take the baton and be the new fall guy.

But I will never let that happen.

'I'm going to share something with you, Maddy, and I want you to really listen to me.' I shift in my chair so I'm facing her. 'I've told you before about my little brother who died. His name was Corey and he had an accident and fell onto some rocks, remember?'

She doesn't nod again, but I can tell she's listening.

'Well, what I didn't tell you was that I've always believed it was *my* fault that Corey died. I dozed off, you see. I was ill and fell asleep when I should have been looking after him. But today I found out that it wasn't my fault after all. Someone else was there that day, someone who could have stopped the accident.'

Maddy stares at me with wide eyes.

'I took the blame all these years because other people said it was my fault.' I sigh, realising I'm probably not making much sense to my exhausted ten-year-old daughter. I grasp her hand. 'What I'm trying to say is that sometimes other people will do anything to get you to take the blame for something. They confuse you, lie to you until you really believe that somehow it *is* your fault. Do you understand?'

'Yes.'

'I know you better than anyone else in the world, and you're a good girl, Maddy. I'd really hate for you to blame yourself because you think it's the right thing to do.' I squeeze her hand. 'You're kind and clever, and you have your whole life ahead of you.'

I can only hope that that's still the case. Any kind of redemption is hanging by a mere thread now.

'It's not too late, Maddy,' I add. 'If you can tell us what happened in Bessie's house, we can help you. All you have to do is tell the truth… *your* truth, not someone else's.'

A single tear rolls down my daughter's soft, pale cheek.

There can't be a worse feeling than this. Desperately wanting to save your child and being so utterly unable to.

Everyone says the truth will always shine through and eventually it has. The truth about Corey's accident is finally out. But at this precise moment, I'm wondering how something so ultimately powerful as the truth can be so easily hidden. So effortlessly, it seems, for all these years.

Most of all, I wonder if we will ever find out the truth of what happened in Bessie Wilford's house.

56

The village

She was doing it again, failing to follow proper procedure. But what harm could it do now?

Dana liked and trusted Juliet Fletcher, and although it clearly irritated Lizzie every time she said so, she didn't believe Maddy was capable of killing Bessie Wilford, regardless of Brianna's accusation. It just didn't stack up.

What harm could helping Juliet do, really? Dana knew that given a bit more leeway and time, Neary would be willing to explore other avenues of inquiry. But for now, the pressure to name a firm suspect was tremendous.

Legally, Neary had almost come to the end of his allowed interrogation time, and Superintendent Fry was gearing up to charge Maddy with manslaughter. Fry herself was bowing under pressure from *her* superior, who was subject to public outrage and press condemnation at the fact that they hadn't already charged the girl.

Dana found it both disturbing and intriguing that the community and the press were so willing to ignore the fact that the two girls were vulnerable ten-year-olds, instead casting them as wicked young murderers in the ilk of Mary Bell and the killers of little Jamie Bulger.

Although Brianna could well be released, the fact that she had been present when Bessie Wilford was attacked still condemned her in the eyes of the world and a later charge could be made when the details became clearer. Dana knew from experience that Brianna would probably be hounded and the family forced to move away from the area.

Despite her bleak thoughts, she smiled to herself as she got into her car and headed towards nearby Kirkby-in-Ashfield. She was looking forward to this evening. She and Lizzie had decided to have a pizza and movie night.

It felt so good to have someone to chew the cud with at the end of the working day, instead of staring at the wall with only a glass of red and a Spotify playlist for company.

Lizzie had said she liked spending time in Dana's house, describing the small village terrace as cosy and comfortable in comparison to her own place.

Dana felt a warm glow when she said things like that. She liked being in a position where she could offer Lizzie a homely place to spend time together. Orla had been a high-flying lawyer with a fancy duplex pad in Nottingham's expensive Lace Market district. Dana had never felt quite good enough, nor quite clever enough, when she'd been with her.

Now it was the other way around. Lizzie made her feel competent and protective, and Dana found she very much liked feeling that way.

She took a right turn onto a side road and pulled into a small parking area behind a new low-rise office building. The words *Ashfield Angels* were picked out in a fancy bronze-coloured script against the black background of the large rectangular sign that spanned the building. Quite unfortunate, Dana thought, that something about it was reminiscent of a funeral parlour.

She entered the building and walked across the small waiting area to a smart beech desk, where she announced herself to the young receptionist.

'Dana Sewell to see Stephen Wade.'

She presented her lanyard ID, signed the visitor book and then took a seat as requested, looking around the foyer.

The walls were freshly plastered in sparkling white and hung with monochrome prints of various cities of the world. Leafy potted plants prospered and quality home interior magazines and Ashfield Angels leaflets were fanned attractively on low tables.

It occurred to Dana that home care for the elderly was the business to be in these days. She reached for a glossy leaflet.

Seconds later, a tall, rangy man with black hair and a grey-flecked beard appeared breezily from a door at the side of the reception desk.

'Dana? Come through.' They shook hands as she followed him through the door. 'Stephen Wade, MD. Good to meet you, hope I can help.'

'Thanks for agreeing to see me.' They entered a spacious office to the right and Stephen indicated for her to take a seat. 'I shouldn't take up too much of your time.'

'No worries. It's nice to take a break from rota spreadsheets, if I'm honest.' He wafted a hand at the giant slimline iMac monitor in front of him.

'Nice place to work.' She glanced approvingly through the floor-to-ceiling window that overlooked fields at the back of the building. 'Everything's so nice and new.' She gestured at the computer. 'No expense spared.'

He nodded. 'Business is good. People are living much longer, you see, and generally have a good quality of life. But they start to struggle with the day-to-day tasks like cleaning, laundry, light gardening. That's where we come in.'

'It's a real need you're filling,' Dana agreed.

'And I could fill it three times over if I had the staff.' Stephen rolled his eyes. 'That's the rub, getting reliable people.'

'Speaking of staff, that's why I'm here today. I'm involved with the Bessie Wilford case.'

Stephen's expression turned grim. 'I know all about it. Heartbreaking stuff. Bessie was one of our regulars, and none of the staff had a bad word to say about her.' He frowned. 'You know I've already spoken to the case detectives about this? I gave them a list of names, staff who've visited Bessie in the last three months.'

'Yes, and I appreciate you giving us a bit more time. Did she have a named employee who was her regular home help?'

'No. We can only guarantee the same person if they book someone at least three times a week. Bessie was more ad hoc than that. In fact, she hadn't put a help request in for about three weeks.' He pressed a button and the printer behind him began to whirr. 'Here's the list I gave the police. There are only four names on it, and I've included their work mobile numbers.'

'Thanks so much.' Dana was delighted he'd volunteered the list without her having to ask or be creative about the reason she needed it. 'I won't take up any more of your time.'

In the car park, she looked at the note in her hand.

Four names that meant nothing to her and the police had already spoken to them all. But she'd done her bit for Juliet.

Maybe they would mean something to Juliet or Chloe.

57

Dana sighed as she took in the queue of traffic in front of her. The council had been working on widening this stretch of the road for what seemed like months, and yet there appeared to have been little progress. Every time she drove by, three or four workers in reflective jackets seemed to be standing around having some kind of tea conference.

She had about an hour to herself before she had to get back for Maddy Fletcher's final interview. Before joining the gridlocked traffic, she'd stopped off at the small artisan bakery in Papplewick village and bought one of their delicious four-cheese pizzas, which she'd plate with a tomato salad later. She hadn't been able to resist a rather splendid-looking lemon drizzle cake for dessert although she knew Lizzie would put up a weak complaint about the calories she'd be consuming.

Lizzie had been working at Dana's house all day. She was trying to get a new business venture off the ground, something to do with a referral service for health professionals. She had fully explained it, but to Dana's shame, her mind had been too full of the case to take it all in properly. She'd make it up to Lizzie tonight and push the case out of her head. There was nothing more she could do for Maddy Fletcher after today.

Infuriatingly, when Dana drove into her road, she saw that the guy who'd moved in next door about a month ago had again parked his Kawasaki motorbike in front of her house. He had a black BMW motor too, which was taking up the space in front of his own house.

Muttering to herself, she parked a few doors down and walked back, opening the front door quietly and shutting it softly behind her so she could surprise Lizzie, who'd set up her office for the day on the kitchen table at the back of the house.

She crept past the stairs and was just about to shout out comically, 'Honey, I'm home!' when she realised Lizzie had her phone clamped to her ear.

'I'm so sorry, Juliet,' she was saying, her voice breaking with compassion. 'It sounds like you're going through hell.' She fell silent again as she listened. 'Yes, I suppose so, but it's like dripping-tap torture, isn't it? It just keeps going, never stops… OK, well if you don't want Josh to come to the juvenile centre, then you could pick him up from my place. Shall we say in twenty minutes? Are you coming alone? I really need to speak to you about something anyway. It's time… it has to be today.'

Dana stood for a moment, speechless. Trying to piece it all together.

Lizzie and Juliet *knew* each other? How could that be? Possible connections wouldn't come.

Lizzie made another call.

'Hello, is that the *Herald*? Can you put me through to the news desk, please? I have some new information on the Bessie Wilford case.'

Dana stepped back into the shadows, spotting Lizzie's handbag on the hall table. If her heart continued pounding at this rate, it would surely burst. She felt sick to her stomach as she heard Lizzie's bright, confident voice speaking again.

The way the press seemed to get to know everything about the case in record time… Dana herself had fed Lizzie the details. Why on earth had Lizzie got herself embroiled in the case like this? Why was she playing a double game with the press and Juliet? More to the point… how did the two women even know each other?

She started putting together seemingly unrelated incidents.

The day Dana had met Lizzie at the spinning class had been a complete accident… hadn't it? She was a psychologist, for God's sake, she would have known if someone was pretending to be genuine. Besides, that had been at least two weeks before the attack on Bessie Wilford, so it couldn't possibly have anything to do with it.

Maybe Lizzie was just one of those people who found intense pleasure from playing the puppeteer role. Controlling events from behind the scenes and then reacting to them, like tipping off the press and then appearing to be as shocked as anyone else and offering comfort to Juliet. Had she engineered 'bumping into' her at some point, too?

Dana picked up the handbag and moved stealthily back into the front room, where she checked that her own phone was on silent and wouldn't give her away.

Lizzie's handbag was well organised, unlike Dana's, which she'd been threatening to clean out for the past year. A hairbrush, another phone, which she saw was locked with a passcode, a bunch of keys, a black leather purse and a foil packet of paracetamol tablets. She fished out the purse and quickly unfolded the front section. Nothing unusual there: credit cards, debit cards – and a driving licence.

She pulled it out and glanced at it. *Elizabeth Chambers.*

Strange seeing Lizzie's full name like that, and something buzzed in her head, like she'd heard it before.

A strap of some sort had hooked itself around the purse, and Dana shook it free impatiently. It was attached to a laminated lanyard. She extracted it from its tangle and inspected it. It featured a familiar black and bronze colour scheme.

Ashfield Angels
Carer name: Beth Chambers

Beth Chambers had been one of Bessie Wilford's carers. And wasn't she also Juliet's friend who was taking care of her son and the business?

Checking that Lizzie was still on the phone, she replaced the contents, put the bag back on the table and then, her whole body trembling, she let herself back out of her house as stealthily as she'd entered.

58

Juliet

I calculate I have enough time to sort this out with Beth before Maddy's final interview in about an hour's time.

I drive to her house on automatic pilot. I don't register the journey at all as my thoughts are focused on Maddy probably being charged today. It's all I can do to keep breathing.

Beth had sounded a bit weird on the phone, and she's looking after Josh. I haven't spoken to him since she picked him up and it would be just like Beth to keep something from me – like if he was unwell – to stop me from worrying.

I pull up in front of her small terrace and rush around to the back door. It's ajar.

'Beth,' I call urgently. 'Beth?'

She appears at the kitchen door, smiling. I take a deep breath.

'I thought I'd pop in just to say hi to Josh before I go back to the juvenile centre.' I try to say it casually, but my voice comes out strained.

'He's sleeping at the moment,' she says slowly, and smiles, an unhinged expression spreading over her face.

'Can we wake him up?' I can't stop the rising panic in my voice. 'I really need to wake him up, because if I don't get back right away, the police will come looking for me so they can interview Maddy.'

There's no chance of that; they'll just get Carol and Seetal to sit in with Maddy on her interview but it's the first thing that comes into my head.

'I know the game's up,' she says. 'I know Dana heard me on the phone. I heard a noise and saw her driving away.'

'Dana?' I frown, not understanding. Is Beth unwell herself? She's never met Dana so far as I know. 'You know, I can take Josh with me after all. I bet you could do with a break yourself.'

I've been dying to tell Beth about Corey… that I wasn't to blame after all these years but I can sense now is not the time. She seems confused, disorientated.

'Josh isn't here. I gave him a little something to help him sleep.'

'What? Where is he?' I step forward, feeling a bit light-headed. 'Is he OK? What have you given him?' Maybe I'm jumping to conclusions and she just means some warm milk or something.

It occurs to me that each time I've spoken to Beth on the phone, Josh has always been too busy watching Netflix to chat. My neck muscles tighten.

'I want to see him, Beth. If he's unwell I'll need to take him to the doctor.'

'He's OK… for now. You'll have to take my word for it. But let's not talk about Josh, let's talk about *you*. You and your heartless family.'

My heart is thudding against my chest, but I have to try and keep calm. There's clearly something very wrong with Beth. I've never seen her like this before; she's usually so rational and calm.

With rising panic, I realise that I've left Josh in the care of someone who has possibly had some kind of a breakdown.

'Beth,' I say gently. 'Are you feeling OK?' I place my hand on her upper arm, but she shrugs it off.

'All you ever bang on about is this supposed kinship we share because our brothers both died. You never knew how I've despised your mother ever since my brother's death.'

A jolt like electricity shoots through my torso.

'Why would you blame my mum, Beth? She was part of the team who cared for Andrew when he was admitted after the accident.'

Beth gave a bitter laugh. 'Cared? That's hardly the right word for letting someone *die*.'

She's making no sense whatsoever, and my patience is wearing thin. I need to see my son right now.

'Andrew died of the injuries he sustained in the accident, you know that's true.' I turn back to her. Again I make a real effort not to raise my voice, but I'm firm. 'Before we talk any more I want to see Josh.'

'You'll see him all in good time. First I have some things to say that you need to listen to very carefully.'

I rush to the kitchen door and shout upstairs. 'Josh?'

'I told you, he's not here,' she says, folding her arms. 'Trust me. You'll want to hear what I've got to say.'

I grab her hand. 'Beth! Stop this now, or I'll call the police.' All thoughts of keeping calm are forgotten now.

She laughs, shakes me off. 'Call the police. Let them hear everything I have to say. In fact, while you're at it, call the press, too. They'll have a field day.'

I doubt the press are interested in her ramblings about poor Andrew's death. She's deluded. But Neary and March will help me get my son back, I know that. I fumble in my handbag for my phone.

'It's always been family first with you, hasn't it?' Beth sneers. 'Even though they treat you like a second-class citizen. Blame you for what happened to Corey when it was never your fault at all.'

I stare at her, disbelief prickling every inch of my skin. *Beth knows it was Chloe who was responsible for Corey's accident?* How is that even possible?

'Did you know that Bessie Wilford was the ward sister on duty the day Andrew was brought into hospital?'

'How do you know that?' I frown, trying to get to grips with all this. 'You *knew* Bessie Wilford?'

'I went to her house in a carer capacity a few times. She'd been diagnosed with Alzheimer's. Now *that* really turned out to be a blessing in disguise.'

I stare at her. She's not making any sense, and in the meantime Josh is possibly drugged somewhere. What if he chokes… or wakes up somewhere strange and panics? I *have* to call the police. I pull my phone out of my bag and open up my call list for Neary's direct number.

'Do you know how Alzheimer's works, Juliet?' She's conversing in this casual tone, as if we're just having a regular chat over coffee. 'Bessie had a near-perfect memory for years ago; it was just the more recent stuff she had a problem with. When she said she worked at the hospital – mad old bat thought she was still there, actually – I asked her about my brother on the off chance, mentioned your mum's name, too.' Beth's face screws up with disdain. 'Bessie remembered the day Andrew was brought in perfectly. She told me his injuries were too severe and there was nothing they could do for him.'

For a moment I see a glimmer of my friend again. She seems so vulnerable and sad. Getting angry with her obviously isn't helping and isn't getting me closer to seeing Josh, so I try a different tactic.

'Beth, this has raked up all your sadness about Andrew. You're bound to feel bad.' I shake my head. 'But you've never told me or the police that you knew Bessie. Why not?'

'Do you know what Bessie told me? She said they could've tried one or two procedures but they all knew he was too far gone. So a team decision was made and they did nothing.' Her hands ball into hard fists. 'They did *nothing*.'

'I'm sorry you're feeling so bad, Beth, but Bessie was old, and as you say, she had—'

'Her distant memory was clearer than yours or mine!' Beth retorts. 'And when I found out about Corey, that's when something snapped inside me. It felt like someone flicked a switch. Both Bessie and your mum were part of that team. They were instrumental in letting Andrew die. And then Corey, too… I can't handle it.'

Her hands fly up to her head, pressing hard against her temples.

Corey… Andrew… who exactly is she talking about? She's in a bad way.

'I'm giving you one more chance, Beth.' I hold my phone up in the air. 'I want to see Josh right now or I'm calling the police. Nothing you're saying is making any sense at all. '

With lightning speed, she snatches it from my hand and tosses it into the sink, which is filled with soapy water.

'You idiot!' I plunge my hand in and fish around for it. When I pull it out and shake off the excess water, the screen is predictably black and unresponsive.

Instead of screaming at her, I turn and walk towards the door. I'll knock on a neighbour's door and ask them to call the police.

'You're as bad as them,' Beth says, following me, jabbing me hard in the back. 'Your sister, your parents… you are *all* liars, the lowest of the low. You must've laughed so hard behind my back, called me a gullible fool believing Andrew never suffered… but not now.' She smiles. 'Now, none of you are laughing. I've ruined all of your lives. Your business is finished, and the villagers hate each and every one of you.'

In that one sentence she reveals who has been informing my customers and also the local press. She's probably behind the terrible online reviews for InsideOut4Kids, too. How could I have trusted her so blindly? There must have been so many signs if I'd only paid attention.

'Beth, you're making no sense. I'm a victim here, just like you. I didn't know about Andrew and I didn't know until today that

Chloe was responsible for Corey's fall. They all lied to *me*, and now I find that you knew all about it too. Did Chloe tell you?'

Her face is twisted as she looks at me with utter contempt.

'Bessie Wilford told me. Her husband Charlie was best friends with your dad since they were at school together.'

Bessie Wilford *again*? A dark uncoiling of something too awful to describe starts in my lower abdomen.

'Ray confided in Charlie to assuage his own guilt about going along with your witch of a mother and protecting her favourite eldest daughter.'

I hate what my family did to me, but I'm not about to share that with Beth and fuel her crazy hate-fest.

'You sicken me, all of you. Even you, Juliet.' She continues, 'You made your sister a director in favour of me, the person who encouraged you to start the business in the first place...'

'And you know I was grateful for that!'

'But not grateful enough, it seems. Not grateful enough to give me a job when it took off. You knew I was struggling financially.' She took a breath, got control of herself. 'But I digress. Your dear family only told you part of the truth today. You want the whole story?'

I take the final couple of steps and reach for the back door as she takes her phone out of her handbag and presses a couple of buttons.

She places it on the table in front of me. I look at the photograph that fills the screen.

'Meet George,' she says.

A smiling young man sits at a table covered in playing cards. He's holding one up at the camera and smiling. One side of his mouth droops slightly, but he's got a cheeky look about him, and he's handsome.

I look at Beth vacantly.

'I don't know who this person is.' I'm tired of her games. The only thing I want is to see my son. Now.

'George lives at an assisted living centre in Edinburgh,' Beth says, watching me. 'When he was five years old, the manager of the place told me, he suffered a fall in which he incurred a head injury and suffered a bleed to the brain. His family gave him up for adoption because they couldn't cope with his subsequent disabilities.'

Her words sound far away and my legs feel weak.

'George is your brother's new name, Juliet. Corey didn't die; your parents lied to you and had him fostered. All this time he's been alive and living in Scotland.'

The ground falls away from me.

59

'I had to punish them all, don't you see that?'

I slump down on a kitchen chair and Beth stands over me. My friend's kind face, the happy demeanour I love so much, is no longer in existence. Her features twist into a hard knot.

'I had to ruin everything for you all, and I'm sorry you and Maddy are the worst casualties of that. There are members of your family who deserve it more. But I was angry with you too.'

'Angry with *me?*' I feel like I'm fading away, drifting. I need to see Josh, need to make sure he's safe and get back for Maddy… but everything feels too far away. I can't get the face of the boy she has on her phone out of my mind. His eyes…

'For being so stupid, so gullible. For making it so easy for them to ruin people's lives… Andrew's, Corey's. They had to be stopped.' She shakes her head. 'Your mother was as guilty as Bessie Wilford in neglecting my brother at the hospital, but having Corey adopted was even worse. Your dad told Charlie that it nearly killed him to do it but that your mother made him choose between Corey and her. She threatened to kill herself rather take on a disabled child with all the stress that entails. And all this time, Bessie Wilford and her husband, before he died, knew and they protected the Voce family. Bessie was as guilty of abandoning my brother and Corey as they all were.'

Even through the fog of my shame and sadness, it sounds just like Mum to choose a peaceful life over having Corey back home. But why did Bessie keep their secret? It's so sad.

'Even that old woman had more than me, do you know that?' Beth was jumping from one thing to another. She's definitely been in no fit state to look after Josh. 'Bessie was losing her mind but she could still pay her bills and had valuable items sitting around the house she'd forgotten were there. It was the final humiliation.'

'Did you have anything to do with Bessie Wilford's death?' I ask her quietly.

'It's true I visited Bessie a few times unofficially, shall we say, extracted every detail I could about Andrew and about Corey. She even knew where Corey lived after all this time, can you believe that? Your dad apparently visited him secretly without ever telling Joan. I found him easy to find.'

I think about Dad's periodic trips away to Scotland. All this time he's kept the secret to himself? Let Corey grow up without us around him? How could my kind, loving dad have been so heartless underneath?

I look at Beth, her face puffy, her features twisted, like a mask of hatred has been fused to the best friend I've known and loved for so long.

'I was burning up inside, trying to control my fury and plan my revenge.' She forced the words out in one long stream between gasping in air. 'But I knew I had to force myself to wait for the right opportunity to cause maximum damage. I started by sending anonymous texts to the phone number Bessie showed me she had for Brianna. Spooking them out a bit but promising them there would be terrible consequences if they told anyone. Brianna wasn't supposed to have a phone, but she'd asked if she could have the one Bessie's daughter gave her ages ago and she'd never used.'

So the phone I found doesn't belong to Maddy; it's Brianna's. Maybe she just gave it to Maddy to keep safe.

Beth looks pleased with herself. If I listen for a few more minutes, maybe she'll stick to her word and tell me where Josh is. If I can get the truth about what happened to Bessie, maybe it could stop Maddy from being charged.

'Then yesterday morning those two spoilt little girls skipped down the street near Bessie's house.' Her smile stretches into a grimace.

'I rang earlier that day, put on a crotchety old voice and asked them over for biscuits and lemonade but not to tell anyone. Only interested if there's something in it for them, those two.' She grins again. 'Like mother, like daughter, it seems.

'Turned out Bessie's house was a treasure trove beyond my wildest dreams. Nearly five grand in notes hidden under the spare-room bed. Can you believe that?' Greed glittered in her eyes like black diamonds. 'Loads of jewellery on her dressing table, and genuine artwork in the cupboard under the stairs.'

'The girls didn't hurt her, did they?' I can feel something shifting inside me, trying to untether itself. 'You tried to frame them.'

'Well that's not strictly true. It all worked out far better than I anticipated,' Beth continues. 'I gave Bessie a little something to help her sleep. Brianna played a trick on her to startle her, and the silly old bat woke up suddenly, tipped out of her chair and hit her head on the tiled hearth.'

'You were there?'

'Oh yes. I stepped out from the hallway then and told them that Bessie had a son, a violent man who would kill their families if they breathed a single word about what had happened. I told them the only way of getting out of the situation was to remain completely silent. Not to say a word to anyone, even the police. I said if they didn't breathe a word, I'd speak to Bessie's son and get them off the hook.' She laughed. 'So gullible, the pair of them. Would never have worked on an adult but they just swallowed it all without explanation. Touching really.'

I press my hand to my mouth, sickened by the thought that Bessie was hurt because Brianna startled her, but also by the fact that Beth was present all along, coolly observing proceedings instead of getting her help. The level of fear the girls must have suffered was off the scale.

But something doesn't quite fit. There's still a niggle at the back of my mind.

Then I get it.

'Hitting her head on the hearth is one thing, but the detectives told us Bessie was battered to death. That's quite a different take on it.'

Beth's face darkens. 'I never planned to kill her. I just wanted the girls to get into trouble for assaulting her, something bad enough to take your mind off the business so I could move in on it. But the business was just an aside; more importantly I wanted to destroy your twisted family unit, expose all your lies. I could've done that without killing her. But the silly old bat woke up, didn't she, after they left. Just as I was packing the money and jewellery into my holdall.'

'But she had dementia. You could have just walked away; nobody would have believed her if she'd told them what had happened.'

'It's true she had dementia, but it's something that comes and goes in the early years. There are periods of lucidity when the brain functions like normal.' She scowls. 'Just my luck she woke up lucid. I might not have had to hurt her had she remained clueless. As it was, the heavy brass lamp on the table came in very handy.'

I squeeze my eyes shut, willing the vision of the scene to leave me.

Instead of a feeling of euphoria at this final confirmation that Maddy did nothing wrong, a wave of something powerful and all-consuming engulfs me. In the space of a few seconds, I grieve for Bessie Wilford and her family, feel regret at staying so blind for so long, and feel a searing heat of fury against Beth for what she's put our girls through.

'As I said, I've been grooming the girls with the anonymous texts for a while now. They were very nervous, particularly Maddy. Brianna's a bit tougher, like her bitch of a mother.'

I think about Maddy's disrupted sleep, hearing her moving around in the night and going downstairs to find her sitting in the living room in the dark, staring into space with that haunted look on her little face. In her last interview she'd talked about someone asking her to do bad things and I simply thought this was Brianna. But if it was Beth… Maddy would be beside herself with confusion and fear.

She's always trusted Beth, known her all her life. Although she didn't know who was sending the texts, Beth knew enough about *her* to tap into what scared her.

'And you did all this to avenge my brother, who isn't even part of your own family?'

Irritation flashes across Beth's face.

'I did it for *my* brother. For Andrew. He lost his life, had no choice in the matter thanks to the neglect of the hospital staff. Your family had a little boy who was still very much alive, and yet they tossed him aside like a piece of rubbish. I couldn't let them get away with that.'

'Beth, did you inform all our customers and suppliers about the scandal, set fire to the unit… get our contracts cancelled?'

'You're so trusting, Juliet, you made it easy.'

A sudden noise makes me jump, and we both turn at the sound of feet scuffing on the hardwood floor. Dana appears, her face pale. 'I tried to call you, Juliet,' she gasps, staring at Beth. 'I heard everything while you were on the phone to Juliet… Lizzie, Beth… whatever your name is.'

Beth laughs. 'Had you fooled, didn't I? I couldn't believe how easy it was to get your attention that day at the gym, but I was only ever interested in your connection to Neary.'

'But we met two weeks before this case. You couldn't have possibly known I'd be involved.'

'I couldn't know for certain but I could hazard an intelligent guess. The newspaper interview you gave was a gift, telling everyone how amazing you are at building a rapport with local kids in trouble and how you work with Neary on cases involving children.' Beth smiled. 'It was pretty obvious that if two local girls carried out a terrible crime, your services would be called for. I'd seen you at the gym a few times before you were suspended. It was a gift when I saw you in that class. I'd have done it all without you anyway but the chance of having an insider view of the case was too good to miss.'

The expression on Dana's face tells me she's crushed. She obviously really cared for Beth... or the woman she knew as Lizzie.

'Beth. Where is Josh?' I growl, strengthened by Dana being here with me now.

We all turn to commotion outside. Dana opens the back door and two uniformed police officers burst into the room. I cry out with relief when I see DI Neary behind them. A grim DS March follows him in.

'She's got Josh somewhere... she's drugged him,' I shout.

'Check upstairs,' he instructs the first two officers.

'I'll follow them up, sir,' March adds before turning back to a third officer still standing outside the back door. 'Get an ambulance here in case it's needed.'

My hands fly up to my face. Does she think Josh could be...

'Juliet, are you OK? You're not hurt at all?' Neary asks, his voice full of concern.

I shake my head and look over at Beth. 'The girls didn't kill Bessie, it was her.'

She smiles to herself, as if she's silently congratulating herself on a job well done. It's as if she's in another world entirely, no sign of any conscience at all.

The officers' boots thunder up the stairs and a few seconds later I hear March shout down.

'He's here sir, he's drowsy but conscious.'

'Josh!' I start towards the stairs and Dana grabs my arm.

'Let them deal with it, Juliet. They'll bring him downstairs safely.'

'The ambulance is on its way, sir,' I hear the officer behind Neary say.

I stagger back, let Dana sit me down on a kitchen stool. I feel dazed and sick.

I don't know how I didn't see the signs with Beth… I think it's the same reason I missed so many other signs the people I love were giving off: my obsession with work. My naïvety when it comes to my family and their motives.

'How come you never realised Beth was Bessie's carer?' I ask Neary and he frowns, looks apologetic.

'We did what we could in a very short space of time, Juliet,' he says. 'I had an officer speak to the carers on the list we had and they all checked out. We had two girls back at the station covered in Bessie's blood and that's where we focused our efforts.'

It's not good enough but I can't help feeling a twinge of sympathy for the guy. It feels like a week ago but Bessie Wilford was only attacked yesterday and there's only so much ground Neary can practically cover in that time.

I never suspected Beth and I knew her the best… or thought I did. If she'd told me she'd done some care work for Bessie, I *still* wouldn't have thought a thing of it.

Dana shuffles uncomfortably beside me. Beth… Lizzie… completely fooled her, too.

Beth was my best friend. I truly believed she had my back. I can't really blame others for not seeing through her.

Commotion outside again and then paramedics rush past the kitchen door and run upstairs, directed by Neary.

'I need to go up there to see Josh,' I say frantically.

'Let them do their job, Juliet,' Dana urges me. 'They can treat him far more effectively if they're left to get on with it.'

'Maddy's waiting for you to take her home.' Neary says quietly as his officers handcuff Beth.

I smile at that. The words I honestly had begun to believe I'd never hear.

'Staff at the detention unit are in the process of informing your husband and family what's happening here. I've asked them to keep everyone there until we get back.'

'They're no family of mine,' I hiss. I feel hot and empty inside when I think about my parents and sister. It feels like something has sucked out all my organs and replaced them with fury and disbelief.

I hear footsteps coming downstairs and stand up in terrified expectation.

'Josh is going to be fine,' DS March says, walking into the room. 'He's been lightly sedated, but they say he should soon recover.'

'Told you he was OK,' Beth taunts me. 'You worry too much, Jules.'

I fly at her, fingernails extended, and feel Neary's strong arms pull me back.

'Don't, Juliet,' Dana says darkly. 'She's simply not worth it.'

The fury drains and I feel so weak. I stagger back and lean against the kitchen counter. Minutes later, the paramedics appear in the doorway, carrying my boy on a small stretcher and a blast of energy whooshes back into me as I fly towards him.

'Josh,' I whisper as I stroke his pale face. 'I'm so sorry. I love you.'

His eyelids flicker slightly.

'He'll be fine, Mum,' the jovial paramedic says kindly. 'He's been given a mild sedative but it's wearing off now. A good meal and a session on his Xbox and he'll be good as new,' he quips as they carry my boy out to the ambulance.

Now that I know Josh is safe and that Maddy and Tom are waiting for me back at the unit, I can breathe.

But still one thought dominates, filling me with both sadness for the lost years and pure happiness for the future, all mixed together in a powerful rush.

My brother is alive.

ONE MONTH LATER

60

Juliet

Our lives are like the aftermath of a battlefield, but we're getting through it.

Tom and I sat down with Dana and he told me everything. How when Chloe approached him to tell him the truth about Corey's accident, he made the decision to keep it from me.

'I'm so, so sorry I chose to make that call,' he apologised, reaching for my hand. 'I knew you had so much pressure on with the business, and you were taking medication again… I was convinced it would tip you over the edge.'

'I had a right to know,' I told him.

'You did. You absolutely did and I see that now, but at the time… I thought it would break us, Juliet. We weren't nearly as strong as a couple as we used to be.' He shook his head. 'Chloe was panicking more and more that you would find out you'd taken the rap for Corey all these years, and I ended up being her reluctant confidante.'

'I was so certain, when I saw you in the car together, that you were having an affair,' I admit.

'I would've jumped to the same conclusion, I'm sure,' he says magnanimously. 'But it wasn't a lovers' tiff you were witnessing.

I'd finally snapped and insisted we had to tell you the truth about Corey. I only wish I'd done it sooner.'

He hangs his head and clutches my hand before continuing.

'But there was never anything more between us. And she never told me your brother was still alive.'

I believe him.

Apparently when Dad last visited George in Edinburgh, the staff there told him that a woman called Beth had also been to see him a couple of times – had said she knew George from long ago.

'Chloe didn't know until a couple of months ago that your parents had put Corey up for adoption,' Dana explained. 'Ray only told her after he found out about Beth's visits. He knew she would probably find out and at least had the decency to forewarn her, finally. Chloe approached Beth and asked her to keep what she knew to herself until she could muster the courage to tell you. And Beth held it over her, demanding money, telling her to neglect her admin duties in the business.'

'Chloe never told me Beth was involved. I just thought Chloe herself had finally broken after all the years of keeping the truth to herself of how Corey fell that day,' Tom added. 'I'd *never* have let Beth have involvement with Josh and in your business affairs if I'd known what was happening. I'd like to think I would have suspected Beth for framing the girls for Bessie's death but truthfully, it probably wouldn't have occurred to me. That level of wickedness would be hard to imagine from someone who has been your friend for so long.'

When I found out the facts, I knew in my heart that Chloe had been a victim of our family just the same as me. She was young too, at the time it happened; of course she would have felt bound to follow Mum and Dad's instruction to stay quiet about Corey's accident. She was playing her own role in our dysfunctional family unit.

But she has been an adult for a long time now and she could have reversed that decision. She could have done the right thing and told me the truth at any point.

Should we continue to give our parents control over our lives as adults and respect old family rules, or do we work to reach a stage where we make our own decisions? Chloe chose the former. And because of that, I can't be near her right now.

I need space to work through my whole life being a lie.

She's said she understands, and maybe in time we can find a way to begin to repair our relationship. I don't honestly know right now but a part of me hopes that might be possible.

Moving away from the village has meant Maddy and Josh both starting at a new school. Josh has already made new friends, and Maddy is getting there. Both seem remarkably resilient, though Maddy sees a therapist once a week. She's been able to understand how she and Brianna did some things that were wrong, like stealing money from Mum's purse. It could have been a way of coping, maybe a cry for help, who knows?

Mercifully, Josh has virtually no recollection of what happened in Beth's house after she drugged him. Before that, he says, things were just normal and he was allowed to watch back-to-back Netflix movies and eat pizza as Beth had initially promised.

Beth is being held on remand pending her trial. She has written to me from prison. It's not a flowery letter full of remorse, far from it. She still holds her grudges as strongly as ever but she did tell me accusingly her lawyer is expecting she could receive a twelve-year sentence… and could be out in six, with good behaviour, Neary tells me.

She has asked me to visit her but I haven't responded. She is part of my past now, as my parents are. Mum has also shown no remorse and is furious with Dad for visiting Corey… George, as he is known now.

Dana emailed to say she'd seen Brianna and she is well. Chloe has allowed her to have some counselling sessions and of her own accord; Brianna confessed she'd thrown the ring she removed from Bessie's hand into the hedgerow as they left. The ring has now been recovered and returned to Bessie's family.

Dana said Brianna and Chloe still live with Mum, but Dad has left home. Nobody knows where he is, but apparently Mum gets the odd postcard from Europe.

My lovely dad. A man I never really knew at all.

THREE MONTHS LATER

61

It's an ordinary-looking building, just a small two-storey block on a road behind a busy high street.

The manager shakes my hand.

'I'm Eileen Boyd, very pleased to meet you. You don't know how happy I was when Dana called me,' she says, beaming. 'The staff were overjoyed to discover you existed.'

I am giddy with anticipation, sick with worry at this long-awaited visit somehow going wrong. It all had to be done properly; Corey – or George, as he now thinks of himself – has had to be prepared so he understands who I am.

Dana takes in my expression and squeezes my hand. 'Everything is going to be fine,' she says, reading me like a book as usual.

Tom has taken a week off work to look after Maddy and Josh, and he's also offered to do some research into assisted accommodation around the East Midlands area, should everything go well here in Edinburgh.

I've started up the business again under another name, and have even managed to salvage some of the contracts that were cancelled. I'm just biding my time to see how it goes, but for now, being with my husband and children is what takes priority.

Dana and I follow Eileen along a corridor and up a flight of stairs to a carpeted landing. She stops at a door and opens it to reveal a large communal lounge area with a big television and comfy sofas at one end and a few scattered tables and chairs at the other, where people, most of them young, are sitting playing cards or board games. She walks over to the window, where she stops and turns.

From here, we can see the whole room.

'There's George, in the blue and white striped T-shirt,' she says quietly. 'He loves Monopoly.'

He's sitting side-on to where we stand, playing with three other people, his brow furrowed with concentration.

His hair is light brown, the same colour exactly as Chloe's. My heart jumps when I see that the tuft of hair that would never stay down when Dad brushed it is still there on the crown of his head.

He is of average build and his forearms look lightly tanned, as if he sits outside in the sun quite regularly.

He's counting his Monopoly money when he suddenly seems to sense he's being watched. He looks up and I take a sharp breath in.

His eyes are the exact same shade as my own. I knew this but I'd forgotten it. He looks at all of us in turn, and then his gaze comes back to me. I smile, and he smiles back, looking slightly puzzled as if he's trying to recall something.

Eileen walks over to the table.

'Sorry to disturb your game, George, but I wanted to introduce you to Juliet Fletcher.'

He looks at me. I look at him and hold out my hand, trying to keep it steady.

'Hi, George,' I say. 'Nice to meet you.'

His eyes flick over my face and he smiles. I think he recognises me. After all this time, I think—

'I've just got the last station,' he says, looking down at the board. 'I have all four now.'

His words are slightly slurred, but he can speak perfectly well. Close up, I can see the small scar at the side of his mouth where next door's puppy nipped him as they played on the floor together.

'Juliet's come all the way from Nottingham to say hello, George,' Eileen tells him. 'Remember we talked about her visit?'

'Very pleased to meet you,' he says, and I can tell he's itching to get back to his game.

'If I come back tomorrow, George, I wondered if you'd like a walk around the park… and we could have a game of Monopoly too. It's been a long time since I played.'

'Yes, that sounds fun,' he says. Then he looks at me – I mean, really looks at me – before he asks, 'Are you my sister?'

'Yes, George,' I say, making a tremendous effort not to dissolve into tears of happiness. 'I am your sister and you're my brother.' I reach for his hand. 'And I promise you this. Nobody is ever going to keep us apart again.'

'My sister. *Juliet*,' he whispers, and squeezes my hand.

To hear him say my name feels like plucking a star from the coldest night sky and holding it against my heart for the briefest moment.

So many lies, so much deceit and wrongdoing, not knowing who or what to believe. But this… this is real. My brother is right here in front of me, living and breathing.

It's the only thing that matters.

We've been given another chance to be together. To live our lives and love each other.

One thing is certain: we've a lot of catching-up to do.

Me and my brother George.

A LETTER FROM
K.L. SLATER

Thank you so much for reading *The Silent Ones*, my ninth psychological thriller. If you enjoyed it, and want to keep up to date with all my latest releases, just sign up at the following link. Your email address will never be shared and you can unsubscribe at any time.

www.bookouture.com/kl-slater

The Silent Ones was inspired by several historical news stories that left a question in my head: if two children committed a terrible crime and fell silent, how would that be resolved? What would be the reaction of the families involved?

Then a nice little complication posed itself: what if the children were cousins and their mothers were sisters? I got to thinking about how a dilemma such as this could easily set families against each other.

Even in happy families, we learn to tolerate each other based on years of getting to know each other, and anticipate how we'll react to certain situations. But such a crime could fracture all that, exposing old secrets and stresses within the family unit.

And this was my starting place for writing *The Silent Ones*.

The book is set in Nottinghamshire, the place I was born and have lived all my life. Local readers should be aware that I sometimes take the liberty of changing street names or geographical details to suit the story.

I know you hear this a lot, but reviews are so massively important to authors. If you've enjoyed *The Silent Ones* and could spare just a few minutes to write a short review to say so, I would so appreciate that. I'd love to hear what you think, and it makes such a difference helping new readers to discover my books for the first time.

I also love hearing from my readers – you can connect with me via my website, on Facebook or on Twitter.

Best wishes,
Kim x

 KimLSlaterAuthor

 @KimLSlater

KLSlaterAuthor

 www.KLSlaterAuthor.com

ACKNOWLEDGEMENTS

Firstly, huge thanks to Lydia Vassar-Smith, my editor, for her first-class expertise and guidance during the editing process. Thanks to *all* the Bookouture team for everything they do, especially Kim Nash and Alexandra Holmes.

Enormous thanks to my agent, Camilla Bolton, who is such a valuable support to me and also to Roya Sarrafi-Gohar. Thanks also to the rest of the hard-working team at Darley Anderson Literary, TV and Film Agency.

Massive thanks as always go to my husband, Mac, and my daughter, Francesca, for their love and support. To my writing buddy and fellow Bookouture author Angela Marsons for always being there.

Special thanks must also go to Henry Steadman, who has managed to do it yet again, designing a mind-blowing cover for *The Silent Ones*.

To eagle-eyed copyeditor, Jane Selley, and proofreader, Becca Allen. Thank you both for your skill in helping to polish up the book in the final editing stages.

Thank you to the bloggers and reviewers who do so much to help make my thrillers a success. Thank you to everyone who has taken the time to post a positive review online or taken part in my blog tour. It is noticed and much appreciated.

Last but not least, thanks a million to my wonderful readers for their continued loyalty and support.

Made in the USA
San Bernardino, CA
12 August 2019